BIG
Temptation
ROBIN L. ROTHAM

Ellora's Cave
Romantica Publishing

What the critics are saying…

ಸ

5 Stars "I just can't say enough good things about this book. One of the absolute best books I have read in the last year! The steam rating is off the charts! Robin L. Rotham just keeps getting better and better!" ~ *JasmineJade.com*

An Ellora's Cave Romantica Publication

www.ellorascave.com

BIG Temptation

ISBN 9781419958847
ALL RIGHTS RESERVED.
BIG Temptation Copyright © 2008 Robin L. Rotham
Edited by Sue-Ellen Gower.
Cover art by Dar Albert.

This book printed in the U.S.A. by Jasmine-Jade Enterprises, LLC.

Electronic book Publication December 2008
Trade paperback Publication February 2009

With the exception of quotes used in reviews, this book may not be reproduced or used in whole or in part by any means existing without written permission from the publisher, Ellora's Cave Publishing, Inc.® 1056 Home Avenue, Akron OH 44310-3502.

Warning: The unauthorized reproduction or distribution of this copyrighted work is illegal. Criminal copyright infringement, including infringement without monetary gain, is investigated by the FBI and is punishable by up to 5 years in federal prison and a fine of $250,000. (http://www.fbi.gov/ipr/)

This book is a work of fiction and any resemblance to persons, living or dead, or places, events or locales is purely coincidental. The characters are productions of the author's imagination and used fictitiously.

BIG TEMPTATION
ഔ

Trademarks Acknowledgement

The author acknowledges the trademarked status and trademark owners of the following wordmarks mentioned in this work of fiction:

Acura: Honda Motor Co., Ltd.

Animal Planet: Discovery Communications, Inc.

Beck's: Brauerei Beck GmbH & Co. KG Kaiserbrauerei GmbH & Co. OHG

Ben & Jerry's: Ben & Jerry's Homemade Holdings, Inc.

Burger King: Burger King Brands, Inc.

Cheerios: General Mills, Inc.

Dumpster: Dempster Brothers, Inc.

Giorgio: Giorgio, Inc.

Grand Marnier: Societe Des Produits Marnier-Lapostolle

Heineken: Heineken Brouwerijen B.V. Private Limited Company

Hershey's: Hershey Foods Corporation

Honda: Honda Motor Co., Ltd.

Hoover: The Hoover Company

Incredible Hulk, The: Cadence Industries Corporation d.b.a. Marvel Comics Group

James Bond: Danjaq S.A.

Kansas City Chiefs: Kansas City Chiefs Football Club, Inc.

Looney Tunes: Warner Bros., Inc.

M&M's: Mars, Incorporated

Mercedes: Daimler Chrysler AG Corporation

Oreo: Kraft Foods Holdings, Inc.

Oscar: Academy of Motion Picture Arts and Sciences Corporation

Reeboks: Reeboks Sports Limited

Road Runner: Time Warner Entertainment Company, L.P.

Sooners: The Board of Regents of the University of Oklahoma

Sprite: Coca-Cola Company, The

Suburban: General Motors Corporation

Tiffany: Tiffany & Company

Viagra: Pfizer, Inc.

Wendy's: Wendy's International, Inc.

Wheaties: General Mills, Inc.

Wile E. Coyote: Time Warner Entertainment Company, L.P.

Prologue

Maybe he should call Dad.

Barrett fidgeted with the candy-wrapper bracelet Kristi Farnham had fastened on him at recess, scooting it around his tanned wrist over and over as he stared at the white-painted panels of his parents' bedroom door. The only sound in the sun-speckled hallway was his own loud breathing. He'd knocked and yelled at her about four thousand times, but Mom wouldn't answer.

Riding his bike home from school today, all he'd wanted was to Hoover down the rest of the Oreos with about a gallon of milk and watch cartoons. Now all he wanted was for his mom to open this door and tell him everything was okay.

Why wouldn't she answer him? She never slept through the baby crying. Even when she was having a really bad day, she never just let him cry.

When Barrett bounded through the front door a while ago, he'd heard his little brother screaming his head off and found him right here in the hall. Dusty must have finally made it over the gate because there was a big carpet burn on his forehead. Barrett had picked him up and hugged him, rocking and talking to him until he calmed down. Then he'd taken him downstairs and planted him in front of the Looney Tunes with some Cheerios on a paper towel and a sippy cup of milk.

He'd been up here trying to wake Mom up ever since, but she wouldn't and his stomach was starting to hurt. His knuckles were hurting, too, even though he'd switched hands a couple of times.

He gave the doorknob one last try but it was still locked. "Mom!"

Not knowing what else to do, he headed back downstairs on shaky legs and wiped his palms on his jeans before picking up the telephone in the kitchen. Gripping the receiver hard, he ran a finger up the phone list on the wall and dialed the third number from the top.

"Good afternoon, Mahoney, George and Butcher, how may I help you?"

"May I please speak to Anthony George?" Barrett winced. He'd used his most grown-up voice but he still sounded like a ten-year-old kid who was about to start bawling.

"May I tell him who's calling, please?"

"His son, Barrett."

"Hi, Barrett. Hold for just a moment and I'll put you through."

It seemed like he spent forever twirling the kinked-up phone cord around his index finger before his dad answered.

"Hey, big boy—what's cookin'?"

Relieved to hear that friendly greeting, Barrett blurted, "Mom's asleep and she won't open the door."

"Did you knock?"

"About five million times. Dusty got over the gate, 'cause he was on the floor screamin' in the hall and I got him some milk, but Mom still won't wake up."

"Did you open the door and look at Mom?"

Barrett's stomach squeezed. Dad didn't sound so friendly now.

"It's locked."

"Son, listen to me." His dad talked really fast now. "Police and firemen are on their way to you right now, and I want you to let them in, okay? I'll be there in five minutes."

He didn't even say goodbye.

Barrett hung the phone up and trailed into the living room. Dusty was climbing the stairs, so he picked him up and carried him back over by the TV. There were Cheerios all over the carpet and the napkin was shredded.

"Hey, don't eat that," he groaned, swiping a ball of chewed-up paper towel out of his brother's drooly mouth with a finger and wadding it up in the scraps. "Don't worry—Dad'll be here soon and everything will be okay."

Everything will be okay. Why didn't he believe that? He had a bad ache in his stomach, like last Christmas when he'd puked up his guts and had the Hershey squirts for two whole days. Mom had been acting really weird for a long time, almost since the baby was born, and he missed her being happy. He missed her shooting hoops with him and watching him wrestle and singing that dumb song about the teddy bears having a picnic. All she did now was cry and yell and hide in her bedroom.

The Roadrunner led Wile E. Coyote over the edge of another cliff, but Barrett could hardly breathe, much less laugh. His eyes kept wandering to the stairs. What was taking the firemen so long?

Suddenly his dad slammed into the house. Leaving the front door hanging open, he raced past both of them and took the steps two or three at a time. Dusty tried to follow, so Barrett scooped him up and started after his dad.

He was on the second step when he heard a loud crash. Tightening his grip on the baby, he hauled butt up the stairs.

"Oh God, no!" his dad cried. "Jesus, Karen, please no!"

Barrett was running now, huffing with the weight of the toddler in his arms, fear turning his bowels to water. It was really bad, he knew it was really bad. Stumbling over the splintered bedroom door on the floor, he landed in the middle of the room and stared into the master bath.

"Jesus Christ, Karen, why? Why? Oh God, why would you do this?" His dad was hugging his mom on the bathroom floor, and he was bawling, too. "I love you so much, Karen, please don't leave me!"

Mom didn't have any clothes on and there was red stuff all over the place. Was it blood? Barrett couldn't see her face behind Dad's chest, but she wasn't moving.

"Mommy?" He was too big to call her Mommy and he never did any more, but he was so scared…

"Barrett!" His dad looked up at him, his face twisted and red. "Oh God, son, please take Dustin downstairs and tell the firemen where we are."

Barrett didn't want to go. He took a step toward the bathroom, the baby in his arms fussing at being squeezed so hard. "Is Mom dead?"

"Barrett, don't look! Just go tell—"

Masculine voices calling out and the thunder of running feet echoed up the stairs, but he couldn't take his eyes off his mom's body, so limp and white on his father's lap, until he was shoved out of the way by all the men who crowded into the bathroom.

His dad came out and plucked Dusty from his arms. Sinking to his knees, he held them both tight against him. His clothes were all wet and smeared with red, and he smelled weird and he was shaking so bad…

"Oh God, Barrett, I'm so sorry," he sobbed against Barrett's neck. "So sorry."

Barrett's stomach twisted as he stood there watching the men try to save his mother. It was too late. He knew it. He'd waited too long.

Tears burned in his eyes and he blinked hard. It wouldn't do any good to cry now—she was gone. His mom was gone and she was never coming back.

Swallowing the sickness in his throat, Barrett wiped the back of his hand over his mouth and felt Kristi's bracelet scrape his cheek. Without bothering to look at it, he tore the braided cellophane off his wrist and let it tumble down his father's back to the floor.

Chapter One

෨

Hotels were just like people—you couldn't tell from the way they looked that something was seriously wrong inside.

Shifting his Suburban into park, Barrett left the engine running while he inspected the Mahoney Tower Tulsa. Sunlight reflecting off the building's copper windows made him squint even through his sunglasses, but from what he could see, it looked like business as usual. A few cabs and a limo were lined up in the parking circle, and a uniformed attendant manned the valet stand despite the brutal heat of an August afternoon. If the lush, manicured lawns and blossoming flower beds were any indication, other employees were hard at work, too.

That didn't mean there wasn't some kind of weird shit going down in the hotel.

Glancing at the dashboard clock, he put on his regular glasses and stowed the sunglasses in the overhead compartment. Then he gathered up the employee files from the passenger seat and shoved them into his soft-side briefcase. He'd had to skim them on the drive from Kansas City, since he'd barely walked in the door when Carla dropped the case in his lap, but judging from what he'd read, there was probably more going on here than just the disappearance of the general manager.

His stomach rumbled. Too bad he hadn't stopped for something to eat on the way down. Burger King beckoned from across the street, but it was too late now. The staff meeting had started ten minutes ago. Not that he minded being late—employees' reactions to his tardiness were always interesting—but he wanted to look around the common areas before he made his appearance.

Tucking the briefcase behind the passenger seat, he braced himself and shut off the engine. Without cool air blasting him from the vents, he broke into a sweat before he even got the door open. Shit, and he'd thought Kansas City was bad. Why couldn't it have been the San Francisco manager who disappeared? Or Seattle? The coast was great this time of year.

By the time he made it through the revolving door, sweat was rolling down his temples. Fortunately, the lobby felt like a meat locker. It was a wonder his glasses didn't fog over in the chill.

Whistling through his teeth, he shoved his hands into his pockets and took a little stroll around the main level. The Tower was scheduled for a facelift next winter, but it still looked pretty damn sharp. From the high, coffered ceiling to the marble-tiled floor, everything gleamed like it was well taken care of. Shiny greenery fluttered in the breeze from the fountain, the cherry furniture in the conversation groups glowed from a recent polishing—hell, even the nap on the area rugs stood at attention like it had never been walked on.

The scents of lemon oil and coffee filled the air, and as he passed Mirabella, his stomach growled urgently at the savory aroma drifting from the restaurant's closed doors. Damn, he didn't know what was cooking, but he sure as hell knew where he was eating tonight.

The elevator dinged and the doors slid open. Inside, a blonde in a cheap business suit was too busy putting on lipstick to get out, so like the gentleman he occasionally was, Barrett stuck a hand out to keep the doors from closing. When she saw him in the mirror, her eyes widened. Rolling her lips as she put the cap on the tube, she looked his reflection over thoroughly before turning.

"Hi," she said with a seductive smile, dropping the lipstick into her purse.

He grinned back. "Isn't this your floor?"

"Not if you don't want it to be."

"Honey, this is definitely your floor." Barrett let his smile grow hard and hers disappeared at once.

"I was just leaving," she said as she swept by.

She didn't look back but strutted directly through the front door to a waiting cab. Barrett rolled his eyes at the cloud in her wake. Nothing said "working girl" like a shitty Giorgio knockoff, and hell if she didn't smell like she'd just bathed in the stuff—right after she humped the Chiefs' starting lineup. Hopefully some punk would be kind enough to put a bullet in him before he got that desperate for sex.

"Can I help you, sir?"

Barrett focused on the front desk. The spit-shined coed behind the counter wore a pleasant smile, but she watched him with wary eyes. He didn't blame her. His monogram wasn't BIG for nothing, and he probably looked like he was sizing up the joint for a robbery. The girl's stock went up a couple more points when he realized her finger was poised over the alarm button.

"I'm Barrett George."

Her eyes flickered over his clothes. "Oh, I'm sorry," she said. "I didn't recognize the— I mean, we expected you at..."

Pink bloomed in her cheeks and he grinned. "No problem—I'm used to it. So, no Friday casual around here, huh?"

"No, sir." She reached for the phone. "The rest of the staff is up in Summerhall F. I'll call up there and—"

"Thanks, but I'll head up and introduce myself in a minute." He ambled over and rested an elbow on the desk's cool, polished surface. Checking out her nametag, he said, "So Amanda, did you see the lady who just left?"

"Hand-me-down suit, loud purse, slutty shoes?"

He stifled a smile. There was nothing wrong with her powers of observation.

"That would be the one," he said. "Is she here a lot?"

She bit her lip. "Define a lot."

I'll take that as a yes.

"Never mind. Any word on Alderton?" At her mute headshake, he straightened and touched his fingers to his brow in a small salute. "Carry on."

Since his knee was stiff from the long drive, he bypassed the elevators and headed up the curving staircase, wondering what other nasty little surprises awaited him. That rumble in his stomach was turning to a burn, so he pulled a roll of antacids from his pocket and peeled off a couple, grimacing as he chewed them up. He liked wintergreen, but all they'd had at the convenience store this morning was fruit-flavored.

At the top of the stairs, Barrett hung a left into the conference wing and headed down the hall. Voices drifted from the open door to Summerhall F, so he slowed his approach to get a preview of the conversation.

"I don't know how long he's going to be here," a whiskey-smooth female voice declared. "All they said is that Mr. George will be the interim GM while a new management team is assembled."

That had to be the hotel's accountant, Jillian Fox. He took a covert look around the door frame and nearly purred in appreciation. A redhead, his favorite flavor. She leaned against a table at the front of the room, her posture patently defensive. Though her short-sleeved shirt was buttoned almost to her throat, her crossed arms framed a promising abundance of feminine flesh, and her trim calves stretched a long way between the conservative hem of her business skirt and a pair of low-heeled pumps.

Tall, stacked, and a redhead—shit, it was like he'd phoned in his order ahead of time. Too bad they were working together. Maybe after he'd wrapped up this case, he'd spend a night or two unwrapping her.

"What's that supposed to mean, *new management team?*" a man asked. The asshole tone raised Barrett's hackles, but he couldn't get a look at the speaker without revealing his presence. "What the hell's the matter with the old management team?"

Jillian's eyes bugged as she threw her hands up. "*What* management team, Darwin? Our general manager's been AWOL for almost a week now and we haven't had an assistant manager in over three months."

Ah, Darwin Patton. His was one of the files that had caught Barrett's attention.

"Hey, money lady, don't get all snooty on me. We have a tight team right here and this place is running just fine without some corporate fancy-pants sticking his nose into things." After a few murmurs of agreement, he continued, "Why'd you have to go and call them, anyway? We'll probably all be out on the street looking for another job once this new team shows up."

"Gee, I don't know—maybe because the pay period ends next week and there's no one in-house to sign our checks?"

"You could have signed them."

Barrett's brows went up. Hell of a suggestion from the security chief.

"The last time I checked, forgery was against the law, Darwin, but thanks for the vote of confidence."

"Oh, come on. It's not like you'd be—"

"Drop it, Darwin."

There was a little grumbling and then someone said, "Miss Fox?"

"Yes, Berta?"

"Can you tell us anything about Mr. George?"

Barrett was tempted to step in, but he made himself wait. Jillian Fox had handled the security twit without any help and he was reasonably sure she wouldn't blow his cover. Besides, he wanted to hear what she had to say about him.

* * * * *

Jillian shook her head at Berta's question. "I've never met the man."

"But have you heard anything?" Mike asked.

Actually, she'd heard from one of the executive secretaries in Kansas City that the hotshot investigator they were sending down had a reputation for being a hard-core player, but she wasn't inclined to pass on that bit of news, especially at a staff meeting. And since Barrett George apparently wanted to play secret agent man, she even had to keep the fact that he was a hotshot investigator to herself.

It really *was* lonely at the top.

"Not a word," she said flatly. "I assume the executive suite is ready, Berta?"

"Sorry I'm late," came a deep baritone from the door.

Jillian jumped to her feet, silently cursing the heat that rushed to her cheeks. A mountainous man in horn-rimmed glasses and a polo shirt was strolling toward her, his hands shoved into his pants pockets. Good Lord, Abby had said he was tall, but she hadn't mentioned he was built like a linebacker. She'd expected more of a low-rent James Bond, but obviously her concept of a hard-core player needed updating.

Maybe Abby had meant to say hard-core *football* player — the guy had definitely been eating his Wheaties.

But no, she'd said specifically, and with obvious relish, that he was a breast man, a detail that had taken some of the shine off Jillian's excitement at finally getting a little help down here. She'd been tearing her hair out for weeks and the last thing she needed was some corporate Lothario talking to her chest for an indefinite period. Her mother had always been flattered when good-looking guys couldn't drag their eyes from her cleavage long enough to notice she had a brain, but nothing turned Jillian off faster.

Except maybe being spied on. How long had he been out in the hall listening to them talk?

Swallowing, she forced a smile. "Mr. George, I presume?"

"Live and in person." His disarming grin was no doubt designed to put everyone at ease, but it made her wish she'd worn her blazer. "You must be Jillian Fox."

He pulled a sun-browned hand from the pocket of his khakis and offered it to her. Fighting the urge to wipe her damp palm on her skirt first, she shook it firmly.

Unbelievably, his bright green gaze remained firmly focused on her face. She'd totally psyched herself up to ignore a subtle but insulting inspection of her figure and hide her distaste for the man behind a plastic smile. The fact that he seemed more interested in deciphering her expression threw her off big-time, and she lowered her gaze to his square chin in self-defense.

It was stubbly. Either he hadn't shaved today or he was one of those guys who had to do it twice a day. The masculine shadow went halfway down his thick neck, and below, a smattering of dark hair sprouted in the open collar of his shirt. The way the hunter-green cotton hugged his wide shoulders and round biceps left no doubt that he was in very good—

Her eyes widened as they jerked back up to his. Oh hell. She'd been checking him out, and the amusement sparkling in his eyes said he'd definitely noticed.

Talking while she ground her teeth wasn't easy, but she pulled it off. "Nice to meet you, sir."

"Call me Barrett."

I don't think so.

Jillian straightened her spine and pulled her fingers free of his, reaching immediately for the bulky ring of keys on the table.

"Tag—you're it." She dropped them into his hand and headed for the rear of the conference room. She could feel his gaze boring into her back, and though she'd been walking successfully for nearly thirty years, she became excruciatingly aware of her gait. Trying to minimize the sway of her hips, she slipped into a glide step, only to realize it didn't work nearly as well in pumps as it had in her marching shoes.

Crap! This was just one more reason why she'd never even considered entering a pageant. The minute she was the center of attention, things that she usually did by rote—things like walking and breathing—suddenly took intense concentration.

Just walk, for God's sake – it's not that hard!

Since most of the aisle seats were occupied, it took an eternity to reach a vacant row. She slipped into a chair at the back and put her hands together in her lap to still their trembling while she tried to get her breathing under control. What in the world was wrong with her? He was just a man. A *womanizer*. She had no business letting him affect her this way. After all, she had another date tomorrow night with Paul Danner, the doctor of her dreams. She should be concentrating on letting *him* affect her this way.

"Pretty quiet around here today," Mr. George commented. He stood right where she left him, both hands in his pockets once more.

Mike held up a hand. "Michael Greeley, sales. We've got two large groups checking in after six."

"Guess I'd better make this quick, then—thanks, Michael."

He flashed a toothpaste-commercial smile and Jillian's heart skipped a beat. She tried to fix Paul's kind, patient face in her mind's eye and was dismayed to realize she couldn't quite recall it.

"Hi, I'm Barrett George," he continued. "I'm a Scorpio, I've got a degree from Notre Dame, and my turn-ons are contact sports, horror novels and imported beer. My pet peeves are square pizza, round ice cubes and telemarketers who think my name is George Barrett. I've been with MGB for almost five years now and I look forward to getting to know all of you. Any questions?"

There were a few muted giggles and snorts, but no one said anything.

"Moving on. Has anyone heard anything from Arlen Alderton?"

Jillian didn't expect any affirmative responses but glanced around anyway. Everyone looked studiously ignorant.

"All right, then is anyone having any problems that I need to address immediately?"

After all the crap Darwin had given her, she'd expected him to jump right in with a list of grievances, but he just sat there trying to look cagey.

"In that case, I'll just make a few comments and turn all of you except the department heads loose." He jingled whatever was in his pockets and then strolled across the front of the room, scanning the crowd as he talked. "First, I looked around on my way in and the hotel seems to be in great shape. Corporate will appreciate hearing that the mice kept right on working while the cat was away, and I mean *appreciate* in a way you can spend, come next payday."

"I can live with that." Phil's comment provoked a chorus of laughing agreements.

"Second, in order to make the transition as smooth as possible, I'm going to try and get things squared away here before the new management team arrives. To that end, I'll be making inspections and doing spot audits and interviews, in addition to the day-to-day stuff."

"So what kind of time frame are we looking at, Mr. George?" At the raised brow, Phil hurried to add, "Sorry, Phil Breton, F&B manager. I guess what I'm really asking is if any of us should be...considering other employment options."

"Definitely not, Phil—and I'd like everyone to call me Barrett. The Tower was already understaffed before Alderton jumped ship, so you really need the three managers they're sending down."

He held up a hand and the relieved hum of chatter ceased instantly.

"Last, at least for now, I'm going to put a brainstorm box in each of the employee locker rooms and ask you to stuff them full of ideas and concerns—if there's something you'd like me to know but don't feel comfortable talking about, put it there. Don't worry about how far-out an idea is or that I'll try to compare handwriting or use some new-fangled CSI gadget to track you down—I just want a little good old-fashioned honesty and ingenuity to spark some positive changes around here."

Jillian blinked. For an investigator posing as interim GM, the man was awfully proactive. And he certainly knew how to project an air of authority. Project, hell—he radiated authority. She'd seen his type before—he was a man who'd accomplish his goals, no matter what the cost, and wouldn't take no for an answer.

There was absolutely no reason why the idea should make her bones vibrate. He didn't appear to have set his amorous sights on her, and even if he did, she she'd never had any trouble saying no and making it stick.

"If no one else has any questions," he concluded, "everyone but department heads can take off."

Their gazes collided across the crowded meeting room and she sucked in a breath.

So why did she suddenly feel like taking every bit of her vacation time?

* * * * *

The department managers stayed in their seats as the rest of the employees filed out and Barrett had to work to keep his gaze from gravitating to Jillian. Or more specifically, to her chest.

Shit, he could spend hours at a time, *days* at a time, with his mouth latched onto tits like hers. No way in hell were they silicone—his brief glance when she'd dropped her gaze during their handshake had been enough to assure him of that. Succulent and round, they lay against her ribs like a pair of homegrown grapefruits and he'd had to clench his hands against the urge to test them for ripeness, to peel her out of that cotton blouse and get a taste of her nipples. Just one taste, just enough to hold him until he could get her into bed, enough to stave off the sexual starvation he'd endured for the last few weeks.

Barrett's stomach resumed its growling even as his cock stirred. The heartburn had cooled but he was hungry and horny, a potentially embarrassing state of affairs when he was standing up here addressing a crowd.

Willing away the sexual reaction, he waved the scattered managers forward. "Everyone move up here. This isn't church—you don't get to fill the back row first."

Jillian was slow to react, but she eventually took a seat behind the tall guy in a maintenance uniform.

Hiding from me.

This time it took concentrated effort to clamp down on the blood rushing to his cock. He could have felt her reluctance from the next county and it brought every predatory instinct he possessed screaming to life. She wanted to be chased and he was just fine with that. A lot of times, the chase was the most exciting part of a sexual interlude.

He sat fully on the table, disregarding its groan of protest at his weight.

"Okay, you all know who I am, now tell me who you are. And stand up so I can see you." That ought to make them all feel conspicuous enough to miss any movement behind his zipper. "Just name, department and length of service is fine—you don't have to tell me your turn-ons and pet peeves."

The security chief went first. Even if his attitude with Jillian hadn't already landed him on Barrett's bad side, the guy would have made a crappy impression. The self-important way he hitched up his duty belt when he stood called to mind Barney Fife, and when he announced his name and title, he looked around like he expected applause. It took every ounce of Barrett's self-control not to roll his eyes—Alderton must have been on mood-altering drugs when he hired this bozo.

Patton wasn't the only employee who rubbed him the wrong way. Something about the front desk lady and one of the F&B managers told him he was going to have plenty of background checks to run when he wasn't doing the GM shuffle. Issuing any necessary pink slips would be up to the new managers when the time came.

After everyone else had introduced themselves, he leaned way over to the side and raised his eyebrows at Jillian. She blinked back at him, tucking a stray curl behind her ear.

"But you already know who I am."

"Humor me."

It was hard not to grin when she half-stood, still fiddling with that curl, and mumbled her introduction in a quick monotone before slouching even lower behind the maintenance chief. She looked annoyed, which produced a big twitch in his boxers. Okay, so maybe he wouldn't wait until he'd wrapped things up here to do a little Fox hunting.

"So here's the plan," he said, casually pulling his sore leg up and resting his ankle on the opposite knee. "For now, I'd like us all to meet every morning at ten—not for long, just fifteen minutes or so—to touch base and share any developments. I also want to have lunch with each of you, one-on-one, so that we can get acquainted and discuss any concerns that you might have. I assume Alderton had a secretary who's still holding down the fort?"

"Penny Rutherford, and yes, she's still carrying on with whatever she can." Jillian's muffled comment drifted to him.

"Excellent. She's my secretary now, so everyone needs to call her and make an appointment. That'll be all for today." Of course, his retiring little accountant was the first to beat a path to the door. "Jillian, if I could see you for a moment, please…"

She froze and then stepped to the side without turning so that the rest of them could get by.

"I'll tell Penny to reserve the first appointment for you," he told her as he sauntered over. Peering into the hall to make sure everyone was out of earshot, he continued, "Since you're the only one who's in on my investigation, I'd like to set up some strategies for gathering information."

She finally turned to look up at him. "I usually bring my lunch. We could just take a few minutes in your office sometime."

Amused by her continued resistance, he was opening his mouth to push back when she let her eyes fall away from his. It almost looked like she was bowing her head in deference, and out of nowhere, the word *submissive* whispered over his nerve endings.

Barrett stiffened. Oh hell, was she into the lifestyle? Did she think that just because he had a domineering personality, he was a Dom?

The idea gave him the heebie-jeebies. Not that he didn't enjoy bending a feisty lover to his will once in a while, but he'd dabbled in the scene enough to know that dominating a real submissive came with the kind of responsibility that sucked all the fun out of it. As far as he was concerned, nothing killed a boner faster than looking into the worshipful eyes of a sub.

Testing the waters, he said in a firm tone, "We're meeting away from the hotel, Miss Fox."

Jillian's gulp was audible and, rather than flushing with excitement, she took on an unhealthy pallor under the freckles.

Okay, so she wasn't a sub, but Barrett frowned. Jesus, was she actually afraid of him? He'd caught her checking him out earlier and assumed that the attraction was mutually combustible, but maybe not. Maybe she was intimidated by his size. Hell, maybe his scars bothered her. It was a rare reaction, for some reason he had yet to figure out, but it happened.

His jaw tightened. Shit. Of all the times for a woman to be squeamish about his face. He really wanted to fuck her.

On the other hand, he was running an investigation here and she was a hotel employee, which made for a potential conflict of interest. His quick glance at her employment record hadn't raised any red flags, but you never knew. It wouldn't be the first time an employee had blown the whistle on some illegal activity in order to preempt an investigation and divert suspicion away from herself.

Fuck. Why hadn't he thought of that before he let his hormones run amok? Time to put his aching balls on ice, at least for the moment. Once he had a better picture of what was going on around here, he'd explore whether or not getting Miss Jillian Fox into the sack was a salvageable proposition.

But he was damned if he'd back off his declared intention to meet alone with her now. That would set a shitty precedent.

"Make the appointment for Monday, Jillian."

She nodded. When she continued to stand there like a prisoner facing the firing squad, he sighed and reached to flip the row of switches, throwing the room into semi-darkness. "You can go now."

She was out the door before the echo of his words died.

* * * * *

Her watery knees barely made it around the corner before giving way. Jillian sank against the wall, hands folded over her fluttering stomach, and took a few deep breaths.

Shit! So much for being able to say no and make it stick. She'd caved to his will like a sandcastle in the surf. Now she really wished she could take her vacation time. If he made up his mind to go after her, she was so doomed.

"Miss Fox, are you feeling all right?"

She jumped, swallowing a squeal. Berta Martinez stood at her elbow, her round face creased in concern. "I'm fine, Berta." More deep breaths. "Just hungry—you know, low blood sugar, stuff like that. I'll be fine after I get a snack."

"Oh, you poor little thing!" Berta gripped her arm and dragged her down the hall. *Poor little thing.* The woman had to be kidding—she was the one who needed a stool to put paper towels in the dispensers. Jillian tried dragging her feet, but Berta was having none of it, pulling her along until they reached the vending machines. Gesturing at one, she said, "You get something in your stomach right now. That low blood sugar can be dangerous. I know—I've been a diabetic for ten years."

"Honestly, I—"

"Here." Berta dug a dollar out of her skirt pocket and shoved it into a slot. "You pick out something."

Sighing in defeat, Jillian turned and studied the selections. Normally she bought pretzel sticks or baked potato chips, but—

Her stomach growled suddenly. Gee, maybe she really *was* having a blood sugar issue.

Drawing another deep breath, she began to relax. Something sweet sounded good for a change.

"Okay—thanks, Berta. I owe you a dollar."

Shaking off the sense of impending disaster, she pushed the button and watched as the package of M&Ms cranked forward on its spindle. It hesitated at the end for a moment and she held her breath in dismay. The degree of relief she felt when it finally toppled over and fell into the tray was so ridiculous, she laughed out loud.

"That was a close one!" she cried.

Berta looked at her like she had a screw loose, so Jillian mumbled her thanks and grabbed the M&Ms. After tearing the corner off the package, she set out for her office, popping the chocolates into her mouth one at a time.

As she walked and nibbled, the shaky sensations in her legs and stomach began to ease and she held up the little brown bag, eyeing it with new respect. She was feeling more like herself already.

Doomed, she snorted. What kind of attitude was that? She was a fighter. Okay, usually in a fairly passive way, but she was fighter. Barrett George was nothing more than a temporary nuisance and all she needed to deal with him was a temporary plan.

Maybe she'd just have to avoid being alone with him for the next couple of weeks. That shouldn't be too hard, since there was a mile-high stack of work on Mr. Alderton's desk awaiting his attention. And she'd accumulated a lot of sick days over the past three years—no reason she couldn't take one or two if the need arose. She'd just do her best to fly under his radar and hope that he'd forget she existed.

She almost pumped her fist in the air as she pushed open her office door. *Yes!* She had a plan. Life was always better when you had a plan.

Smiling as she plopped down in her executive chair, she poured a dozen or so of the colorful little candies into her palm and tossed them all into her mouth at once.

Chapter Two

The screen was starting to blur, so Barrett tossed his glasses on the desk and heaved a big sigh as he scrubbed his hands over his face.

Shit. He'd sifted through thousands of emails since six o'clock this morning and found nothing. Not the good kind of nothing, anyway. Judging by the lack of chatter in the days after Alderton pulled his disappearing act, a lot of employees knew a lot more than they were telling. Corporate would be thrilled.

Slouching deeper into the leather chair, he yawned and stretched before lacing his fingers behind his head. There was only one email folder left unopened, and something in him balked at going there. Reading Jillian's email would just give her one more reason to dislike him. She already avoided him like a dental drill, bailing on meetings and calling in sick and his gut told him it didn't have anything to do with Alderton. In fact, she appeared to be the only employee besides Penny who'd made any effort to track the guy down.

No, this was something personal, an idea that both annoyed him and turned him on. After Jillian skipped work on Monday, he'd tried to dial back the forcefulness and play up the teamwork angle with her, but it hadn't put her any more at ease. Hell, she'd even found herself a hotel blazer to hide behind and worn it every day in the middle of a brutal fucking heat wave.

What was she so afraid of? Had his reputation proceeded him? If so, which one? He had a history of cleaning house in both boardrooms and bedrooms.

Then again, what if his gut was wrong? What if her avoidance tactics *did* have something to do with Alderton's disappearance? Was he getting so egocentric that he imagined every woman in the world quaked in fearful anticipation of his oversized charms?

Snorting, he slipped his glasses back onto his nose and nudged the mouse to cancel the screensaver. Jillian knew he was conducting an investigation, and she wasn't stupid—she had to expect that he'd check her out just as thoroughly as he did the other employees.

Not surprisingly, her inbox was empty. Even when she didn't show up at the office, she was efficient.

A scan of the subject lines in her deleted file made him grin, and he clicked on the latest series of messages.

From: Cherry Fields
To: Jillian Fox
Subject: Condolences on the Big 3-0!

You know I'm kidding, sweetie! Today is the official first day of your sexual prime, and something tells me the arrival of the Big Guy is anything but a coincidence. Speaking of which—is your little chocolate binge showing any sign of letting up? ;-)

I'm sorry about missing your concert tonight. Now that Roly-Foley is planning on "helping" me with the open house—yeah, right—I'm half-tempted to duck out. I would, if I hadn't put so much work into selling this monster. (Sigh.) Oh, well. Why don't we just have lunch at the Tower today? You know how the heat and humidity bring out the beast in your hair.

C

From: Jillian Fox
To: Cherry Fields
Subject: Re: Condolences on the Big 3-0!

Thanks, I think. And nice try, Cher, but I can see right through you—I'm not letting you within a mile of this hotel until he's gone. I don't trust either of you. Let's just stick with the plan, okay? (And would you please not peddle your harebrained sexual theories on the company server? You never know who's rummaging around in here.)

Dr. Egan just emailed me—the concert's been postponed because of HVAC issues. He tried to move it outdoors… OMG, can you imagine the headlines? Heatstroke on the Brown! Dozens Dead, Hundreds Hospitalized—Conductor Declared Non Compos Mentis! <g>

Anyway, I'm going to stay home and play beautiful music to my hair. Think that'll tame it?

J

From: Cherry Fields
To: Jillian Fox
Subject: Re: Condolences on the Big 3-0!

Of course the heat wouldn't bother Dr. E—it looks like he and King Tut used the same embalmer. <g>

And fine, have it your way—Manuelo's at 1:00. AGAIN. You never let me have any fun! One of these days, come hell or bad hair, I AM going to meet the Big Guy. How else can I offer you any meaningful advice about how to handle him? And no, I don't think anything could tame your hair.

C

From: Jillian Fox
To: Cherry Fields
Subject: Re: Condolences on the Big 3-0!

I already know how to handle him—with great caution, and preferably from a great distance.

J

Barrett sprawled back in the chair again, his grin widening.

I don't trust either one of you.

Anticipation kicked him right where he liked it best, and he let fingers slide down his fly to press on his tightening balls. Trust, he could live without—sex, he couldn't, and it looked like relief was finally in sight. Yeah, the starchy little redhead was into him after all. Fighting it tooth and nail, but definitely into him.

He scanned those telling little messages again, trying to read more between the lines than he already had. Assuming he was the Big Guy in question—and come on, who else could it be?—the two women had obviously discussed him before. The reference to Jillian's chocolate fetish was damn intriguing. He'd noticed that she downed M&M's with a frequency that would eventually transform her from voluptuous to voluminous if she didn't watch it, but he hadn't suspected it had anything to do with him.

Until now.

His grin erupted into a chuckle. What a chump! He'd known from the start the attraction was mutual, but he'd second-guessed himself and let her get away with playing her little game of hide and seek, put his gonads in the deep freeze thinking she really couldn't stand him.

Well, she could consider that game officially over because what he'd just read was initiating a major meltdown. If he were smart, he'd wait until this assignment was winding down to pursue her, but he was already feeling the strain of going too many weeks without a good, hard fuck.

Trolling at nearby bars hadn't provided any relief—the only halfway appealing women had required more effort than he cared to put forth after a sixteen-hour day. As a result, he'd spent the last few nights gnawing on antacids and jerking off to some extremely raw fantasies of a certain red-headed accountant.

Jillian was probably smart not to trust him, especially if she was looking for a ring. *Crappily ever after* was not on his agenda. But the kind of sexual energy that arced between them didn't come along every day and he was damned if he'd let a few prissy ideas on her part put a damper on it. He needed to get past her defenses, and armed as he was with this inside information...

Barrett grinned. He was going to nail her to the wall.

* * * * *

Jillian let her forehead thump onto her desk with a groan, and then did it twice more, trying to shake out a few petrified brain cells. In the past two hours, she'd combed through last month's F&B receipts three times and still couldn't figure out where the shortage was coming from. Normally she wouldn't sweat forty dollars so heavily, but this was the fourth such incident this month. Something was screwy somewhere.

"Are you all right, Jillian?"

"Mr. George!"

She jerked upright and started shuffling her chaotic financial reports. The Big Guy stood in the doorway, watching her.

"You caught me," she managed to joke without blushing. "I was just punishing the receipts for being forty dollars off."

"Oh yeah?" He looked amused, just as she'd intended. He also strolled into her office and eased his massive frame into one of her conference chairs, which she'd not intended at all. "What would you do to them if it was forty thousand?"

"I'd spread them on the pool deck and dive onto them from the penthouse balcony."

"That'd show 'em, wouldn't it?"

"Well, sometimes you just have to let them know who's boss." She reached out to snag a couple of M&M's from the bowl on her desk as he stretched out his long legs and folded his hands over his belly and generally made himself right at home in her space.

"Funny you should say that. I was just thinking the same thing on my way to your office."

Jillian gulped down her half-chewed candy and watched him warily.

"You were?"

"Mmm-hmm." He leaned forward in the chair, elbows on his knees, and for the first time, she noticed the pale, jagged scars that crisscrossed the upper part of his face. His shaggy dark hair covered some of them, and the bulky glasses and aggressive nose had a way of distracting the eye, but she still couldn't believe she'd overlooked such extensive scarring. He was obviously no stranger to pain, a concept that suddenly made him seem even more dangerous.

"Take you, for instance," he continued.

"Me?" *Uh-oh.*

"You." His celery-green eyes, magnified slightly by the lenses, were unblinking as they snared hers. "If I've got my facts straight, Penny has set up a lunch interview for us twice in the last week and both times you've begged off."

Jillian grabbed a whole handful of M&M's and started popping them into her mouth one by one as she tried to think which tack to take here. If she weren't certain it would cause her a lot more grief, she'd remind him very politely that he wasn't really her boss.

"I did notify her in advance that I wouldn't be able to make it yesterday. And I had a family emergency on Monday."

"That doesn't change the fact that you're the only department head I haven't gotten acquainted with over lunch."

How could she argue with that? She could hardly tell him the truth, that getting acquainted with a man like him was rock-bottom on her list of fun things to do. Lower than visiting her brother in the state pen. Lower than getting a pelvic exam. Lower, even, than having her taxes audited. The last week had done nothing to lessen her bone-deep conviction that getting further acquainted with Barrett George would be hazardous to her mental health.

"I was the first one you talked to when you got here." She flashed a conciliatory smile. "And we've talked every day since then, except for Monday. We're as acquainted as we're going to get." She sucked in a breath. "What I mean is, we're as acquainted as anyone here."

He cocked an eyebrow at her. "If that were true, you wouldn't still be calling me Mr. George. And don't bother soft-pedaling the truth, Jillian. You meant what you said the first time."

Shit, shit, shit! So much for flying under his radar.

"Mr. Alderton felt that a certain level of formality helps employees to better maintain a proper customer service attitude," she defended.

"Mr. Alderton is a stupid fuck on a power trip," he countered with a pointed look. "If he'd gotten a little friendlier with his staff, we might have a better idea of what he's been up to and where he's gone."

That might be true, but his unprofessional use of profanity made her teeth clench. His use of that particular word made something entirely different clench. God, she'd put off having sex way too long if just hearing the man say it had that kind of effect on her. She should have jumped on Paul Danner while she had the chance last weekend. If there'd ever been a time to throw caution to the wind and put the moves on a man, that was it.

But had she? Hell no. When his hesitant kiss on her front porch had failed to elicit any clenching except that of her fingers on the doorknob, they'd said goodnight there.

He hadn't asked her for a third date.

"That's your opinion," she fired back.

"Yes, it is, and it's my opinion that should concern you at the moment, Miss Fox."

"Now who's on the power trip?"

His eyes narrowed and Jillian had to work not to bite her lip, had to work harder to maintain eye contact. She knew that was the wrong thing to say the minute the words left her mouth. Why, oh *why*, did he make her act so out of character? Defiance wasn't her thing. She was the helper, the diplomat, the woman with a knack for becoming invisible when the situation warranted—she would never purposely throw down the gauntlet in front of an arrogant bastard like him because there was just no way he wouldn't pick it up.

Her heart slammed against her ribs, two or three beats for every tick of the wall clock, and she wondered if he could hear it in the deafening silence that ensued.

"Evidently we haven't gotten to know each other at all," he said in a silky voice. "Perhaps you should consider having lunch with me today as a means of rectifying that."

Jillian winced. "I have a lunch date already."

"Ah." He sat back with a knowing nod. "That's right, it's your birthday, isn't it?"

"How did you know that?"

His smug look should have warned her.

"I read your e-mails."

"I beg your pardon?"

Jillian froze with disbelief, but her brain raced, trying to remember exactly what she and Cherry had talked about lately. The concert, her birthday, lunch…*him*. Good Lord, what had they said? She was pretty sure she hadn't mentioned him by name, but had Cherry been as careful?

"Yeah, but don't feel singled out. I've been through everyone's, looking for clues about what the hell's going on around here."

"Well, that just makes me feel so much better about it." She allowed annoyance to creep into her tone. Corporate investigator or not, he had no right to…

Okay, he had the right, darn it. *Note to self: No more personal mail on company server.* "Did you find anything incriminating?"

"Just that you're thirty today. And that your concert tonight has been canceled, which means you don't have any excuse to wiggle out of a dinner appointment instead of lunch."

His expression said he wouldn't take kindly to a refusal, but she couldn't seem to help herself.

"What if I've made other plans since then?"

It took every ounce of willpower she could muster to look him in the eye and not cringe in anticipation of his reaction.

Barrett George rose to his full, incredibly intimidating height and leaned over her desk, splaying his gigantic hands on the blotter. He kept on leaning until his face took up her entire field of vision and his coffee-tinted breath kissed her hot cheeks. Her fingers clutched the armrests and blood roared in her ears at the sensory overload. She desperately wanted to concede the staring contest, but found herself unable to.

Without looking away, he reached to his right and pressed several buttons on her phone, and she was impressed when his secretary actually answered on the intercom. As hard as she was shaking, she probably couldn't have hit the correct buttons looking right at them.

"Jillian can't make lunch today, Penny, but she's agreed to work me in tonight. Would you call Baylen Butcher at Chartreuse and ask if he could make room for us this evening?"

Jillian blinked twice. Uh-oh. That "work me in" had precipitated more than just clenching down there. God, she needed to find another suitable boyfriend, like yesterday.

"Sure, what time?" Penny asked.

"Six."

"I'll see what I can do."

He didn't move away after she disconnected.

"Let me give you a little tip, Miss Fox." He bared his textbook-straight teeth in a smile made all the more ominous by its brilliance. "Don't ever play poker with me. You'll lose your shirt."

* * * * *

Jillian fell into the relative dark of Manuelo's entry with a sigh of relief that would have ruffled her bangs, if they hadn't been plastered to her sweaty forehead. Once through the inner doors, she was blasted with a wave of air so cold it sent a chill down her spine. As unobtrusively as possible, she reached under the collar of her jacket and pulled the damp silk of her blouse away from her back.

Spying Cherry's shining blonde head in the far corner of the crowded dining room, she waved and brushed past the hostess with a quick smile.

"Okay, you win," she declared as she slid into her chair. "The next time it's over a hundred, we're eating at Mirabella."

Cherry grinned. "Oh, so I'll be the only one who has lunch looking like a wrung-out washrag."

"That'll be the day. You always look gorgeous."

Their waiter appeared almost immediately.

"The usual today, ladies?" he asked as he filled their water glasses.

"Yes, thanks."

"Cancel that, Tod," Cherry said, arching a perfect brow. "It's Jillian's birthday, so we're having blended margaritas."

"A margarita, then, no salt," Jillian said. "But I still want my chili rellanos."

Tod grinned at her. "The margarita's on the house for the birthday girl."

Cherry showed him her dimple. "What about mine?"

"Yours, too," he assured with a wink.

After he hustled off to put in their order, Jillian snagged a corn chip and dipped it in her salsa, eyeing the festive gift bag in the adjacent chair.

"Let me guess," she said, munching on the chip. "That's a crotchless panty set for the blind date you're setting me up with."

"Nope," Cherry said with a sly smile.

"No blind date or no crotchless panties?"

"Neither."

Tod returned and Jillian gnawed the inside of her lip while he served their margaritas. Twelve years with Cherry, first as college roommates and then as best friends, had taught her to be wary of those Mona Lisa smiles. She'd smiled like that during their junior year at OU, right before she got even with a two-timing boyfriend by plying him with tequila shooters until he passed out and then spray-painting his privates a nauseating shade of pea green.

Cherry lifted her glass. "So," she asked, taking a sip, "any news from Dr. Downer?"

"Danner," Jillian corrected with a frown. "And no, he hasn't still called—thanks for the reminder."

"He was all wrong for you anyway."

"Please. He was perfect for me."

"Perfectly boring," Cherry snorted. "Did he even have a pulse? I know I didn't after two minutes of conversation with him."

"Paul has a very soothing personality," Jillian defended.

"Snoozing, you mean."

"Oh, forget it." Jillian scowled as she took a big gulp of her margarita. She and Cherry had always had totally opposite tastes in men, but at least she had the grace to keep her opinions to herself.

"Okay, then how's the Big Guy today?"

Jillian narrowed her eyes. "I don't want to talk about him, either."

"You do, too."

"Excuse me?"

"Oh, come on," Cherry insisted. "You're dying to talk about him and you know it."

Jillian opened her mouth to deny it and then pursed her lips. Damn it, Cherry was right—she *was* dying to talk about him, but she had no idea where to begin.

Cherry sighed. "Jillian, why don't you just admit the man's hot and get it over with?"

"He's not hot," Jillian said uncertainly. "He's a player."

"Because he's *hot*."

Okay, so maybe it was stupid to keep denying it. "Your point, if you have one?"

"You're not your mother."

"I know that!"

"So why are you eating a pound of chocolate every day when what you really need is sex?" Jillian gasped, but Cherry blazed ahead, "You haven't gotten laid since college, Jill, and you need to do something about it."

"Sorry to interrupt, ladies," Tod broke in easily, sliding a steaming plate in front of Jillian. "But these are really hot."

God, they couldn't be any hotter than her cheeks at this moment. Staring down at her plate, she mumbled, "Thank you."

"Hey, no problem. Let me know if there's, uh...anything *else* I can do for you."

Jillian's eyes widened. Had he just made a pass at her?

She risked a peek from under her lashes and, sure enough, the sun-bronzed server was looking straight at her. His slow smile as he set Cherry's plate down froze the breath in her throat and she quickly dropped her eyes to her plate again.

"Ooh, remind me to leave him an extra tip," Cherry murmured as he walked away. Then she laughed out loud. "You should see the look on your face! Loosen up, Jill. I'll bet he could make you come, if you gave him a chance."

"Very funny," Jillian hissed, ripping her napkin off her silverware. "I don't need to come."

"Honey, I think that's exactly what you need. Do you remember the last time you went on a chocolate bender?"

"Yes, I do, and that has nothing to do with this. I was depressed then." She took a big bite of the cheesy Mexican potatoes, hoping the subject was closed.

No such luck.

"You were *depressed* because Evan Cowdery was a dud in the sack, and you needed to come then just as bad as you do now."

"Aren't you going to eat before it gets cold?" Jillian asked desperately.

"When I've said what I have to." Cherry did take the time to unwrap her silverware before continuing, "Jillian, what happened to your mother is not going to happen to you. Letting yourself enjoy some mind-blowing sex with a man isn't going to turn you into a nympho any more than drinking that margarita is going to turn you into an alcoholic. You just don't have an addictive personality."

Jillian ate more potatoes.

"But until you figure that out for yourself, I think you should at least try to take care of your needs with something other than chocolate." She grabbed the balloon-covered gift bag and set it on the table. "Which is why I bought you these."

Oh, great. There couldn't possibly be anything in there she wanted to see, much less take home. Ignoring the bag now, she took another swig of margarita before stuffing her mouth again.

"If you don't take it, I'm going to leave it here on the table for Tod to open."

Jillian swallowed the bite whole.

"I'll open it at home," she promised quickly. *Like hell.* If it was what she thought it was, she'd drop it in a Dumpster on her way home.

"There are several different kinds of dildos and vibrators in there," Cherry confirmed, "and before your eyes roll back in your head and you start foaming at the mouth, I want you to listen to me."

Jillian sighed. Did she have any choice?

"I don't know why you're so freaked about sex toys. I haven't been shy about the fact that I use mine on a regular basis, though you've never really believed it." At Jillian's skeptical look, she added, "See? Even now, you doubt me. I know you think I've got some *wow* guy tucked into every corner, but honestly, the pickings can get pretty slim sometimes, and like I've said over and over, a girl has to be willing to take matters into her own hands. If you can figure out what trips your own trigger, you'll have better luck helping some guy figure it out, too.

"So take these," she concluded, shoving the bag over farther, "in the spirit they're intended."

Jillian arched a brow. "Are you done?"

"For the moment."

"Good. Thank you," she added dutifully, setting the bag on the floor beside her chair.

"For the advice or for shutting up?"

"Take your pick."

Cherry's laugh turned several heads. "You know you love me," she said. "Oh, and don't throw that away without even looking. There are a couple of other things in there, too."

She started chatting about the evening's open house as she dug into her enchiladas and Jillian finally started to relax. Most of her meal was gone already and she'd barely tasted it. Oh well. The margarita was really good anyway.

She tensed immediately when Cherry said, "I feel really bad that you're going to spend your thirtieth washing your hair."

Oh hell. To tell or not to tell?

"Uh, my plans have changed a little," she said reluctantly. "Mr. George came to my office this morning and kind of strong-armed me into having dinner with him."

After a stunned silence, Cherry scolded, "Jillian Fox, that's the kind of thing you're supposed to tell me right away!"

Then she brightened. "But woo-hoo! I'm so excited for you. If he's the player you say his is, maybe you won't be needing my gifts after all."

She was damned no matter which way she responded to that one, so Jillian ignored it. "Didn't you hear me? The man coerced me into going out with him."

"Just out of the blue, huh? He's never asked you out before?"

"Um, not exactly."

"Um, what *exactly* does that mean? Has he or hasn't he?"

With a sigh, she explained about the aborted lunch dates.

Cherry grinned, shaking her head. "You do realize that only reinforced his determination to meet with you."

"I know. It was stupid, but I just…"

God, how could she explain a visceral reaction she didn't understand herself? Considering how this morning's little skirmish had ended up, the idea of having dinner with Barrett George had her on the verge of breaking out in hives.

"You just need to let him take you to bed, is what you just," Cherry said.

"Let him—" Jillian snapped out of her rumination. "For God's sake, Cherry, he invited me to dinner, not to look at his etchings. It's just a little get-acquainted session like he had with the rest of the department heads. He'll probably be in a hurry to dump me at the hotel so that he can go off and find a real date."

"Keep telling yourself that, Jill. Meanwhile, I hope you're wearing some decent panties." Her eyes sparkled. "I'm betting he's into them before the evening is over."

Refusing to react to that pulse-tripping wager, Jillian glanced at her watch with relief. "Much as I'd love to sit here and argue with you, I've got to get a move on or I'll be late." She tossed back the last of her margarita and stood up.

"Well then, don't forget that, just in case." Cherry pointed at the bag on the floor. "And Jillian…"

"What?"

"No M&M's. You'll spoil your appetite."

Chapter Three

At five o'clock, Jillian powered down her computer with a heartfelt sigh. The rest of her year had better be significantly less hellish than today or she might not make it to thirty-one. As if tussling with the financials, losing a battle of wills to the Big Guy, and being presented with an outlandish array of sex toys hadn't been enough to ruin her birthday, all that walking in the sticky heat had frayed her pantyhose and rubbed a fiery rash on the insides of her thighs. And the worst was yet to come, no doubt.

The smartest thing for her to do would be to sneak out of the hotel through the fire exit and never come back. She was supposed to meet Mr. George in his office at five-thirty, and at the moment she felt like a preschooler about to advance from playing with matches to handling weapons-grade plutonium.

Damn it, where was the Castleton file?

Pawing through the pile of bulging folders and unfinished reports on her credenza, she finally found the file and put it back in its hanger. God, she was losing it. She'd better pull her head out in time to blaze through payroll on Monday or she'd be pretty unpopular around here come Wednesday afternoon.

Jillian eyed the addictive little candies on her desk as she finished up the filing. *No M&M's, my ass.* She could probably devour the whole bowl without registering the slightest dip in her stress level.

Could it be true that eating so much chocolate was just sublimating her need for sexual fulfillment? It certainly seemed that no matter how much she ate the last few days, she never really felt satisfied, which was why she was considering switching to elastic waistbands and control-top hose.

But sex-starved or not, she was still dead certain that letting Barrett George anywhere near her would be the biggest mistake she could ever make. He supposedly wasn't even forty yet, but something in his eyes told her he'd already seen and done more than she would in a dozen lifetimes. He was a human iceberg, and the ten percent of him that showed was enough to scare the wits out her. Whatever was under the surface scared her even more.

Which didn't explain why everything south of her navel contracted with need every time she so much as thought about his huge, brawny body. Lord, she could be going down like the Titanic tonight.

Going down...

Uh, no. She was not going there. Ever.

She hoped.

God, she didn't even have to wonder if he was the type who would demand something like that — and insist on returning the favor. He'd obviously never met a boundary he didn't push.

Jillian sucked in a dismayed breath. Crap, her panties were getting wet just thinking about the coming evening.

The gift bag in her cargo hatch loomed large in her mind's eye and all at once she understood why a last-ditch effort to "take matters into her own hands" might have been an acceptable idea. Why hadn't she listened to Cherry sooner? She could have called in with a minor emergency and stopped at home, taken one of the godforsaken things out of the bag for a test drive.

Prurient curiosity had made her take an extended peek before tossing it into the back. A couple of the toys looked relatively unassuming, possibly non-invasive in nature, but the rest just blew her mind.

The rubbery replica of a penis, which she'd immediately dubbed Mt. Fleshmore because of its freakish size, seemed fairly straightforward in its purpose—*fill 'er up!* The second was less obvious. It was actually two bullet-shaped things attached by wires to a dual control, and she didn't even want to think about where they might fit. The last one was obviously designed for advanced users. Long and thick and made of tinted plastic, it was curved at the end and equipped with enough knobs, folds, nubbles and prongs to look...hazardous. And fascinating. What were they all for?

"Shit!"

Slamming the file drawer, she raced to lock the door, thankful, for once, that her office had no windows. She fumbled in her workout bag and pulled out a pair of plain but not-wet panties. It was humiliating and nerve-racking to have to wipe herself with tissues in the office—Mr. George carried that set of master keys with him at all times. But it was more private in here than in the public restroom down the hall.

Stuffing her wet panties and ruined hosiery in the bag, she tied her Reeboks and straightened her skirt.

She'd have to make damn sure they took separate vehicles. While she doubted the man would care to fold himself into her Honda, she wasn't taking any chances on his getting an eyeful of Cherry's gifts. The idea of riding in his Suburban might have been all right if she weren't suddenly so concerned about his effect on her in an enclosed space.

Definitely separate vehicles.

* * * * *

"We can take my Suburban," Barrett told her as they made their way down the curving staircase toward the lobby. A boisterous group was checking in and the noise level was unusually high. Jillian skirted the crowd, waving goodbye to the harried desk clerks with a sympathetic grin. He liked that she didn't hold herself apart from the entry-level staff.

"I thought we'd take both vehicles," she said firmly after they'd pushed through the revolving door.

Barrett crooked a smile. "If you insist."

Damn. He'd spent the last six hours alternately beating down a major hormone uprising and imagining everything he could do to her in the spacious confines of his SUV. Which meant it was probably for the best that she'd vetoed his suggestion.

Walking behind her across the blazing parking lot, Barrett took time to appreciate the view. He fell back a step and surveyed her from the tenuous knot of curly red hair at her nape to the oddly sexy sneakers she'd changed into. Even under that baggy jacket, she was enough to make him sweat.

Then it hit him — she'd lost her panty hose in the hours since lunch. Shit. Separate rides was definitely a smart idea. During his sophomore year in high school, a sheriff's deputy had caught him fucking a cheerleader in the back seat of her father's Mercedes and made him lean over the trunk with his shorts and underwear around his ankles while he made out his report. Knowing the cruiser's dashboard camera was probably recording a big ol' full moon had made Barrett smirk back then. It wouldn't be so amusing now.

"Oh, man! I can't believe this!"

Jillian was staring at her Honda's rear passenger tire, which was flatter than last night's Heineken.

"No biggie," he assured her. "I'll take care of it."

"I can't ask you to do that, Mr. George. I'm a big girl and I know how to change a tire."

"You didn't ask, Jillian, I offered, and if you don't quit calling me Mr. George, I'll have to do something about it."

He was almost disappointed when she didn't rise to the bait.

"Oh, fine — *Barrett*," she puffed crossly. "I can change my own tire, but thank you."

"That's better, but still not quite right. You're supposed to say, 'Thank you, Barrett, for changing my tire.'" He held up his hand when it looked like she was going to fuss at him. "Forget it, Jillian, there's no way I'm going to stand here and watch you change a flat in hundred-degree weather, and in a skirt, no less." Then he grinned. "Hell, I don't know why I'm even bothering to argue with you. I'll bet you can't even get the lug nuts off."

"Just watch me."

Jillian tossed her purse and workout bag through the passenger door, then shrugged out of her jacket and draped it over the seat. Stalking to the rear of the SUV, she yanked open the side-mounted door.

When a colorful bag toppled from the cargo area, she let out a muffled screech and dived for it like a defensive lineman after a loose ball. She managed to catch the bag just as her knees hit the ground, but the force of her grab sent its contents tumbling onto the hot concrete and skittering beneath her vehicle. Everything happened so fast, Barrett hadn't even begun to react when he saw the horse-hung dildo, still in its hard plastic wrapper, skid under her bumper.

For one excruciating instant, they both froze, Jillian on her knees and Barrett with his bugged-out eyes glued to the spot where that dildo had disappeared. He dragged his gaze upward with some reluctance and found that Jillian had turned her face so that he couldn't see it. That didn't mean he couldn't see the vivid color staining her right ear and cheek, though.

"Uh, Jillian..." he started.

Multiple reactions were vying for prominence within him. He was too jaded by years of no-holds-barred sex to be embarrassed himself, but he couldn't help feeling for her. Amusement was welling, too, and he bit the inside of his lower lip, managing to suppress all sound, if not the shaking of his belly.

At the same time, incredulous anticipation made one hell of a hard-on spring up to test the stress limits of his zipper. Something huge would be shoving into Miss Jillian Fox, all right, but it damn well wouldn't be battery-operated. Not tonight, anyway.

Working to smooth out his roughened edges, he asked mildly, "Are you okay?"

"Please tell me you didn't see anything," she begged in a hoarse voice.

Now, if he were a better man, he'd give an Oscar-caliber performance right about now.

"Sorry." If he tried to say any more than that, he'd laugh out loud. Or spell out in coarse detail why she wouldn't be needing that particular apparatus any time soon.

Jillian groaned and covered her face with her hands. "Go away!"

"Are you okay?" he asked again. "You hit the ground pretty hard."

He tried to pull her up to get a look at her knees.

"I'm fine," she insisted in a gravelly tone, keeping her face averted. She shrugged his hand off her elbow and hugged the bag to her chest.

"Why don't you let me get that stuff for you," he suggested.

"I'll get it!"

He watched with a grin as she shoved the bag under the bumper, completely out of sight, and stuffed everything back inside. The temptation of her raised ass in its conservative navy skirt was almost more than he could resist. His palms actually tingled when he imagined skidding the fabric up and inspecting those fleshy globes. Hopefully she'd do something to earn a good, hard spanking this evening.

"Birthday present from your lunch date?" he inquired over her shoulder as she stood up and stuffed the bag into the depths of the cargo area.

"Yes!" She turned and planted her palms against his ribs, trying to shove him out of the way without meeting his eyes.

"Aren't you going to show me the rest?" he baited, holding his ground for a moment.

"No, you jackass! Get out of my way."

Oh yeah, she was in a temper now. He stepped back, letting her snatch up the jack and scurry by, refusing to watch as she crouched in front of the tire. Taking a deep breath, he strolled a few feet away, gazing absently at the reflective copper windows of the Tower. The damp heat of her hands through his shirt had twisted the knife blade of desire in his gut and he wondered if she'd noticed the boner thrusting behind his placket. His libido was definitely on a hair-trigger now. Not that he'd ever had trouble getting it up, but he'd almost reached his flash-point already and they'd barely touched. He should have taken a few minutes to lock the office door and take the edge off. The way he felt right now, it would be a miracle if he hung on long enough to bring her off before giving in to his own volcanic arousal.

That was, assuming he was able to talk her into bed tonight. If he failed, he deserved another long night alone with Rosie Palmer and her five sisters.

What the hell was taking her so long?

Barrett finally turned and had to roll his eyes. She was standing there by the rear door, reading the directions printed on the underside of the jack cover.

"Jillian," he said, grabbing the tire iron from its perch on the edge of the cargo bay. "Here. Just show me that you can get one lug nut off. If not, you're riding with me and I'll change the tire after dinner. Maybe things will have cooled off a little by then." In more ways than one.

Looking hot and annoyed, she took the iron from him and approached the flat once more.

"Shouldn't I jack it up first?"

"No, Jillian, you shouldn't. If you do, the wheel will move around when you try to loosen the lug nuts."

"Oh."

* * * * *

Okay, God — now would be the perfect time for a tornado to drop down and suck me into the sky.

First, this devilish man had gotten a glimpse of her personal pleasure arsenal, and now he stood watching as she examined the smooth, nut-free surface of the wheel without a clue. Shit! Where in the bloody hell were they? And what good did a college degree do her when she couldn't even find the lug nuts on her own damn tire?

"Uhhh…"

"Sometime today would be nice, Jillian."

"Um, well…"

"Is there a problem?"

She cleared her throat. "I, uh, just got this car a couple of weeks ago…"

"And you don't have the foggiest idea what you're doing," he finished.

"That would about sum it up, yeah."

"Good. Let's go. I'm ready for a beer."

Jillian lurched upright.

"Hey, what about my tire?"

Barrett stood there, hands pulling the pockets of his khakis tight over his crotch. His very full-looking crotch. The crotch she had a hard time dragging her gaze away from.

She almost wished she hadn't bothered. Despite his clunky prescription sunglasses, the rat was the picture of smug satisfaction. Jillian saw her own reflection, red-faced and stringy, in his lenses and wished, for once, that she were a lesser woman. She'd like nothing better than to slap that grin off his scruffy face, glasses or no.

"I told you I'd change it after dinner." He turned and walked off. "You coming or what?"

"Or what," she muttered under her breath, sticking out her tongue at his retreating back.

Since the aggravation twisting through her now was better than the humiliation that had consumed her earlier, she used the adrenaline rush to throw everything back into the rear end. Hesitating, she glanced behind her to make sure Barrett wasn't watching and then reached into the gift bag.

Past the lumps of plastic packaging, past the slim volume of erotic bedtime stories, way in the bottom corner, lay the jeweler's box. Pulling it out, she flipped it open and heaved a sigh of longing. The blue topaz earrings, with their cleanly cut stones and heavy gold settings, glinted temptingly in the sun. So gorgeous. They, at least, she truly appreciated. She wanted to wear them but refused to look like she was primping for him.

Sighing again, she dropped them back in the bag and slammed the door with a disappointing thud. She'd hoped for a resounding boom, but they just didn't make cars like they used to.

God, what was he thinking about all those sex toys? What was he thinking about her? Jillian groaned out loud as she trudged toward the passenger door. Life was so unfair! She'd never even considered using one of those things—well, at least until this afternoon—and now the man was probably imagining she diddled herself silly every night.

Every molecule of oxygen left her body at the thought. Barrett George was definitely the kind of guy who'd get off on fantasies of women doing that. Of her doing that.

Jillian shook herself. Just because the toys might have given the aggravating man an idea or two didn't signify anything about her, no matter how it felt. She wasn't that kind of woman.

She stalled as long as she could, straightening her hair and squeezing back into her low-heeled navy pumps, and generally trying to assemble herself into some variation of normal. Barrett's white Suburban pulled up behind her and, deliberately taking her time, Jillian fished around in her purse for nothing in particular and then did the same in the front seat of her car while he idled behind her. She could hear classical music drifting through the Suburban's open windows.

"Find what you were looking for?" he asked when she finally wandered over. Good Lord, the man had been standing here waiting to open her door. Now she felt guilty. Sort of.

"Yes, thank you."

"Good." He climbed in and rolled up the windows, since the fan had started blowing cool air. "So, is Chartreuse okay with you?"

"Fine." She buckled up and stared out her window as he turned into rush-hour traffic. The warmth of the leather seeping through her blouse reminded her of the jacket draped over the passenger seat of her Honda. She felt even more exposed without it, but couldn't bring herself to ask him to go back.

Actually, she would have been excited about going to Chartreuse with anyone else—intimate and expensive, it was the kind of restaurant that generally required reservations weeks in advance. But the ambiguity of the situation had her biting her nails, especially now that she knew for certain Barrett must be speculating about her sexual practices. This was supposedly a business dinner, but she couldn't shake the feeling she was being stalked by a hungry predator. Surely he hadn't met with Wayne or Berta or Darwin at such a posh restaurant.

Then again, who knew? Maybe he ate that way all the time and she was getting all worked up over nothing.

Right now, the French horns flaring urgently in the background made her wish he'd turn off the music, or at least switch to something less...dramatic. Like reggae, maybe. Or a good polka. No, make that talk radio. Music affected her mood, sometimes deeply, and classical music held particular sway over her. Holst was powerful—at times heartbreakingly beautiful, at others nerve-racking—and the sound system in the Suburban was superb. If she sat there and listened long enough, she'd either melt into the leather or bounce right out the window.

Jillian stole a glance at him. They were stopped at a light and he appeared to be deep in thought. His profile was appealing, even with the stubble and the scars and the boxer's nose. Maybe even especially with them. What would he look like without the glasses?

Her tummy fluttered. Probably the only times he didn't wear them were when he bathed and when he slept. One thought led to another and the flutter intensified. Jeez, how juvenile was that? She was thirty years old, for crying out loud, not some preteen drama queen.

His head turned her way and she instinctively pretended to be fascinated with something outside his window. Okay, so maybe there was a little bit of preteen drama queen left in her. It was reasonable to assume that sooner or later, her inner nympho would beat the stuffing out of that sniveling little teeny-bopper.

Then she'd really be in trouble.

Chapter Four

Barrett suppressed a grin as he followed Jillian through the ornate leaded-glass door he held open for her. As he'd expected, the lady was having quite a time and they hadn't even made it to the table yet. Her vengeful dawdling back in the parking lot had allowed him a few more minutes to enjoy an unrestricted view of her charming backside. The short-sleeved pink shirt she wore had clung to her back, revealing the band of a plain white bra. He would have been surprised and perversely disappointed to see anything else. Somehow, the dichotomous image of this conservative woman pleasuring herself with such an excessive dildo held boundless erotic appeal.

"George, reservations for two," he informed the hostess.

Though he said nothing, Barrett didn't miss Jillian's shiver when his hand slid into the small of her back, propelling her through the maze of tables.

At six o'clock on a Friday evening, every seat was occupied and several servers in black and white uniforms danced hushed attendance on their guests. The low hum of conversation and occasional tinks of silverware on china were accompanied by tastefully quiet chamber music. They passed through another archway into a second, smaller dining room, then took a carpeted staircase up to the narrow balcony overlooking the main dining area. There were only a half-dozen tables up here, set far enough back from the open rail that they weren't on display for the diners below. All were occupied but one.

There were times when knowing how to act like a gentleman came in very handy. Although the four-top was set with two places on a corner, both facing the rail, Barrett suspected Jillian would have taken the seat opposite his if he hadn't seated her first and taken the place to her left.

He was surprised to hear her request a Cabernet he was partial to himself, though he didn't order the same. Wine sometimes gave him a headache and he had no intention of torpedoing his evening before it had even begun. Instead, he ordered an imported dark beer.

"So, tell me about yourself." He stretched his legs under the table and crossed his ankles.

Jillian looked startled. "What would you like to know?"

Now there was a question. He wisely settled on, "Are you originally from around here?"

"I grew up near Ponca City, but I was actually born here in Tulsa." Amusement softened her expression a bit. "My mother was here visiting my aunt when her water broke all over the front seat of the car and she wound up delivering me in the emergency room at St. Francis."

"Were you premature?"

"Not more than a few days—Mom just assumed that my due date was set in stone and proceeded accordingly. All those popular pregnancy manuals hadn't hit the shelves yet, I guess, and she's never been real big on taking doctors' advice."

"My mom had the opposite problem," Barrett said without thinking. "I was so late and so large, they had to do a C-section to get me out."

"How big were you?" Horror etched her features.

"Oh, just a fraction of what I am now," he murmured. "Twelve pounds, four ounces."

"Good Lord, I'll bet she was miserable."

"Yeah, I imagine three extra weeks of pregnancy is every woman's worst nightmare. My folks had planned to have more than two of us, but they decided to hang it up after my little brother. Together we weighed as much as four babies."

"For God's sake, how much did he weigh?"

"Thirteen pounds even. But Dustin's a shrimp now."

"I'm sure I'll regret asking this, but what's your idea of a shrimp?"

"He's six-four."

"I'll bet nobody ever picked on you guys when you were kids," Jillian marveled.

"Just Dad."

"He must be pretty tall, too."

"Until Mom died, he seemed like a giant to me. After that, he kind of shrunk." Barrett looked out over the balcony. What in the hell had made him tell her all that?

"I'm sorry."

"That's okay. It's old news." Barrett studied the crystal chandelier, schooling his features into a careful blandness.

After an awkward silence, Jillian blurted, "My dad took off when I was five."

If the subject hadn't been so serious, Barrett might have smiled at her look of consternation. Evidently he wasn't the only one uncomfortable with making personal revelations. His had made the burning in his gut flare up.

"That must have been rough." He pulled a roll of antacids from his pocket and chewed a couple.

She shrugged, frowning as she watched him. "I don't really remember much about that time. When I got older, I wished we could move to a new town so I could pretend he'd died. Somehow that seemed preferable to being deliberately left behind."

Their server arrived bearing drinks, which was fine with him since the conversation hovered much too close to places he didn't feel like revisiting at the moment. They took time to order and then Barrett hoisted his bottle.

"Here's to getting acquainted."

Radiating uncertainty, Jillian sipped without comment. Barrett studied her in silence as he took a few pulls from his beer, unwilling to resume their earlier discussion. He could think of plenty of conversational gambits—you didn't get to be general manager of a cosmopolitan hotel, even on a temporary basis, without being skilled at shooting the shit—but Jillian's past held zero interest for him right now. It was her immediate future, say the next six to twelve hours, that was on his mind.

He should work harder to keep a lid on his mounting sexual appetite, but even doing nothing more inviting than holding her chair down, she was becoming a dangerous temptation. The knot in her hair appeared to have worked loose once more and strands of it were curling at her nape and around her lightly freckled face. He'd had a lifelong fascination with redheads and this one pushed every one of his buttons in a big way. The fact that he hadn't gotten laid since Memorial Day wasn't helping, either.

"So you're from Kansas City?"

She was on edge again. Was her sixth sense tattling about his renewed arousal? He followed her lead with a sigh, letting his eyes linger on her lips. Jillian Fox had very fuckable lips.

"Born and raised in the suburbs," he confirmed. "Got my BA in criminal justice and since then I've worked at several other Mahoney hotels, including the ones in Boston and Chicago." There—now she had his whole life story, at least as much of it as he was going to share.

"Wow, you're quite the globetrotter."

"Sounds like you might be interested in a little hotel-hopping yourself."

He was surprised when she shook her head. "Not right now."

When she didn't elaborate, he prodded, "Why not?"

"I have...commitments here," was all she would say. She lifted her glass and then frowned when she realized it was empty. Oh yeah, she was still nervous as all hell. While she concentrated on looking anywhere but at him, he studied her, noting the pink cheeks and the glittering eyes and the breasts that rose and fell just a little too rapidly.

Jillian Fox was becoming aroused, right before his eyes. It was a miracle his hard-on didn't knock the table over.

She fiddled with her silverware until she realized he was staring, then parked her hands in her lap. Realizing there was no way he'd be able to put her at ease, he gave up trying and granted himself the pleasure of just watching her squirm. She'd be plenty relaxed after he made her come five or six times.

"I didn't expect you to listen to Holst," she finally tossed out. "The Jupiter Suite is my favorite. Of course, that's everyone's favorite."

Actually, his brother had left that disc behind when he borrowed the Suburban for a camping trip, but Barrett wasn't about to say so. He tended to favor rock, but he wasn't averse to some country. He'd put the classical in for her, hoping it would help her unwind a little. There was usually classical music or soft pop drifting from the CD player in her office and he'd heard her humming along several times. What he hadn't expected was to find the classical music so…stirring. It had taken some concentration to stifle his physical reaction.

"How often do I do what you expect?" he asked. Not as often as she'd like, no doubt.

Barrett couldn't help but grin when she didn't answer.

* * * * *

An hour later, Jillian was warming a snifter of Grand Marnier over her coffee. She'd bypassed dessert in favor of the fragrant orange liqueur, hoping it would help ease the tension knotting her neck and shoulders.

Unlike her, Barrett had seemed completely at ease with the lack of dinner conversation. Every time his knee brushed hers under the table or their fingers met at the salt shaker, he'd murmured "Sorry," smiling at her without the least hint of apology. She'd avoided meeting his gaze any more than she had to, but her eyes had strayed his direction again and again during the prolonged silences. His hands were huge, and he'd wielded a knife and fork with surprising delicacy. Heat had curled in her belly as she watched him savor his New York strip—the muscles bulging in his forearms as he sliced off bite after leisurely bite, the powerful bunching of his jaw as he chewed, the smooth rippling of his throat as he swallowed…

She'd had to swallow, too, since saliva had pooled under her tongue, and of course he caught her. His *I know you want me* smirk had made her fingers tighten on the stem of her wineglass. The arrogant ass was lucky she hadn't thrown her wine in his face.

Then again, she should probably have thanked him for acting like the womanizer he was. If he'd put on a self-effacing front, she might not have remembered that she was supposed to be avoiding him until it was way too late.

Barrett lifted his snifter of brandy and then paused. "You know," he told her over the rim, "there was a chocolate torte on the dessert tray."

"There was a pretty sharp knife on it, too," she snapped as a blush seared her cheeks. Then she looked away, biting her lip. *Way to overreact, Jillian!* The man had no way of knowing her chocolate cravings had anything to do with him. Did he?

One peek at his face confirmed the worst—he was smiling like the cat who'd swallowed the canary. Bastard. She wouldn't have been surprised to see little yellow feathers sticking out of the corner of his mouth.

Well, if he thought she was going to just fall at his feet, he could—

"Oh my God! Jillian!"

That familiar squeal tightened her neck muscles into marble.

Oh my God! Cherry! If she'd set this up somehow, Jillian was going to take her pinking shears to that little schemer's coveted Seller of the Year blazer.

"Hi, Cherry." She forced a bright smile. "What are you doing here?"

Cherry stood by their table with a portly gentleman Jillian could only assume was Roly-Foley.

"You'll never believe it," she breathed. "We had a purchase agreement within the first hour, and for twelve thousand over the asking price!"

She was bursting with energy, bobbing from foot to foot in her excitement.

"Mr. Foley, the sweet thing, is treating me to dinner to celebrate. He has a standing reservation here on Friday evenings. Oh, I'm sorry," she rushed ahead. "Farrell Foley, this is Jillian Fox, my best friend and part-time tether to reality. And I believe this would be…"

Barrett stood up and shook Foley's hand. "Barrett George." Then he reached for Cherry.

"Cherry Fields," she gushed. "It's so nice to finally meet you, Mr. George. Jillian has told me so much about you."

Barrett slanted a look at Jillian and grinned. "Now that surprises me, since she's never mentioned you." He still held Cherry's hand. "Please, call me Barrett."

Blushing furiously, Jillian sputtered, "Well, I—there's never been—"

Cherry ignored her, making no move to retrieve her hand from Barrett's. "Naughty man," she murmured, peering at him through her lashes. "I'm sure the two of you have better things to do than talk about me."

Something unpleasant slithered through Jillian's rib cage at the picture they made. Cherry, all golden and willowy, with her heart-shaped face and tilted cornflower eyes, and Barrett, casual yet commanding in a navy polo and khakis, his dark head inclined her way in unconcealed interest…

The slithering was probably fear of what Cherry would say to him. Or maybe even a bit of envy at her friend's easy acceptance of male attention.

It definitely wasn't jealousy.

"Why don't you and Mr. Foley join us for a drink," Jillian suggested, her anxiety at being alone with Barrett suddenly soaring again.

"We'd hate to intrude on your evening," Foley began.

"Not at all." Barrett pulled out the open chair next to his for Cherry, who quirked a brow at Foley.

"I guess a drink would be all right." The rotund realtor settled to Jillian's right with a look that said he'd rather not. "After all, it's not every day," he boasted, laying a beefy hand on Cherry's shoulder, "that one of our agents closes such a spectacular deal."

Cherry directed a toothy smile his way, but Jillian read danger in her eyes. She had a feeling Mr. Roly-Foley was in for a disappointing evening.

"Why, thank you, Farrell." Cherry shrugged out of her jacket, effectively dislodging his hand. Then she turned her million-dollar smile on Barrett. "And it's not every night we get to check out Jillian's new boss."

* * * * *

At any other time, Farrell Foley would have annoyed the hell out of her. Tonight, however, the conversation hog was just what the doctor ordered for her thinly-stretched nerves. His neat bourbon languished untouched as he droned on *ad nauseam* about every spectacular deal he'd ever closed. Cherry tried to give Barrett the third degree whenever Foley drew a breath, but he always managed to deflect her less-than-subtle parries with a smile and lob the conversational ball back into the other man's court.

The only real break in Foley's monologue came when the restaurant's owner stopped at their table.

"Barrett," he said with a smile, extending a long hand when Barrett stood up. "I couldn't believe it when Tara told me you were in town. How long are you here?"

"Two or three weeks, probably. Unless something big comes up."

Jillian, swirling her Grand Marnier, tossed back a hasty gulp when the vision of a particular something big coming up suddenly appeared in her mind's eye. Her nose and eyes watered, though she managed to keep from choking on the potent liqueur. Barrett didn't miss it. His eyes glittered as he made introductions and she could tell he was having a hard time containing his amusement.

Although he didn't come close to Barrett's extraordinary height, Baylen Butcher was tall and lean, and not to put too fine a point on it, breathtaking. Movie-star material. His picture could be used in the dictionary to illustrate flattering adjectives from A to Z, and just for fun, Jillian started ticking them off mentally while the two men visited. *Assured, beguiling, cordial, delicious, elegant, fine, golden…* Just like Cherry. They'd make a stunning couple.

Glancing at her, Jillian narrowed her eyes. Cherry's expression was beyond bored as she checked her watch.

"So, racquetball on Monday, twelve-thirty," Baylen was saying. Then he grinned. "Sorry I can't stay, but I've got a date in twenty minutes and she gets a little impatient when I'm late."

I'll just bet she does, Jillian thought as he walked away, leaving a momentary silence in his wake. She glanced at Barrett, and the speculative look he gave her as he signaled for the check sent a frisson of pure panic down her spine.

When his attention was diverted by the server, she shot an urgent glare across the table and Cherry jumped to her feet at once. "Would you please excuse us for a moment, gentlemen?"

Jillian barreled into the ladies' lounge without bothering to see if Cherry was behind her and was immediately calmed by the Mendelssohn nocturne trickling from a number of tastefully camouflaged speakers. Art deco wall fixtures cast a warm, diffuse light that was multiplied and yet muted by smoky floor-to-ceiling mirrors.

The quiet intimacy pulled a sigh of relief from her and she kicked off her shoes the instant the door closed. Squishing her naked toes into the plush carpeting, she crossed and dropped onto the floral sofa with a low moan, rolling her head back and forth to work some of the tension from her neck.

"God, what a nightmare!" she moaned.

Cherry gaped at her in the mirror as she rinsed her hands under the automatic faucet.

"Jillian, you dope — get over it! That divine man is out there sharpening his utensils and you're the next course."

At Jillian's startled look, Cherry rolled her eyes. "Well, I'm not blind, silly! He's been doings things to you in his head all night and I'll bet a few of them would make even me blush. I'm telling you right now, if you don't sleep with him, you're going to regret it for the rest of your life. I'm going to regret it for the rest of your life. And you said he was weird," she snorted, applying a fresh coat of pale lipstick. "Hell, if you don't sleep with him, I will, and you can go home with Roly-Foley."

"Fine, you take him then." She steadfastly ignored the little voice in her head growling, *You do and you die.*

"Yeah, like you wouldn't totally tear my hair out if I did," Cherry said.

"I would not!"

"And anyway, he wants you, not me."

"Well, that's too bad because I don't want him." She *didn't.* She'd made up her mind to say no and make it stick, and she was damn well going to stay the course. Why even take a chance on winding up like her mother?

"Oh, please. And I don't want to win the lottery and buy an island in the Caribbean." Cherry turned and leaned her hips against the vanity table. "Jillian, you want Barrett like you've never wanted any man and you damn well know it. So take him already! It doesn't have to be a big deal if you go into it with your eyes open. Just make up your mind to use him for exactly what he is—a convenient and very hot body—and afterward kiss him goodbye with a big, satisfied smile on your face. If you're still conscious," she added with a grin. "Something tells me he's the type to take everything a girl's got."

Jillian grimaced. That was exactly what she was afraid of.

"You make it sound so simple."

"It is simple, Jill. You go right back out there and let that towering tank of testosterone take you wherever and *however* he wants to. I doubt you'll even have to do anything—he's definitely the dominant type. Just let him take the lead."

"I honestly don't think I can," Jillian cried around the rock in her throat. "Every time he makes any kind of move in my direction, I freeze up or start arguing with him, and it's like it's all totally out of my control. Please," she pleaded. "Just tell me you'll give me a ride back to my car. If I have to ride back with him…"

Sorrow was plain in Cherry's expression.

"Oh, Jillian…"

* * * * *

Judging by the relief on her face and the chagrin on Cherry's, their little powwow in the ladies' had provided Jillian with some way to dodge being alone with him for the rest of the evening. The idea put his hunter on full prowl.

"Sorry we kept you waiting," Cherry apologized.

"No worries, ladies. The server just came back with my receipt." Barrett's smile wasn't faked, and hopefully it didn't look too predatory. Jillian's maneuvering both amused and aroused the hell out of him. She wanted some serious arm-twisting and he was ready and willing to provide it.

He didn't have to wait long to find out what her game was. Cherry still had an apologetic look on her face. He had a feeling she'd tried to talk Jillian out of it, bless her perceptive little heart.

"I hope you don't mind, Barrett," Cherry said, "but I'm just so excited about this deal that I'll never be able to sleep tonight and I thought, since it's Jillian's birthday and all, a girls' night at my place would be the perfect thing." She practically winced as she said the words, and his smile widened. "Jillian said she'd keep us company for a while and then ride home with me, if that wouldn't bother you."

He grinned. Liberating Jillian's car keys from her purse while they were gone had been a wise move indeed.

"Of course not," he said easily. "It's nice to know she has such good friends."

He nearly laughed out loud at the looks on their faces — Foley's was put out and Jillian's totally relieved. Cherry was suspicious, but trying not to smile. He winked at her as he tucked the receipt into his wallet and returned it to his back pocket, then stood up.

"Well, congratulations on the deal, Cherry. It was nice meeting you both." To Jillian, he said, "Thanks for joining me tonight. It's been very enlightening."

Right before he hit the stairs, he jingled her keys over his shoulder and called, "I'll just leave these at the front desk after I change the tire."

Chapter Five

༄

It was a full minute before the implications of his parting comment hit her between the eyes like a ball pean hammer.

"Dammit, Barrett!" she snarled. Giving Cherry the evil eye, she grabbed her purse and took off without another word.

Cherry's "Hey, what'd I do?" followed her down the stairs.

She slipped on the third step from the bottom but made a quick recovery and hot-footed through the still-crowded dining room as quickly as was decent. If she didn't catch him, the bastard would no doubt drive right to her car and go straight for the gift bag.

She tumbled into the driveway just as he was pulling up and they looked at each other through the open passenger window. His left wrist was draped over the steering wheel, the gold watch strapped around it glinting red in the fading sunset. He wasn't smiling and he didn't say a word. He was daring her to get in.

Damn it all. If she did it, if she climbed into that vehicle with him, he'd think she was running up the white flag and proceed accordingly. Her heart began to knock painfully and she swallowed, trying to take a deep breath. She could do this. She'd beat him off with her purse, if she had to. If she wanted to…

Her feet moved forward without conscious direction and then she was sitting next to him, knees tucked firmly together, eyes straight ahead as he pulled away. The snick of the doors locking made her pulse spike, but Jillian said nothing. Instead, she spent a few minutes pulling herself up by her mental bootstraps.

Why in the hell was she so nervous, anyway? She didn't have to have sex with him, and even if she did, it wasn't like she was a virgin. She'd had Evan Cowdery's Tab A in her Slot B plenty of times and it just wasn't any big deal. Unless she counted the psychological discomfort of having her space so thoroughly invaded. Oh, and the pressure to produce something she wasn't capable of.

Jillian had never understood why women got so breathless and giggly over sex. Besides being sloppy and undignified, it posed unacceptable risks while offering no discernable payoffs—with the possible exception of offspring, which she was definitely not in the market for right now.

Worse, it was excruciatingly intimate and at the same time profoundly superficial. Even now, the memory of Evan's face contorting above her made her feel embarrassed and slightly sick. His grunting pleasure had had nothing at all to do with her, at least not on any level that she could relate to— he'd simply gotten into a hot lather over her body, used it to stimulate his penis 'til he humped up and came, and then been insulted when she hadn't enjoyed herself.

Ugh.

What made this time, this *man*, so different? And why this pinching ache in the portion of her anatomy that she was now fairly certain was Barrett's objective? Even as she concentrated on it, the pinching intensified right at her body's opening, and she nearly whimpered. It wanted to know the intrusion of his Tab A in a very bad way, obviously.

Oh God—what if there was a wet spot on the back of her skirt? She shuddered, horrified and yet perversely thrilled at the thought of him noticing such a thing. He wouldn't laugh, she knew that much.

"So, did you get anything else good for your birthday?" His lazy inquiry made her jump. They were waiting to turn right onto Garnett and he glanced at her, his eyes as unreadable as ever in the dusky pink light, his lips quirked in a knowing grin.

The words *not yet* nearly slipped from her lips. Good God, she couldn't even believe she'd almost said that. Why would she say that? She'd never been a flirt and wasn't about to start at a time like this. She should be telling him to mind his own business.

"Uh...a pair of earrings," she stammered instead, hating the heat that crept up her neck. Why was she even answering him? "And my aunt sent me a blouse."

"And did you treat yourself to something?"

Was he suggesting she'd bought the toys for herself?

Ignoring the hot blush that seeped into her cheeks, she managed a saccharine smile. "Just dinner with you."

"Hmm..." The narrowing of his eyes told her Barrett had caught her almost unintentional little jab. He gave her little time to celebrate hitting her target.

"You seemed quite taken with Bay."

Jillian's heart bumped as the image of a lion stalking a gazelle on the great Serengeti popped into her head. Barrett George would be right at home on Animal Planet.

"I wouldn't say taken," she started. Then she shifted uncomfortably. *Taken.* It was his word, so why did it sound like she'd come up with a blatant double-entendre?

"Good-looking bastard, isn't he?"

Jillian swallowed. She so did not want to answer that question. Her little gazelle heart was galloping away.

"If you go for the type."

"And you don't."

"I don't go for bastards, no matter what they look like." She kicked herself even as she worked up another dead-pan smile. What in the hell had gotten into her? Barrett wouldn't let attitude like that go unanswered. If she were smart, she'd beat a hasty retreat before he went for her jugular.

"What type do you go for, Jillian?" His voice was smoother than cream, trickling down her hollow, breathless insides and making her long for...

"Safe," she croaked weakly.

"I find that hard to believe." Barrett's sideways glance lasered into her. "It looked to me like you might be interested in a little three-way with Bay."

Jillian's breath froze in her lungs as the lion finally pounced, taking her down with barely a whimper. His implicit "and me" turned her body to fire and ice simultaneously. She needed to open her mouth and deny his taunting observation, needed to take him down a few dozen pegs, but she was so out of her league!

Too late, she realized it was totally insane to try to one-up such an aggressively sexual man. He was obviously baiting her, but oh God, the shocking image of herself being serviced by those two just wouldn't subside. Heat exploded in her abdomen and her joints felt weak.

"Yeah," she found herself murmuring with a cottony mouth, "but he and Cherry both had dates tonight."

Barrett's long, rumbling chuckle dribbled straight into her underwear.

The hotel was in view now. Soon he would be changing that tire. Her keys were probably in his pocket, and they'd be as toasty-warm as his body when he handed them to her.

Don't think about his body! God, she needed to get a grip on herself before she was attacking Barrett instead of the other way around. Why in the world did this man affect her so disastrously? He looked like Stephen King on steroids, for crying out loud.

She heard Cherry's voice. *Keep telling yourself that, Jill.*

Okay, so maybe Stephen King wasn't a total turn-off.

They pulled into the vacant space next to her Honda and Jillian reached for the door handle before they'd even come to a complete stop. Damn! It was locked. Feeling like an idiot, she fumbled frantically for the right button. His vehicle was so dif—

"Jillian." The engine was still running when his palm slid over the back of her neck, under the stray curls that tickled as he brushed them aside and pulled her toward him. She countered with instinctive backward pressure, but he was insistent. The strength of his fingers on that sensitive skin made her whimper.

"It's just a birthday kiss," he murmured.

She wouldn't look at him. Just a kiss. Yeah, right. She'd never enjoyed kissing any more than she'd—

Warm lips met hers over the console before she could pull away. He smelled like every forbidden daydream she'd ever had, hot and spicy and masculine, and oh, wow, did that beard stubble send shivers into her southern countries. Her ribs pressed against the leather armrest as she leaned into the sensation. Barrett's lips were soft and enticing next to the roughness of his cheeks. They rubbed firmly on hers as he held her in place, prodding, nipping, drawing a sigh from her. Mmm, maybe kissing wasn't so bad.

Her eyes fluttered shut as his left hand slid up the side of her face to turn her just so. They flew open again when he scraped his teeth over her upper lip. He sucked briefly at the same spot before moving to her lower lip. This time his teeth were sharp, provoking a moan that was half-alarmed. Jillian felt his breath coming hot and fast on her cheek as he pulled much of her lower lip into his mouth and sucked at it like he couldn't get enough. Her pulse ran wild and it felt like lightning bolts were exploding out of every pore on her body.

When his tongue plunged into her mouth, she shuddered and grabbed his thick wrists, and then there was no stopping him. Her mind was wiped clean. Barrett poured into her, a brandy-flavored storm of pure lust that drummed inside her head like a herd of stampeding elephants.

Then he tore his lips away from hers. "What the fuck!"

Jillian blinked in confusion as he turned and lowered the driver's window, letting in a flood of muggy air.

"What?" he barked.

Oh hell, someone was out there. Catching a glimpse of Darwin Patton over his shoulder, she gasped, averting her face and trying to disappear into her seat. Great. That was just what she needed, to be caught necking in the parking lot with the man everyone considered the new boss. And by the chief of security, no less.

"I'm sorry to bother you, Mr. George." Darwin sounded uncomfortable. "But I thought you'd want to know there was another car break-in this evening."

"And you couldn't have called my cell phone?" She could still hear him sucking in air like a bellows.

"I was just going in to call when I saw you pull in and I thought, um...well, when you didn't get out, I was afraid you'd leave." He cleared his throat. "Sorry. I'll just go back—"

Barrett sighed and killed the engine. "Well, you're here now, so let's have it. How many did they hit this time?" He reached for the door handle and Jillian closed her eyes, cringing at the thought of being illuminated by the interior lights. Although he projected an air of bumbling enthusiasm and brown-nosed with the best of them, something about Darwin gave her the creeps. She hated for him to see her in this position.

"Just one, sir."

To her surprise, she remained in darkness when Barrett opened the door and climbed out. He must have hit the dome override button first. Gee, maybe chivalry wasn't dead after all.

"Has the owner been notified?"

"Uh..." Darwin cleared his throat again. "It belongs to Miss Fox, sir. The police are on their way."

Jillian's eyes flew to her SUV.

"Might as well get out, Jillian."

Well, he'd tried. Pursing her lips, she opened the door and slid out of the high seat, tugging down her skirt as she strode behind the Suburban without looking at either of them. Circling the Honda, it took her only a second to spot the smashed driver's window.

"Oh, man," she groaned.

"Is anything missing?"

She heard the locks click and realized Barrett still had her keys. Opening the door, she leaned in, careful of the broken glass littering her seat. Her jacket was still slung over the other seat, but the dashboard shade had been tossed into the back.

"Doesn't look like it," she said. "I try not to keep anything valuable—"

Jillian bit her lip and hurried to the back of the car.

"Damn it!" The bag was gone, along with the earrings she'd so stupidly decided against wearing. She should have known better. Like many area businesses, they'd been having break-ins for weeks now. Bet whoever stole them had gotten a laugh out of the other items in the bag.

"Your birthday present?"

"Hell, yes!" she muttered, blinking to hold the tears at bay.

"I take it there was something more valuable in the bag than just the—"

"Yes!" The urge to cry took a back seat to the urge to clock him with the tire iron.

"You're fully insured, aren't you?" Barrett took her stiff hand and maneuvered her into the driver's seat of his vehicle as a city police cruiser pulled up, lights flashing.

"I'm an accountant," she reminded him crossly, resting her toes on the Suburban's running board and keeping her scraped knees carefully closed.

Barrett grinned at her. "Right."

She watched as the officer made a thorough inspection of the damage and wrote out his report. Darwin flexed his security muscles, playing up his role in discovering the break-in.

"Was anything stolen?" the officer finally asked.

When Jillian hesitated, Barrett volunteered, "She had some birthday gifts that were taken."

The officer looked at her.

"A pair of blue topaz earrings," Jillian spoke up hesitantly.

Barrett's grin bordered on sadistic. "What about the other items?"

"The rest was just a gag gift. No big loss," she assured the officer, glaring at Barrett. If looks could kill…

"We need to have a complete description of everything that's missing. It's important when it comes to getting a conviction down the line." The cop obviously meant business and Jillian gulped, her face on fire. She could feel Barrett's eyes resting on her with unconcealed amusement.

"Come on, Jillian," he coaxed. "It can't be that bad."

Oh, how she hated him!

"Can I talk to you in private?" she asked the policeman, her arms folded beneath her chest. Under normal circumstances, she'd be horrified to have to explain the exact nature of her missing gifts to this handsome young cop, with his military-short blond hair and rock-hard physique. But compared to detailing the bag's contents in front of Barrett and Darwin, it was a piece of cake.

* * * * *

Barrett smiled as the uniformed slab of beefcake gave Jillian a hand down from the Suburban and escorted her to the front seat of his cruiser. He felt no remorse whatsoever. She'd earned every bit of torture he was going to administer tonight and then some when she'd tried to duck out on him at the restaurant. His eyes never blinked as they followed her into the low-slung vehicle, eating up the enticing bit of thigh that appeared as her skirt rode up before the door closed.

Then he scowled. His hands would be busy between those thighs right now if it weren't for the security chief. He'd have to make sure that fucking lamebrain learned some discretion or his career path was going to take a severe and permanent wrong turn.

"Darwin," he said.

"Yes, Mr. George?"

"Call someone to clean all the glass out of Miss Fox's vehicle."

"You got it."

Finally dragging his eyes away from the cruiser, he focused on the other man. "And Darwin…"

Patton raised his brows.

"If any details regarding tonight's…" Barrett chose his words carefully "activities leave this parking lot, you'll be looking for work in another time zone. Do I make myself clear?"

"As glass, sir."

* * * * *

Jillian eyed the headlights in her rearview mirror with increasing trepidation as she drove Barrett's Suburban down Fifteenth Street toward her house.

She'd finally escaped the police officer's relentless questions—the damn things were gifts, for crying out loud! How was she supposed to recite make, model and serial number when she hadn't even gotten a good look, and no, she wasn't prepared to call Cherry for the details—to find Barrett in the process of changing her tire while Darwin supervised the cleanup of her front seat. The oversized dictator was piloting her SUV now, following her home. He'd refused to surrender the keys, claiming it was unsafe for her to be driving it alone, at night, in the city, without a window, blah, blah, blah.

Like she was any safer alone, at night, in the city, with Barrett George...

That kiss had demonstrated once and for all that the man was lethal to her self-control. She couldn't let him into her house or she was done for, one way or the other. Damn the man! If he'd just followed her in his own vehicle, she would probably have been able to race inside with a quick "Goodnight!" — if she hadn't managed to lose him on the way. But he had her keys and probably wouldn't give them up without a very intimate tussle.

Even as her mind scrabbled for a way to get rid of him, her body begged her to reconsider. Although being grilled about her new intimate massagers by a centerfold-worthy cop had dried out her nether regions quite nicely, thank you very much, the crotch of her panties still clung uncomfortably and it would only take one hot look, one hard finger grazing down her cheek, to reopen the floodgates. She had the uneasy feeling that if she slipped off his glasses and stared into Barrett's piercing green eyes, she would see every shameful secret she'd never been able to discover about her own frustrated body.

It was scary how much she wanted that. Oh God, she wanted it so bad, she was shaking and her hands were slick as they gripped the wheel. She had to get rid of him, and quickly, before she gave in and pushed the self-destruct button.

Jillian pulled up to the curb across the street from her house, which was unnervingly dark. Usually she was home well before sunset, at least during the summer. Surrounded by two towering old oaks, a mimosa, and several crape myrtle bushes, and situated in the middle of the block, the house was completely shielded from any street lamps.

Leaving the engine running, she scrambled out of the Suburban and watched him pull into her garage, which he'd opened with the remote. Damn, he was fast!

"Turn it off, Jillian." He rose from the driver's seat and faced her with a challenging stare, feet planted wide, arms akimbo. "I'm not leaving until I've checked your house for intruders."

"Intruders!" A likely story. She pulled the keys out of his ignition anyway and walked across the shadowed street toward him, jacket and purse over her arm. Cicadas still sang their comforting summer songs and a light but humid breeze was finally stirring the low-hanging leaves of the oaks. The sweet fragrance of the mimosa was a balm to her over-stimulated psyche.

Stopping at the mailbox, she asked, "What makes you think I have intruders?"

"Nothing in particular." He watched her step into the meager light from the garage door opener. "But someone broke into your car tonight, and they might have gotten your address off your registration. I'm not taking any chances."

The idea made goose pimples dance up her arms.

"You need to install floodlights and motion sensors over all the entrances. It's way too dark out here."

"I usually leave the porch light on when I'm going to be out after dark." She tried to slip past him, but Barrett put out an arm to halt her progress.

"It only takes one unexpected night, Jillian." His rumbling bass in her ear made her bones hum. "I'll go first."

She should protest. She was a strong, tall woman with a few self-defense sessions under her belt.

What she wasn't was six-and-a-half feet of pure male intimidation. Caving with a sigh, she followed him through the door into her laundry room, which was pitch-black until he flipped on the fluorescent overhead light. He moved ahead of her without hesitation, turning on lights first in her narrow kitchen, then in the dining and living rooms. The wall switch just inside the wide archway to the living room turned on a Tiffany-style table lamp in the far corner, bathing the room with rosy light.

Barrett tested the sliding glass door while Jillian laid her jacket and purse on the pedestal dining table. Force of habit made her kick her pumps underneath then step barefoot to the buffet along the wall to check her answering machine. The big red zero mocked her, as did the stack of bills and junk mail. She wasn't sure what else she'd expected, but it was disheartening to find no birthday greetings waiting for her.

She was thirty years old today and the only person who'd really cared was Cherry. *Pathetic.* She'd lied earlier about the blouse because the naming of a single gift had seemed so damned pathetic. Gifts from Aunt Carol were always late, and getting later every year since she'd moved to London with her new husband. Her mother would have bought her a blouse or some pretty bauble if she were able, but the idea was hardly comforting. And it would be a frosty day in hell before her brother ever gave her anything but a hard time.

Maybe it was time she gave herself something she really wanted. Something she needed.

Barrett's keys were still in her hand. Jillian squeezed them a couple of times and then, without giving herself time to reconsider, pivoted and padded back through the kitchen. Reaching out into the now-dark garage, she aimed the electronic key at the Suburban, listening for the honk to make sure it locked. Then she smacked the button on the wall to her right to lower the overhead door. Leaning her forehead against the jamb, she took a shaky breath, and when she turned, Barrett stood in the dining room, watching her intently.

* * * * *

Was it his imagination, or had she just tucked them in for the night?

He wasn't about to ask. The look on her face was one he'd never seen there before, but he knew it nonetheless. She was ready for him. She might not fully accept it yet, and judging by the widening of her eyes as he advanced on her, hands in his pockets, she didn't. But she was ready for him. And he was sure as hell ready for her.

When he was four feet away, she whirled suddenly, presenting her back, and Barrett stopped. He could see her ribs expanding and contracting with her quick, shallow breaths. Her obvious apprehension concerned him.

"Jillian—" He could hardly believe it, but he had to ask. "Are you a virgin?"

She shook her head without turning and he relaxed. Thank God. He'd have hated like hell to leave, but if she'd said yes, he would have done it for both their sakes.

Wearing a slight smile, Barrett took that final step forward and stopped within inches of her, his groin so very near her backside it made him ache. He absorbed her like this for a moment, closing his eyes and breathing in the scents that surrounded her. Her house smelled like his grandmother's, like home. The subtle hints of bacon and coffee and laundry detergent and lotion were surprisingly soothing.

But Barrett didn't want to be soothed. He concentrated on the smells he'd picked up in her office and in his Suburban, and then in her vehicle, the personal scents that were uniquely Jillian.

The injuries to his eyes, which had rendered him temporarily blind, had forced him to develop his other senses more fully than most, and he'd found scent to be the most reliable—and the most provocative. Jillian always smelled of honeysuckle shampoo and a buttery green perfume. And for the last few days, chocolate.

Tonight, after that impossibly hot kiss, he'd smelled her arousal and it had just about launched him into the stratosphere. God only knew where he'd have stopped if Patton hadn't rapped on the window.

He could still smell her arousal, he realized with a start. And she was perspiring. His hesitation was probably torturing her.

Barrett leaned over her shoulder, laid his face alongside hers, ear to ear, cheek to cheek, and looked down into her shadowed cleavage, inhaling the humid heat billowing up from her skin. He could live happily forever with his face buried in such a fascinatingly soft, carnally evocative cleft. Or his dick buried there.

Jillian jumped when his hands touched her waist and he heard his keys hit the floor. She might not be a virgin, but she was far from seasoned. The realization should make him step away from her. Instead, it led him to edge closer. He'd probably hurt her, but it was way too late to stop now, unless she actually asked him to. It would be a near thing, even then.

Letting his arms slide around and cross over her midsection, he curved his body over her back and pulled her against him, waiting, letting her adjust to his size and nearness. He felt her mouth open on a gasp and stay that way as she all but panted. The sound sent blood pounding through him, and she gave another gasp, obviously aware of his reaction. Her hands slapped onto his forearms but she didn't try to pull away. Instead, her hips shifted anxiously against his.

Barrett turned his head until his lips touched her ear and whispered a promise. "I'm gonna fuck you with that."

Jillian jerked against his arms, moaning "Oh God."

He smiled hotly at her reaction. Her urgent squirming said more clearly than words that she needed to come in a very bad way. Never one to deny a woman something so pleasurable to them both, he slid his right hand down her leg and tugged her skirt up high enough to reach underneath.

Shit, the insides of her thighs were sticky and he didn't even have her panties off yet.

Cupping her through the soaked fabric, he pulled up firmly, forcing a howl out of her. She couldn't seem to stand still. In fact, she couldn't seem to stand at all. Barrett tightened his left arm, supporting most of her weight as he eased his fingers into the leg of her panties and probed through her slippery curls for the perfect spot to set up a hard, fast rhythm. Her moisture bathed him, and the sounds his fingers made as they slid over her were incredible. Jesus, no wonder she was so skittish, and no wonder Cherry gave her a dildo for her birthday. How the hell long had it been since she'd had a decent lay?

Still cheek to cheek with her, he could feel the tears of a terrible need spilling down as she sobbed. He paused in his ministrations, but kept his hands where they were.

"What?" No way. Surely he'd heard her wrong.

"Stop, Barrett, please!" Air was scraping sharply into her lungs between sobs—there was no way she could actually want him to leave her like this.

"Why?"

"I have to use the bathroom!"

That startled an incredulous laugh out of him. She sounded mortified.

"Now?"

"Yes, now!"

What could he say to that? Against his better judgment, he loosened his hold and let his fingers slide away from her. She was off and running in a heartbeat.

He shook his head as he closed the door to the garage and trailed after her, switching off lights as he went and chuckling in spite of himself. Jillian Fox was one strange bird, but you just had to like her.

Chapter Six

She was an absolute fruitcake!

Jillian sat on the toilet, shaking like a leaf and frustrated beyond belief when only a trickle found its way out. She couldn't believe it was happening again. Every time she got close, and this time it had been *insanely* close, her stupid bladder signaled an overwhelming pressure to void, making her sprint for the nearest bathroom.

God, what was she going to do? Barrett was out there waiting for her right now, and she didn't know if she could face him. Bearing down hard, rocking on the seat, she emptied her bladder as completely as she could. After she'd wiped herself up—good Lord, what a mess she was down there—she washed her trembling hands and splashed her blotchy face with water. He must think she was—well, she couldn't imagine what he was thinking right about now. Maybe if she stayed in here long enough, he'd leave.

Yeah, right. He was probably as determined to get his as Evan Cowdery had been. Scratch that—he was way more determined than Evan Cowdery had ever been.

Opening the bathroom door, Jillian stopped short at the sight of Barrett standing at the other end of the hallway, adjusting the thermostat. He'd already shed his socks and shoes, and as he turned to look back at her, he whipped his shirt over his head, tossing it carelessly through the open bedroom door. She felt like a cartoon character slammed in the gut by a wayward I-beam. Carved from a block of granite, the man was even more massive half-clothed.

"Hope you don't mind that I turned it down to sixty," he said easily as he ambled toward her. "I like to get sweaty as much as the next guy, but I try to avoid heatstroke."

Get sweaty. Her pulse went weak and thready when a vision of him sweating over her erased every other thought in her head. A whimper lodged in her throat as she tried to back into the darkened bathroom. As if he dealt with that reaction every day, Barrett simply snagged her wrist in a firm grasp and led her into the master bedroom.

He'd already been in here. The three-way lamps on both nightstands were switched on low and the ceiling fan was doing its lazy twirl over her queen-sized bed. Previously neat and awash with frilly pillows, the bed was now stripped of everything but its floral fitted sheet.

Oh, crap—Barrett couldn't have made it more clear he intended nothing civilized to happen on that mattress, which now looked more like a sacrificial altar. She looked away with a gulp. All her lovely linens and pillows lay on the floor under the window, looking apologetic. *Sorry, Jill,* they seemed to say, *but you're on your own.*

Without a word, he tugged the hem of her blouse out of her skirt and began unbuttoning the pink silk. Jillian just stood there, drawing one shuddering breath after another as she watched his big, tanned hands work with devastating dexterity down her front. Despite her apprehension, she was woman enough to wish she were wearing something a little more slinky. But with a chest like hers, slinky usually translated to droopy, so here she was in her practical white bra, dressed not so much to kill as to bore a man to death.

The blouse slipped off her shoulders to the floor and Barrett wasted no time reaching back to unhook her bra with disconcerting skill. Jillian swayed as he pulled the garment down her arms. There was something so elemental, so innately carnal in baring her breasts to this man that she didn't know if her knees could take it. Barrett's long growl only heightened the primitive reaction, but before she could hide her face in his broad chest, he dropped to his knees in front of her and buried his face in her cleavage, breathing deeply. The glasses he still wore dug into the inner curves of her breasts and she speculated inanely that her sweat and body oils were probably smearing his lenses but good.

Jillian wrapped her arms around his big, shaggy head anyway and held him there, her sighs just as deep. This, she could handle. She could stand here with him this way forever.

At least she thought so, until he turned his head and nuzzled her nipple—then the only thing holding her upright was the band of his arms. The first lick of his tongue drew a whimper from her, and the famished heat of his mouth sucking her deep had her right back where she'd left off in the kitchen—on the verge of screaming or passing out, whichever came first. She thought she'd die as he feasted on her without restraint. His strong suckling pulled raging need from her very core, making her grind her mound against his chest in helpless agony.

Pulling away, Barrett somehow managed to support her as he climbed to his feet.

"You, Miss Fox, have the tits of a goddess," he declared unevenly. He fumbled with the side button on her skirt and popped it right off. "Sorry."

He didn't sound sorry, Jillian thought as he shoved the skirt down over her hips, but she was lost in her arousal and too bemused by his compliment to care.

"Aw, shit," he hissed. "What a picture." Spinning her around, he slid one arm around her waist and resumed the position he'd taken in the kitchen. Jillian stiffened at the sight of their joint reflection in the vanity mirror. No way in hell did she want to watch herself.

"No." She tried to step away, but he held her fast.

"Oh, yeah." Without the impediment of her skirt, his right hand plunged straight down the front of her panties, and the sight of that thick brown wrist against her pale abdomen, disappearing into the white cotton, was enough to trigger palpitations. Barrett's face darkened as he leaned over her back, and even through his khakis and her panties, his arousal was making alarming headway into the cleft between her buttocks.

His fingers didn't hesitate. Two of them surged between her slick labia and worked up and down both sides of her clitoris without mercy as he rocked against her backside. Jillian barely had the time to be mortified by the slurpy sounds his fingers were making—hadn't she just taken care of that?—before she felt the intense pressure building in her bladder and renewed her struggle with real anxiety.

"Barrett, stop!"

"Not happening."

He hunched lower, digging his prickly chin into the flesh between her shoulder and neck while his fingers slid deeper with every noisy, squishy pass, exacerbating that awful burning pressure.

"Please," she sobbed.

"I am *not stopping.*"

"I have to pee!" she wailed.

Barrett paused, his eyes snaring hers in the mirror. "I'm about as far from fastidious as a guy can get, Jillian, so you go right ahead."

Jillian groaned, horrified that his words ratcheted up her excitement one more throbbing notch. Oh God, he was so...*base*.

She jerked, dismayed to feel a twinge of pain when those two fingers shoved deep into her quivering flesh. *Too big, too big!* It was a relief when they withdrew, dragging more of her wetness out and over the sensitive swell of her clitoris. Then Barrett was back to that primitive rhythm, riding her with his palm until she was actually yelling at him to stop, to turn her loose, as she clawed at the arm around her waist.

"Let it go, Jillian."

"I can't!"

He stopped long enough to grab the crotch of her panties and snap the elastic right off her hips, tossing the shreds somewhere out of sight. Without loosening his arm, he fumbled behind her. The clink of his belt buckle and the rasp of his zipper tortured her imagination and she pushed futilely at his forearm, making him tighten his grip. His face was heavy and red against the delicate veined whiteness of her skin.

"Let it go, or we'll have to try something a little more drastic." She was disconcerted to feel his damp fingers separating her right buttock from the left. And then something smooth and hot and very, very large was crowding between them, hovering on the brink of an all-out invasion.

Jillian just about fainted, falling forward to brace her hands on the vanity top, twitching with fear and fascination. Barrett followed her, keeping his hot, hairy chest plastered against her back.

"Let that tight little pussy come for me," he ordered in her ear. "You know it's going to." His damp fingers tweaked her nipple before diving back between her legs. "Come on, baby, I wanna hear you scream."

When his fingers pushed into her again, Jillian sucked in a breath and held it. Something was different this time, *ah, God,* so different! The rhythmic pulsing of that menace from behind, the heel of his thumb sliding against her clitoris, those relentless fingers that felt like they were tugging her pubis toward the floor—together, they whittled away at her self-control, *slashed* away at it like a machete at a cream puff, and the pressure became intolerable. She tossed her head from side to side in urgent denial, but the harder she fought it, the more she needed to breathe…

The pent-up air burst forth and her tortured gasps echoed in the room as her pelvic muscles went lax. A tidal wave of blood surged into her face and chills rose on every inch of her skin.

"*Fuck*, yeah! Do it, baby..."

Every bit of air she managed to suck in emerged in a hoarse scream as release slammed into her like an express train. She leaped against his arm as contractions ripped through her abdomen and thighs, contractions so hard they bordered on painful, and they wouldn't stop, just kept coming and coming, and his hand wouldn't stop rubbing and pulling, and it felt like she was being turned inside out, he was pulling her inside out, and oh God, it was incredible...

Barrett yanked his fingers out of her abruptly and replaced them with his penis, driving into her with a heavy groan. The stress of it, instantaneous and intense, made her cry, "Oh God oh God oh GOD!" His arm locked her hips in place as he rammed home without restraint, over and over again, battering deeper than she'd thought possible, deeper than she could stand. The explicit commentary flooding out of him shocked her even as his rough fingers on her clitoris drove her unwillingly higher.

Jillian couldn't stop the tears that streamed down her cheeks, whimpering now as her body started to contract once more around his impossible girth. Her head banging into the mirror made her arch her back and hook an arm around Barrett's neck, drawing his head alongside hers again. The force of her thighs hitting the vanity's edge rattled bottles and jars all over the surface while wave after wave of painfully brilliant sensation burst through her. Barrett's narrowed eyes glittered as they watched her breasts jump and jiggle obscenely with every thrust, making her burn down to the soles of her feet.

Her lilac candle fell to the carpet as he pushed deep and held, stiffening, groaning. Jillian felt his thighs tremble and then he jerked roughly. She didn't recognize the two dark-eyed, feral creatures who watched her from the mirror.

One last guttural "Fuck!" burst from his lips as his hands closed on her hips with brutal strength. He pulled out, wringing one more contraction from her before he sent the hot rush of his ejaculate up her backbone and onto her neck.

* * * * *

The only sounds in the shadowy bedroom were the hum of the air conditioning unit outside her window and the asynchronous rhythms of their labored breathing.

Jillian's arm slid away from his neck as they stared at one another in the mirror. Her eyes were shell-shocked and fine tremors racked her. Barrett lowered his gaze to the evidence of his total loss of control, gasping for air. He ran one fingertip through the slippery fluid in a slalom pattern down her long back, eliciting a shiver.

"Guess that makes two firsts tonight, huh?" he panted. Jillian's expression turned wary. "You've never come before, have you? You should have told me sooner. I might have handled that…a little differently."

He sure as hell wouldn't have knocked on her back door that way. Good intentions aside, threatening a woman with that particular weapon was pushing the envelope even for him, and he was honest enough to admit he'd half-hoped she would continue to hold out. It was damn disturbing. One of his few unbreakable rules, at least in the bedroom, was to allow the deviant in him out to play only with women who were plainly bent in a similar direction. The fact that he'd very nearly introduced Jillian to something she would no doubt consider the height of kink—and without a condom, for God's sake—wasn't sitting well at all.

As it was, he'd taken her like a fucking animal. Literally. If he'd sunk his teeth into her nape to hold her in place, he would have been the spitting image of a tomcat mounting a female in heat. And she'd been so damn tight, his graceless entrance must have hurt like hell.

He hadn't even kissed her. She deserved better than that.

On the other hand, she'd finally come hard enough and loud enough to drive him right over the edge.

"Do you hear anyone complaining?" The breathless question brought her face back into sharp focus and he couldn't help his wry grin.

"Liked that, did you?"

She regarded him seriously. "You're very bad, aren't you?"

Barrett hesitated. It didn't seem like a good idea to admit he was badder than usual around her. He sidestepped, "And it bothers you that it took a man as bad as me to bring you to orgasm."

Jillian nodded with obvious reluctance.

He leaned forward and breathed in her ear, "Better me than that dildo."

Color flooded up her chest and neck as she recoiled, but he snaked his arms around her waist, refusing to let her flee.

"Simmer down." He caught her ear lobe between his teeth, scissoring delicately, stroking the captured flesh with his tongue. "It's nothing to be ashamed of. You should have been introduced to one long before now, apparently."

Jillian moaned. "You just had to bring that up, didn't you?"

"Cherry's a very insightful woman." Barrett eased his hands upward and lifted the sexy weight of her breasts away from her ribcage. Their bounty, sweaty underneath, overflowed his palms. Watching in the mirror, he squeezed and shaped them, pleased when their large nipples stiffened immediately. Jillian didn't answer, but her pupils dilated once more as they took in the seductive movement of his hands.

"I'm sorry you never got to try it out," he murmured. "Bring home another one and I'll use it on you, if you'd like."

"Only if I get to use it on you first," she fired back, blushing fiercely even as she gasped at his sharp manipulation of her nipples.

"I'll try anything once," he rumbled with a sexy look.

* * * * *

Eager to divert his attention from that particular subject, Jillian asked, "So what was the other first?"

It was a surprise when Barrett dropped his hands with a grimace. She turned and watched as he stepped back, kicking away his fallen pants and boxers. Leaning down, he retrieved his wallet.

"I never forget to use a condom. Ever." He looked her in the eye as he pulled one free of the leather and wagged the foil at her. "I suppose it would be too much to hope that you're on the pill?"

Jillian started. "But you—you pulled out," she sputtered. She could feel the sticky chill of it all the way up her back.

"Yeah, but not before you took the first shot right where it counts."

She bit her lip and covered her breasts with her hands in an instinctive gesture of self-defense, wishing she had a third to send down south. This was bad.

"I take it that's a no?" he asked.

"I've barely known you a week," she said helplessly.

Barrett seemed to have nothing to say to that. His careful study of her was unnerving. The sight of his heavy genitals stirring to life was even more so. It wasn't long before he was standing at attention under her breathless scrutiny and she stared in amazement. And just a trace of fear. Holy cow. It was no wonder she'd felt stretched to the point of rupture. If she'd gotten a good look at him first, she might have put up more of a fight.

"It was a pretty tight fit. Did I hurt you?"

"Uh…" Whatever she'd intended to say was lost in the train wreck of her consciousness. He'd taken that intimidating length of flesh in hand and was stroking up to the head and then slowly back down to the thick base. Again. And again. Pausing with his thumb curved over the base, he massaged the furry sac below with his long fingers.

Her tongue felt almost as thick as that monumental column of masculinity. Come to think of it, so did the vacant lot between her ears where her brain used to live. In the absence of intelligent thought, the thudding of her heart echoed in her ears. When he broadened his stance and took his testicles in his left hand, squeezing and pulling as the other swept up and down his shaft with increasing roughness, Jillian looked on, rooted to the spot by his brazen show. Her nipples prickled under the protective curve of her palms.

Then she realized, much to her horror, that she was panting. Open-mouthed. Like a dog.

Her teeth snapped shut with an audible click and her eyes flew to his face. The damn man was watching her with a smile wide enough to show off his molars.

"Does that mean you're ready for another piece of this action?"

"Um…" Jillian felt the blush creeping up her chest again. She sidled toward the door. "I just…need to…"

Barrett immediately stepped into her path and she drew up short just inches from the tip of his penis, still cradled in his stroking fist. His grin took on an ominous cast.

"I don't think so."

"But…" Jillian's teeth just about punctured her lip. *Shit, shit, shit!* "But, why?"

"You want to clean up."

"Uh…yeah." For Pete's sake, you'd think the man would be relieved to see her head for the shower—she reeked of every bodily fluid known to man, save the one she'd been so worried about.

Barrett stepped forward, brushing that surprisingly delicate skin against her stomach. She couldn't help looking down at his hand as it milked out a large bead of fluid and swirled it around her navel, which meant she totally didn't notice his other hand sneaking forward until a finger brushed into her slickness.

"You'd wipe that all away before I even get one lick? And after all the work I put into making it run out of you? I'm hurt, Jillian."

Heat exploded into her face as his crude imagery stole the breath from her lungs.

"You're a bad man," Jillian accused again in a low voice, even as her nipples pushed insistently against her palms. *So what does that make you?* She was trembling again and would have declared a pressing need to relieve herself, if her previous claim hadn't resulted in that twisted invitation. He was so bad, she couldn't even come up with an adequate word to describe him. "My back is sticky."

In answer, Barrett set his damp forefinger to her breastbone and shoved. Startled, she stepped back, her eyes widening. When he did it again, she took another big step back, crying, "Barrett!"

This time he planted eight fingertips and pushed, making her fall backward onto the bed.

"That's what the sheet is for," he told her, dropping to his knees on the floor between her sprawled legs. "Trust me, there's gonna be come all over it before we're done here."

When she tried to scramble away from him on the mattress, he grabbed an ankle and yanked her back down, drawing a screech out of her.

"Just let me eat you for a while and then you can wash all you want," he promised.

"Barrett George, I am going to kill you," she spat back, pushing up onto her hands and kicking hard as he tried to arrange her to his satisfaction.

Oh no, oh no! He was going to do that to her in this disgusting condition. Anticipation kicked her in the gut even as she tried to kick him in his. Her knee knocked his glasses askew and he released one ankle long enough to set them right again.

"I was trying to be gentle about this, at least," he grunted as she took advantage of the momentary freedom to twist over and scramble to her knees. "But you're exciting the hell out of me, Jillian. Keep offering me your ass and I'm going to take it."

She stilled instantly, then tried to plop back over onto her rear, but it was too late. He'd grasped both ankles and pulled hard. Unable to find purchase on the tight fitted sheet, she slid and slid until her hips were over the end of the bed, and then she kept sliding and the room spun around her. What in the world...?

The next thing she saw was his penis, leaping with arousal, directly in front of her face, his long, muscular legs stretching down below her. Jillian gasped and grabbed for those legs, bracing her torso away from him. Barrett was standing now, breathing loudly, and he had her dangling upside-down, her thighs over his shoulders, those maddeningly strong arms clasping her hips.

Jillian tried to kick the back of his head and he smacked her bottom hard so hard, tears sprang to her eyes.

"Be still." His voice wasn't the least bit harsh, but she heard the threat implicit in his tone. Damn it, there wasn't a thing she could do except hold on and wait breathlessly for him to do whatever he would to her. She'd never felt so vulnerable in her life. Never. Blood pounded in her ears at a frantic pace as she gripped his sparsely furred thighs.

"That's better," Barrett murmured. "I like to eat in peace."

"You're a pig!" Jillian gasped.

"I hope you like pork, then, because I'm gonna feed you a nice big mouthful."

Outraged, she opened her mouth to say something cutting in return. The only sound that emerged was a long, broken groan.

* * * * *

Barrett was in heaven. His world was reduced to Jillian's incredible ass and the succulent pink flesh laid open before him.

Knowing he couldn't keep her this way too long, he dived right in with long, firm strokes of his tongue. Upended as she was, no more of her fluids would find their way out, but he lapped up what he could before tucking his chin down to focus on her clit. Her moans made him want to laugh. She was so damn contrary, it was beyond fun to goad her.

Brimming with anticipation, he taunted her further by rocking his hips forward, pushing his cock into her face. He heard her gasp, felt her nails dig into his thighs as she tried harder to hold herself away.

"Pig!"

He plucked her clit with his lips and she shrieked. He rocked into her face once more.

"Dirty rutting pig!"

"Think you're a real bad-ass, don't you?" He scraped his teeth over her and she howled, smacking one fist against his thigh. He nudged her face again. "Suck my cock, Jill."

"Bite me!"

Barrett obliged at once, clamping her clit firmly between his teeth and flicking the tip of his tongue against the plumped knot. As Jillian bellowed loud and long, he braced an arm behind her lower back and ran his other hand up over her hip. He dipped his middle fingertip into the overflowing well of her pussy and then pressed it between the globes of her ass, once again stopping just short of pushing in. Her arms stiffened, holding her body so far out Barrett had to strengthen his hold and realign his footing to remain upright. He felt goose bumps rise on her flesh and broke out in a few of his own. She was almost there, and incredibly, so was he.

"Suck the head, Jillian."

Just as it occurred to him that he was threatening her again, her utter stillness struck him. She *wanted* him in her ass.

His heart, already pounding with exertion and lust, picked up steam.

"Has anyone ever been in here?" he asked in a harsh whisper, pressing, pressing...

"No, oh God, no one!" she shrieked as he breached her with his fingertip.

"Saved all the good stuff for me, huh?" He didn't back off the downward pressure, advancing into her ass until his spread palm was flush against her cheeks. Jillian moaned continuously, and not in pain. Oh man, he was going to enjoy the living hell out of her. If he had her flat on the bed, he'd give her a finger-fucking she'd never forget. He settled instead for massaging her tender virgin rectum, savoring the shudders that racked her.

"Suck me, Jill," he groaned. "I'm gonna come and I want you to taste it."

After a moment of pulsating silence, Barrett felt the heat of her lips stretch around his bulging head and smiled in agonized triumph. Keeping his eyes shut tight, he fought against the hellacious orgasm pounding for release and concentrated on eating her quivering pussy. Jillian was panting hard through her nose as she rested an elbow against his thigh and wrapped her hand around his cock, squeezing while she sucked at him like he was a giant straw in a super-thick milk shake. The fact that she apparently hadn't given much head only made him love it more, made his balls draw up into tingling, aching stones.

When he could no longer resist the rush, he plunged his tongue deep and ground his sandpapery chin against her clit, tugging with his finger to stretch the muscles ringing her anus.

The sound of her voice screaming his name totally did him in and he jerked roughly, again and again, as he came all over her face.

Chapter Seven

ೞ

Barrett bent his wobbly knees and let Jillian drop onto the bed with a boneless bounce. Her head hung slightly over the foot of the mattress, her eyes closed, her chest rising and falling like she'd just finished a marathon. Her pink cheeks and chin were smeared with his semen, her reddened lips dripping with it.

The way she looked now, he was ready to fuck her again. Immediately. Instead, he crouched down beside the bed and threaded his hands through her tangled hair, supporting her head in his palms. When her eyes opened, unfocused, he rubbed his lips lightly over hers. She moaned softly, one hand rising from the mattress to slide behind his head and hold him to her. Her sweet lips parted and he swept in, engaging her in a long, musky kiss that he never wanted to end.

Whoa – down, boy. Barrett pulled away at once, frowning. Talk about a stupid idea. He was only in town for a few weeks—provided he could pull his head out of his ass long enough to put on a condom. Otherwise, he could be spending a lot more time with Jillian Fox than he planned to spend with any woman, ever.

The idea shriveled his balls.

A snuffle from the bed made him focus on her once more. There she lay, naked on a stripped bed, with the lights on, her head half off the mattress, her hand draped over his neck, and her face covered with come—and Jillian was asleep. He couldn't help grinning.

If he were the decent sort, he'd find a wet washcloth and swipe her up a little before he tucked her in and let her sleep for a while. Unfortunately for Jillian, he was the nasty sort. Oh, he'd let her sleep, but there was no way in hell he was cleaning even a drop of anything off her. The idea that she was lying there marinating in the fragrant amalgam of their emissions satisfied him in some strange and no doubt perverted way he didn't even want to understand. He'd leaned heavily toward the raunchy end of the sexual spectrum from day one, but this was... unfathomable.

Barrett laid his lips gently on her forehead for a moment. He'd put off thinking about it, but it hadn't escaped his notice that his penchant for sexual aggressiveness had escalated to outright dominance tonight. He'd walked a fine line between persuasion and force, and though intuition told him that she'd needed him to apply that element of force, to take away all her control before she could experience the ultimate release, it was just as apparent that she hadn't realized it. He had a feeling he'd really frightened her more than once. If she had submissive leanings, she seemed to be unaware of them, and he'd just as soon it stayed that way.

Then there was his new ass fetish... He smiled ruefully. She'd probably never turn her back on him again. Appearances to the contrary, he wasn't in the habit of insinuating himself into a woman's backside unless she came right out and asked for it. Especially given his size, odds were high she might require surgical intervention or a year's supply of Preparation H afterward if he didn't keep a tight leash on his urges. He was willing enough to oblige the women who wanted it, but he didn't really understand their drive to make themselves vulnerable to such a prospect. There were men out there who didn't know the meaning of the word restraint. But that's how compulsions usually were—senseless. God knew he had a few of his own that didn't bear close examination.

However obscure the reasons, it seemed that his inner deviant had staged a jailbreak and drawn a bead on this inexperienced woman. It was time to round it back up and lock it away before he wound up hurting her. Or jailed on forcible sodomy charges.

But there he stood, unable to peel his eyeballs off Jillian Fox, spread before him in all her glorious vulnerability. His gaze strayed to her breasts, beautifully soft as they spilled out to the sides of her body, then on to her endless legs, one knee thrown out in unintended invitation. She'd hate it that he was looking at her, but the knowledge didn't deter him. Now that she was so relaxed—unconscious qualified as relaxed, didn't it?—he could look his fill, perhaps even feel his fill, if he were careful enough.

But first things first.

After dropping one more soft kiss on her forehead, Barrett grabbed a couple of pillows off the floor and tossed them in the general direction of the headboard, then scooped her up in his arms for the short trip to comfort. He didn't want her waking in a couple of hours—if he could wait that long—with a crick in her neck. The woman really was dead to the world. She didn't stir at all when he laid her on the pillow, which begged the question, *What else can I do with her, unchecked by those pesky inhibitions?*

Because the air had acquired a pleasant chill, he tugged the chain on the fan and covered her to the waist with the light summer quilt he'd thrown against the wall earlier. Her breasts continued to beckon and he paused, leaning over to push them together. Unbelievably, his cock twitched at the sight. *Fucking perfect.*

Barrett smiled darkly at his own joke. Maybe he'd wake her up that way later.

He turned off the lamp by her face and wandered into the hall. Though he'd denied Jillian use of the facilities, he had no intention of depriving himself. Even in the breezy cool of her very efficient air conditioning, he'd broken into a head-to-toe sweat during their workout that would soon render him more rank than a three-dollar bottle of wine if he didn't rinse off.

As he stood beneath the chilly spray, he found himself wondering how she'd wound up in such a needy condition. From the shocked look on her face after their first bout, he had to assume she'd thought herself incapable of orgasm. It must have been way, *way* too long since she'd been laid and whatever maggots she'd hooked up with then had either been totally self-absorbed or a quart low on testosterone.

Why she hadn't learned to get herself off was something else to consider. He and every guy he'd ever known learned to jerk off the minute they started waking up with boners. Hell, even now, he couldn't resist a stroke or two when he was supposed to be rinsing off, and he'd just come twice in barely an hour.

While she was in the bathroom earlier, he'd snooped in the nightstands and found no sex toys, which wasn't surprising considering her horror at being caught with Cherry's gift. Barrett grinned. He'd gotten to her in the nick of time. If he'd waited one more day, she might have brought that thing home and introduced herself to the pleasures of the flesh. Then again, she'd had two hands all her life and never learned to use them, so there was no reason to think the dildo would have been any different.

He opened a shampoo bottle and sniffed. *Mmm, Jillian…* As he squirted some onto his head and scrubbed, it occurred to him that he would have to make sure she knew how to masturbate before he left town, and the idea was all it took to run up his flagpole.

* * * * *

Jillian was in the kitchen having coffee with her mom. Whose kitchen, she wasn't sure—it felt like hers, but it was a lot bigger and had a cathedral ceiling and wall-to-wall windows. She didn't remember Mom getting here, but there she sat across the table, talking about her day as if she'd never been away, and she looked so happy, Jillian's throat tightened with love. Finally! This was how she'd always wanted her mother to look.

The windows faced a wide, sunny meadow with a tree or two off in the distance and a creek splitting it right down the middle. Despite the brightness of the afternoon, the house seemed to be sitting in a shadow. Something didn't look right. She scanned the horizon intently and saw a black funnel drop from clouds that hadn't been there just moments ago. It quickly grew into a tornado that had to be a mile wide, and it was headed right toward the house.

Good Lord, it was for real this time! They were about to be hit by a tornado!

Heart racing, she turned to herd Mom into the basement and saw her out in the garden, bending over the tomato plants. She was frowning—no doubt the tomatoes had blight again. Every time she bought starts from Howard's nursery, they always got blight.

Jillian banged on the window, trying to get her attention, but Mom went right on fussing over those plants. The yard was still splashed with sunlight and it didn't look like the winds had picked up, but the tornado was getting dangerously close to the house and Jillian was becoming frantic. She pounded on the windows with both fists, screaming at her mother to come inside, but it was no use. The roar of the tornado was deafening.

The door—she had to find the door and go out there and get her. Jillian ran down the bank of windows, reaching, searching. There had to be a door here somewhere, damn it, there just had to! It was getting darker now, and she could barely make any headway across the floor as the house began to shake.

Oh God, had her mother already been swept away?

It was so dark, but the wind was starting to regulate, rushing into her ear in great rhythmic gusts, sending chills down her body, making her ache between her legs. She needed relief so badly!

Jillian tried to open her eyes, but everything was too heavy—her eyelids, the air, the body atop hers... She was covered with Barrett, and her thighs were spread wide by his hips and he was in her so deep she couldn't catch her breath. But she could hear the harshness of his as it pumped in her ear, hard and steady, could feel his crisp hair brushing her cheek—had anything ever felt so good?

He was sucking at her, sinking his teeth into the muscle between her neck and shoulder, making her arch and moan. His hands slid under her buttocks and he began to rock, slow and steady, and he didn't stop, even after she was crying and clawing his shoulders at the sensations sluicing through her. Still he rocked, so heavy against her breasts...

* * * * *

Jillian awoke shivering, curled into a ball, her feet so cold they were cramping. Where in the heck were her covers?

She sat up, rubbing her upper arms and blinking against the strong eastern sun streaming through the sheers and the half-closed slats of the blinds. Her bedroom looked like a cyclone had hit it. Jeez, was she developing some kind of psychic powers, where her tornado dreams somehow manifested themselves in her room at night?

Then it hit her. *Barrett.*

She vaulted off the bed and spun around, suddenly breathing hard. There he was, naked as the proverbial jaybird, unjustly sleeping the sleep of innocents. He was stretched out on his back, a pillow wadded up behind his head, one hand on his chest and the other lower, fingertips just brushing his...

Typical man, she snorted, trying not to be shocked and awed by his hardware. Even at rest, it was large enough to look...*unreal*, like the flesh-colored thing from Cherry.

The man had delivered what he promised last night, that was for sure. The promise alone had been nearly enough to make her come screaming in her kitchen. Jillian bit her lip. She *had* come. Screaming. She, Jillian Irene Fox, had finally had her first—and second, and third—orgasm at the hands of the most depraved man she had ever known. No tender kisses, no sweet words, just heat and strength and an unbending will—and one impossibly twisted sex drive.

Barrett George hadn't made love to her, hadn't even pretended to. He'd fucked her brains out, pure and simple.

Make that impure. And *so* not simple.

The memory of that upright sixty-nine popped into her head and she blushed fiercely. God, the man gave a whole new meaning to the phrase *monkey sex*. And she was his monkey. Was there anything she wouldn't let him do to her?

Bracing herself, she turned and looked in the vanity mirror. Ouch. She could have posed for some undiscovered Picasso painting. *Woman Eschews Hygiene*. Or maybe *Debauchery Unbecoming*. No, wait, she had it—*Nude Embracing the Dark Side*.

Whoever the hell that crusty woman was, she needed bathing and brushing in a very big way.

Liquid warmth crept down the inside of her left thigh. Nice. The final brush stroke on a bawdy masterpiece. Could she be any more lovely?

"You have ten minutes, Jill."

Her eyes flew to Barrett's. He was watching her with a hint of squint—his glasses were on the nightstand beside him, but he didn't reach for them. Somehow she'd thought he might look younger and gentler without them. So much for that theory. Now she could clearly see the crinkles and fine scars around his eyes and nose, and if anything he looked even more intent on turning her to the dark side. But she had to admit, without those glasses, he might just succeed. Darn it.

She knew exactly what his dictum meant, and her bristling inner feminist was tempted to take issue with it. Unfortunately, an errant glance at that big hand, which had closed over his erection and was massaging it absently, inspired her still-hungry inner nympho to KO that militant bitch and beg for another serving of what he was dishing out.

Oh, this was so not good, Jillian thought as she sidled around the bed and hurried to the bathroom. Was it possible to grow a backbone in ten minutes?

* * * * *

"I can't come anymore!"

She lay spread beneath him, gasping and tousled and every bit as slick as last night, much to his satisfaction. It had taken all his patience to let her shower first, but jumping her after she'd steeped overnight and developed morning mouth and sheet creases, not to mention a whopping case of bed head, was too cruel even for him.

"Oh, I think you can."

He'd been enjoying her for the better part of an hour, his patience a fortunate side-effect of last night's blistering releases. His slow buildup to detonation had begun at her ears and gradually worked its way down to her tits, where he'd outdone himself. She would have come from that stimulation alone if she hadn't been fighting it so hard again. But, in a mellow sort of morning mood, he'd let her get by with it, knowing he'd make her pay up further down the line. And pay up she had, with clenched teeth and grating cries, her pussy clamping around three of his fingers so hard he'd surged against the sheet, in imminent danger of compounding the stains they'd deposited there last night.

He could tell she was sore from the way she'd flinched when he first pressed his fingertips into her, but he was damned if he could hold back now. Pinning her wrists to the mattress beside her head, he mounted her face-to-face, working his cock into her swollen channel as gently as his pounding blood would let him, glad he'd thought to roll on a condom before she was even out of the shower.

Obviously none too happy with the control he was still exerting over her, Jillian struggled silently against his restraining hands until he quelled her little rebellion with a sharp nip on her earlobe. Though she turned away from him, her whole body leapt in response. Whether she recognized it or not, his domination was part of the excitement for both of them.

Something dark prowling around inside him snarled at the sight of her averted face, wanted to make an issue of it, wanted to force her eyes to his so that he could see what she was hiding. Slamming the door on that something, Barrett settled for trailing his lips across her cheek. He nibbled at the corner of her lips until she turned enough for him to make a thorough conquest of her minty-fresh mouth, a pleasure he'd cheated them both out of until now. But she kept her eyes closed to him, poking at that dark something he was trying so hard to keep caged.

A sound caught his attention. Stilling for a moment, he listened. Someone was in the kitchen, making coffee, from the sound of it. Cherry, no doubt, here for a full accounting of last night's activities.

Fuck.

He broke the kiss and pushed himself up and back until he was sitting on his heels, then grabbed Jillian's flanks and pulled them up onto his thighs. There was no way he was stopping until he was through, but he'd hurry for her sake. Going up on his knees, he held her hips suspended over the bed and pistoned into her fiercely.

* * * * *

"Barrett!"

Jillian was startled and grudgingly thrilled at the abrupt switch to high gear. He'd finally let go of her hands, now that he was too far away to touch. She reached up and grasped the bottom edge of the headboard, unable to do anything but hang there—again—as he bullied her into coming one more time. *Oh, oh, oh...* This position thumped him right against her most sensitive spot and the soles of her feet were beginning to burn again.

She tightened her grip on the headboard until it cut into her fingers, sucking in every breath like it was her last. Her breasts were undulating so wildly with his thrusts, she'd have blushed if she weren't already sizzling with need. This one might kill her.

"Oh, my." The drawn-out syllables shocked the hell out of her.

"Cherry!" God, was that her voice? She sounded like she was about to die… Oh, shit, she was about to die now, now… "Oh please, *now*!"

And he wasn't stopping, oh, no, not Barrett George. He was looking right at her, dark and intent. A scream strangled in her throat as he slammed her over the edge right in front of her best friend, pounding her hard enough to make her skull glance off the headboard. He didn't make a sound when he came.

The jerk.

Cherry wasn't there when she finally dared a look at the doorway. Boy, there was nothing like an unexpected audience to help shake off the after-stupor of a fabulous orgasm. Barrett still had her smashed against his crotch, eking out the last spasms of his own satisfaction.

"Let me go!" she hissed, trying to wrench free. That, of course, made him tighten his grip. When would she learn not to challenge him directly?

He leaned over and planted a smacking kiss on her mouth.

"Now you can go."

* * * * *

His imperious attitude pissed her off, but she didn't have time to deal with it at the moment. After a frantic pit-stop in the bathroom, Jillian strolled into the kitchen as nonchalantly as possible, wearing panties and her prim winter robe.

"Good morning, sunshine." Cherry handed her a cup of steaming coffee. "Sorry about the interruption. I didn't see a car in the driveway, so I figured..." She trailed off, looking all kinds of pleased with herself.

Jillian wondered if she wore a similar expression. After all, she was the one who'd just been laid six ways from Sunday. Unable to help herself, she smiled back, blushing furiously.

"So Cherry," Barrett said, ironic amusement coloring his tone, "what brings you to this neck of the woods, all bright and early on a Saturday morning?" He'd come up behind Jillian and was sliding his hands around her waist. Having experienced this too recently, she immediately seized one of those hands and placed her coffee mug in it, moving so that his other arm was around her back, holding her to his side. She wouldn't have put it past the big oaf to slide hands up over her breasts, just to show Cherry he could.

"Well, I was in the neighborhood," Cherry began, flashing her dimple.

"And thought you'd drop in for a quick peek?"

"Barrett!"

Cherry laughed out loud. "Actually, I would have settled for a detailed description, but this was a lot more fun."

"Cherry!"

"I'm sorry, hon." Cherry handed her another cup. "I shouldn't tease, but y'all were just so darn cute."

"Cute isn't usually the effect I'm going for," Barrett said dryly, sipping the coffee. He'd dressed, except for footwear, and was wearing his glasses again. Oddly enough, she was kind of getting to like them on him.

"Okay, you looked like a total studmuffin," Cherry consoled. "Those claw marks on your shoulders tell the tale of a spectacular night."

"Yeah, I thought those were a nice touch."

Jillian frowned as he took another sip of his coffee. She didn't remember scratching his shoulders—the man had never let her near his shoulders.

Oh, wonderful. He'd come to her bed wearing the marks of another woman's recent good time.

Stiffening, she tried to step away from him, but Barrett grabbed her wrist and held, still sipping casually.

"They are," Cherry nodded. Looking him up and down, she gestured to the box on the counter. "Gee, I'm glad I brought so many donuts—you look like you could eat them all by yourself."

"I'll try to restrain myself." Barrett's fingertips stroked the inside of Jillian's wrist as he set his cup, and then hers, on the counter. "Would you excuse us for a few minutes, Cherry?"

"Of course. Go, go!" She shooed them out of the kitchen.

Dragging her feet all the way, Jillian let Barrett pull her into the bedroom and close the door. When he leaned against it and crossed his arms, she put on a carefully blank face. After all, neither of them had made any claims or promises. She had no grounds for feeling possessive.

The jerk.

"Sorry," he said, "I guess we should have talked about—"

"No need to apologize," Jillian broke in coolly. "Your personal life is none of my business."

"None of your business?" He frowned. "Jillian, what in the hell are you talking about?"

Crap. How could she answer this without sounding jealous?

"It's none of my business who marks you up during sex," she finally said.

"Who marks me..." He shook his head as if to clear it. "You're kidding, right?"

Jillian fidgeted with her belt. "Can we drop this, please? Cherry's waiting."

"Well she can wait a little longer," he said, bracing his hands on his hips. "Jillian, just who in the hell do you think marked me?"

"Well it wasn't me!"

"Did I miss something? Did you sneak out of bed after I fell asleep last night and send in a pinch-hitter?" He whipped his shirt over his head and went to the mirror, twisting to examine his rippling shoulders.

"Very attractive," Jillian said with a little more venom than she'd intended.

Barrett raised his brows at her over his shoulder. "Jillian, I'm telling you, you did this to me."

"Oh, please. I didn't have that much to drink last night." Or did he think she'd been so overcome by his earthy attentions that she wouldn't remember raking furrows in his flesh?

"Well, I didn't have all these scratches when I got here and I obviously couldn't have inflicted them on myself."

"Dammit, Barrett, you never let me touch you, remember, Mr. Domination Freak?" She crossed her arms over her chest and stared back, daring him to deny it.

"Jillian, look at them."

Against her better judgment, she went over to inspect the scratches. They were red and angry, a couple of them deep enough to have drawn blood. She frowned—they weren't even scabbed over yet.

"You really don't remember, do you?" Barrett put a knee on the mattress and leaned over it, searching. "Look."

There were a couple of small smears of blood where he'd been sleeping.

"That's just weird. I could have sworn…"

"Do you remember me giving you this?"

He stood up and turned her to face the mirror. Sweeping her hair back, he drew her robe away from her right shoulder. The purple hickey and faint red circle of tooth imprints toward the back of her shoulder muscle brought last night's dream roaring back.

"Oh my God, I thought I was dreaming," she said. "I *was* dreaming. The tornado dream..."

"Excuse me, the tornado dream?"

"That's what I said." She pulled her robe back up and tightened the belt again. "And before you ask, I dream about tornados a lot."

"Were you in one or something?"

"Not that I know of. Anyway, I was having the tornado dream, and my mom was out in the garden and I was trying to get to her, but I couldn't find my way." She cleared her throat to try to ease the constriction. Jeez, was she going to cry now, too? "You know how those dreams are."

"Yeah, I've had a few." His tone said it was a lot more than a few.

"And then it was dark and you were on top of me and we were, you know..."

"Fucking?"

"Barrett, don't you know any civilized terms for sex?" she asked, exasperated.

His lips quirked. "Sure, but that's my favorite."

"Well, pick a new one!"

"Gee, I'll get right on that," he drawled. "So we were humping in your dream. What else happened?"

"I already told you!" If he thought she was going to talk dirty to him, he could think again. That was his perverted purview.

"You clawed my shoulders, didn't you?"

Jillian bit her lip. "Okay, fine, I guess I did it. Sorry. I'm a pretty heavy sleeper and I'm always kind of disoriented when

I wake up." Obviously her inner nympho was busting out with a vengeance. There was no telling what was busting out of him.

"I'm the one who should be apologizing," he said, grabbing his shirt off the bed and pulling it on again before facing her. "Jillian, I didn't use a condom."

Chapter Eight

Well. Now she knew what was busting out of him.

"Which would explain the flood this morning," she sighed. "Hey, I was asleep—what was your excuse?"

"Look, I really am sorry." He sure sounded a lot more sorry than when he'd popped the button off her skirt. "I'm not used to sleeping with anyone." At her arch look, he added, "I mean actually sleeping. I don't spend the night with my…dates."

Jillian frowned. Was that supposed to make her feel better?

"So," he continued, "when I rolled over in the middle of the night and found you, all soft and warm and smelling like sex, I just…"

"Helped yourself?"

"Basically." He ran an impatient hand through his hair. "Is this going to be a problem?"

"No, it's not." At least not for him. When was the fertile time in a woman's cycle, anyway?

"When is your period due?" he asked.

"About a week," she mumbled, even less thrilled with this line of questioning.

Barrett reached into his pocket and took out that roll again. Antacids? Did he have an ulcer? "Perfect. Couldn't have timed that any better if I'd tried."

"How do you know?"

"Honey, if there's anything I know, it's women's bodies."

"Lovely." Jillian marched to the bedroom door and opened it. "Why don't you go find your own breakfast?"

"I think I'll do that, but not because you're telling me to." He followed her into the living room and put on his socks and shoes, balancing on one enormous foot at a time. Plucking his keys off the dining table—Cherry must have found them—he said, "Jillian, it's probably nothing to worry about."

Cherry, sitting at the table with her coffee and a Tom Clancy novel, looked on, not bothering to pretend she was reading.

"I'm not worried."

Stepping in front of her, he snagged her wrist again. "Yeah, right, you're not worried at all. That's why your pulse is going a mile a minute."

"It's doing that because you annoyed me," Jillian snapped.

"Mm-hmm. Listen, I have to go to Kansas City today, but I'll be back tomorrow." He planted a quick kiss on her lips and drew back, searching her face with those unfathomable eyes. Evidently one wasn't enough for him any more than it was for her, because he leaned in for another long, lush kiss. When she surfaced, she was wrapped around him like a stripe on a barber pole.

"Can I take a rain check on the donuts, Cherry?"

"No problem, big guy," she assured him.

After one more quick peck, he ordered, "I'll be back tomorrow around four. Be ready, Jill."

"For what?"

"Me."

* * * * *

"Have you ever been flattened by a steamroller?" Jillian asked as she pulled up the lid on the donut box. Cherry had brought a couple of raspberry-filled jellies, bless her pea-pickin' little heart.

"Not since Dubbya took the White House," Cherry replied. Jillian ignored her. They'd had to relegate politics to their list of "Do Not Discuss" topics way back in college, but neither of them could resist the occasional potshot.

"Count yourself lucky," Jillian advised, taking a bite right on the jelly hole.

Cherry looked her up and down. "Oh, please! If that's what it looks like, I'll throw myself in front of the next one that rolls by."

"Cherry, I'm serious! The man is an unstoppable force, and this immovable object just about got crushed into oblivion. I swear to God, the things he made me—"

The phone chirped.

"Darn it! Just when you were getting to the good part," Cherry groused. Jillian set her donut on the counter. Caller ID told her it was Barrett, and she frowned, licking glaze off her thumb and middle finger. Five minutes. That must be a world record. Did he forget something?

"Hey, I forgot to tell you that I called your dealership while you were in the shower earlier. Someone will be by at eleven to pick up your car and drop off a loaner."

Jillian blinked.

"Wow. Thank you. I hadn't even thought about that yet."

"No problem."

There was a long stretch of dead air.

"Barrett?"

"I'm here. Sorry, I was just thinking."

"That's okay. I'm a little zoned myself."

"How do you feel about football?"

"Baked or fried?"

He chuckled. "On the gridiron. Kansas City. You and me. Today. Interested?"

Her heart was doing the mambo again.

"Who are we playing?"

"Seattle."

"You're on. When do I need to be ready?"

"Two hours at the outside. Bring an overnight bag."

Jillian pressed the disconnect button on the handset and stood there trying to figure out what had just happened.

"What's he making you do now?" Cherry inquired, tongue in cheek, reaching into the box behind Jillian to snag a maple bar.

"He's taking me to a Chiefs game."

"Oh, you pitiful thing! A night of wild animal sex, a trip to Kansas City, a professional football game…" Cherry shuddered. "What other horrors await you, I wonder?"

"An overnight stay in the maternity ward?"

Cherry's eyes bugged out as she choked on that first bite. Jillian couldn't help laughing as she thumped her on the back.

"Jesus, Jillian, that's not funny!"

She didn't know the half of it.

"It's probably nothing to worry about," Jillian said, sounding even less convinced than Barrett had.

"You're serious?"

"Yes, unfortunately. Last night, we…" She waved her hand. "You know. Without a condom. Twice."

"You're not on anything?"

"Why would I be?"

"And I suppose you didn't ask if he'd been checked recently." Jillian's expression must have said it all because Cherry pulled hard on two handfuls of her blonde hair and screeched, "Arrgh! What am I going to do with you?"

"Well, I didn't exactly plan it." Just saying the words made her stomach churn. God, she couldn't imagine how any woman had the nerve to do something like this on purpose. No wonder her mother had turned into such a mess.

"Have you thought about taking a morning-after pill?"

Jillian pursed her lips. "No."

"You could."

"I know." She picked up her donut and took another big bite, trying not to think.

"You're in love with him."

Jillian shouted "I am not!" around her mouthful.

"Barrett and Jillian, sittin' in a tree…" Jillian advanced with a threat on her face as Cherry chanted, "F-U-C-K-I-N-G."

"You are so not getting the four-one-one from last night."

"Big deal—I saw all I needed to know and then some."

"Thanks for reminding me." Jillian bypassed her, heading to the fridge for a glass of milk. "Actually, I really wanted to talk to you about—oh Lord, about everything, but I've got to get my butt in the tub or I'll never be ready on time."

"Go for it. We can talk while you clean up."

* * * * *

Barrett sat in Jillian's driveway with the motor running, wondering what in the hell he was doing. It was like he'd taken out his list of hard-and-fast rules concerning women and was checking them off, one by one, as he broke them.

Never spend the night with a woman.

Check.

Never fuck a woman without protection.

Check. Check again.

Never lose control while fucking a woman.

Check. Damn it, check again.

Never take a woman further than she's comfortable going.
Check, check, check, check...
Never let a woman fuck with your head.

Ah, the pencil was hovering over the paper on this one. He'd been no more intimate with Jillian's body than he had with any other woman's. He'd told her no more about himself than he'd told any other woman. Well, not much more. And for God's sake, he'd even taken other women to football games practically every week during the last season.

But this time was different. This time he was taking a woman home with him. Home, to his city. Why did that feel like a big deal? And why was taking a woman he was fucking to Kansas City any more intimate than fucking a woman who lived in Kansas City?

It wasn't. And yet...

He opened the center console and peeled a couple of antacid tablets off the roll, barely chewing before gulping them down. Christ, he hoped he wasn't making a monumental mistake here. The fact that he'd given in to the impulse to invite Jillian along was proof positive that his gonads had seized control and were shutting down his higher brain functions. He was in clear violation of a previously unrecognized rule: *What happens someplace else, stays someplace else.*

Fuck.

Jillian opened the front door before he'd even rung the bell.

At least she was prompt.

Barrett couldn't say exactly what he'd expected, but it sure as hell wasn't the red foam finger she crammed in his face. She had on a solid red Sooners tee shirt tucked into a pair of faded blue jean shorts that hit her at a very conservative mid-thigh. Though they displayed a good bit of her lovely legs, he wouldn't have minded if they'd been a little shorter and a lot tighter. But he'd known from the start she wasn't into accentuating her positives. That was okay—he was happy enough to see the tee clinging lovingly to her breasts.

"I take it you plan to root for the home team?"

She shot him a look as she closed the door and checked to make sure it had locked behind her. "It would hardly be polite to do otherwise. Besides, I already had all this red stuff from college."

"I can't believe you kept a foam finger for, what, seven or eight years?"

"I'm kind of a packrat." She stood aside as he opened the rear window of the Suburban, then offered him her overnight bag. "Besides, it's coming in handy, isn't it?"

"That depends on what you plan to do with your finger," Barrett drawled, surprising a laugh out of her. She turned red, too, almost as red as her shirt.

"Nothing so twisted as what you do with yours, I'm sure."

Laughing out loud, he corkscrewed the knuckle of his right index finger into a nostril and wheezed, "I don't know *what* you're talking about."

"I hope you weren't planning on holding hands," she returned primly.

"Typical woman—you'll let me stick my nose in your twat, but you won't chance picking up a booger holding my hand."

"Barrett George!" she scolded, still as red as her shirt and obviously trying not to laugh. But at least she marched around to the passenger door instead of back into the house. Climbing in, she continued, "You need to watch your mouth. This is Saturday morning and there are a million kids in this neighborhood."

"They probably don't even know twat that is," he said as he buckled up. He'd never really yanked a woman's chain like this before. He liked it too much.

"They will by the time you're through with them." After a long pause, she added in a determined tone, "And if you'll recall, I didn't let you. In fact, I did everything I could to stop you."

Anticipation whispered through him. They were just backing out of the driveway and already she was begging for a little smackdown.

"And then screamed my name at the top of your lungs when you came."

"You're still a pig." She looked annoyed now, obviously hating that he was right. Barrett put it in Park halfway into the street.

"And you still want me to fuck you." He stared at her from behind his sunglasses, daring her to deny it.

"I hate it when you say that." She crossed her arms, turning to look out the window. Barrett grinned and put the vehicle back in gear.

"No, Jillian, what you hate is that hearing *you, me* and *fuck* in the same sentence makes you cream your panties."

"In your dreams," she snorted.

"Oh yeah?" Stopped at the corner, he stared at her over the tops of his tinted lenses. "Fuck me, Jill."

He was gratified to hear her suck in a tremulous breath. She bit her lip and refused to look at him when he declared with finality, "Game, set and match."

* * * * *

Jillian heaved a big sigh. She should have just kept her mouth shut. She knew not to poke at the sleeping tiger, but she'd done it anyway, and look where it had gotten her — put in her place and creamed in her panties.

Cherry had insisted that she could have as much power over Barrett as he had over her, but she was damned if she could figure out where to find it or how to use it. Jillian mulled over the discussion they'd had while she was getting ready. The barrier of the shower curtain and the racket of running water had lent a certain anonymity to the situation, allowing her to share her concerns with much greater detail than she might have otherwise.

"Oh my God, I hate you!" Cherry had groaned. "Does he have any brothers?"

"Just one, younger. I think Barrett said his name was Dustin."

"Hmm. I don't know if I'm up for training a younger man."

"Please. If he's anything like Barrett, he won't need any training." Jillian worked shampoo into her hair, deep in thought. "How would you handle a man like him, Cherry?"

"Oh, I'd probably do what you're doing, to start with. Let him play his little domination game for a while, provoke him just to see how far he'd go."

"That's not what I'm—" Jillian winced. That was exactly what she'd been doing. "God, am I sick?"

Cherry burst out laughing. "Jillian, relax! Boys and girls have been playing domination games since Cro-Magnon man dragged his woman back to the cave by her hair. That stab of primal fear can be a total turn-on when you really feel safe with a guy."

"I'm not so sure I feel safe with Barrett," Jillian sighed, turning off the water and reaching for a towel.

"Of course you do. You wouldn't have run after him at the restaurant if you didn't."

Jillian explained exactly why she'd run after him while she toweled off and reached out for her robe. When she drew back the shower curtain, Cherry was wearing a wide-eyed smile. Then she told her about the break-in, and her account of her rosy-cheeked interview with stud-cop had Cherry holding her sides.

"I'm sorry to laugh, sweetie, and I'm sure sorry about the earrings, but that's got to be the funniest thing I've ever heard!"

"Barrett said if I'd bring another one home, he'd... Oh God, I can't even say it." She held out one unsteady hand. "Look, I'm shaking."

"Girl, I'll have a few more in your nightstand when you get home tomorrow."

"You will not!" Jillian cried, aghast.

"Jillian, that's exactly why the man keeps pushing you," Cherry said impatiently. "He obviously knows you well enough to tell when your mouth is saying one thing and your body is saying something else."

"I do not want to be Barrett's sex slave."

"Honey, you don't have to *be* his sex slave to play his sex slave. I say again, you're not your mother." Jillian looked away. Cherry had nailed another one. "That's what's bothering you, isn't it?"

"How can you be so sure I won't turn into her?"

"Because you're already way too strong to become a weakling like her. I doubt a man like Barrett would be the least bit interested in you if you didn't present a major challenge."

"Thanks, I think." She went into the bedroom and started digging in her dresser, very happy she'd taken the time to strip off the bedding and toss it in the washer. The musky odor of sex in the air still seemed overpowering to her, though Cherry didn't comment on it when she flopped into the chair.

"All I'm saying, Jill, is that I can tell from the look in his eye that he's boinked more than his share of hot babes wearing low-riders and showing off belly-button piercings. His type only goes after the retiring ones when they challenge him."

Jillian had to smile—she liked the word *boinked* better than anything Barrett had come up with.

"What you're going to have to do now," Cherry continued, "is learn how to turn the tables on him."

"And just how do I do that?" Jillian pulled on a pair of panties before shrugging out of her robe to dress. She couldn't help smiling again when Cherry groaned with unconcealed envy, her eyes fixed on the purplish shadows marking her hips. It felt really good to be on the receiving end of that emotion for a change.

"Have you ever thought about waxing?"

"Cherry!" Jillian blushed to her roots.

"Hey, I've been doing the Brazilian thing for over a year and I'll never go back."

"Doesn't it hurt?"

"Not that much, especially if they use a topical anesthetic first. And I'm telling you, Jill, it's nice not to listen to guys spitting out hairs."

Jillian screeched. "Cherry, how did you get so naughty?"

"Years of dedicated practice."

Of course. What else?

"You were just about to tell me how to turn the tables on Barrett," she reminded her.

"Right. Two key things here, you lucky little brat, and you have to take them in order or it'll never fly."

"Okay—shoot."

"First and foremost, you have to be honest with yourself. I think that's going to be the hardest part for you, hon, because you're so conditioned to denying your sexuality."

Jillian thought about denying that assessment, but let Cherry continue. "It's absolutely true that knowledge is power, especially when it pertains to sex. If Barrett knows more about you than you do, he holds all the cards. You can start, Jillian," she said pointedly, "by admitting to yourself, even if you never admit it to me or him or anyone else, that you're totally turned on by the idea of Barrett using sex toys on you. I can absolutely guarantee," she added with an arch look, "that he knows it."

Jillian's face got so hot, she turned her back on Cherry to finish dressing.

"Barrett is light years ahead of you experience-wise, and if it weren't for the way he looks at you, I'd be worried for you."

"Well, I'm worried for me." Then she blinked. "How does he look at me?" She couldn't begin to interpret the darkness in his eyes when they rested on her.

"Possessively."

Well, she'd asked.

"So what's the second thing?"

"You learn him." Cherry made that sound so simple. "If I had time, I'd give you a crash course in basic alpha-male behavior, but you're just going to have to pick it up as you go. You need to study him as carefully as he's obviously studied you, learn what makes him laugh, what pushes his buttons, what turns him on."

"And then?"

"And then you use it against him."

Chapter Nine

"Penny for your thoughts."

Jillian's eyes met his shaded ones head-on for a moment, then slid down his Chiefs tee shirt to his lap before returning to the road. She let a slow smile creep over her face, saying nothing, and it wasn't hard to work up a blush.

She could hear his breathing now, and it sounded just a little bit hard, a little bit fast. Hey, maybe she could do this after all. She turned her face to the window before he could see her smile turn to an outright grin.

"I was just hoping it wouldn't be too hot for the game."

"Too hot, huh?" His voice was dripping with suggestion.

"Mmm." She clamped down on a snicker. The man could find innuendo in an IPO prospectus.

"There's a cooler in the back seat, if you get overheated," he told her blandly.

"Think that'd help me?"

That got a chuckle out of him.

"Again," he said, "it would depend on what you intended to do with it."

"Well, thanks. I'll keep that in mind."

"Did they pick up your Honda?" he asked, glancing in the rearview mirror as he changed lanes.

"Yes, thank you. Although how you managed service like that is beyond me. And speaking of service, how in the heck did you get us the best table at Chartreuse so last-minute?"

They were on the interstate now. Barrett set the cruise control and leaned back, holding the wheel loosely in his left hand and settling the right against her headrest.

"Do you know what MGB stands for?" he asked.

It took a minute for Jillian to catch up with him. MGB, as in MGB Hospitality Group, the hotel's parent company.

"Monsters Going Bowling?"

"Not quite," he grinned.

"Men Going Berserk?"

"Closer, but still no cigar. More like Mahoney, George and Butcher."

"Ah. I take it you're the George?" Oh, crap. She was sleeping with… Oh, crap.

"Actually, Dad's the real George. I'm just a cheap knock-off." That should have been funny, but she got an odd vibe when he said it. "Brian Butcher is one of the partners. He's also Bay's father."

"Well, that explains that. And the dealership?"

"Money talks."

Right. The idea that he had greased someone's palm to expedite her car repairs made her uncomfortable, but she didn't say so.

Every word out of his mouth made it more and more apparent that Barrett George was a very complex man. Study him, Cherry had said. Well, there was no time like the present. Jillian tried to figure out how to do that without being too obvious about it. She'd worked so hard to avoid looking at him last week… God, she was so lame. Just sneaking a glance at his huge sneakers had her heart racing. How was she ever going to learn what made him tick if she couldn't even look at him without having a panic attack?

Suck it up, Jillian! So what if a tickle in her tummy told her that scrutinizing him openly might incite him to some sort of perverted retaliation? What could he do to her while they were flying down the highway at seventy—make that seventy-three miles an hour, and on an already tight schedule?

As casually as possible, she drew her left knee up and turned in her seat, ordering her hands to relax against her thighs. Then she girded her mental loins and began the inspection.

Oh Lord, this man took her breath away. Although he'd shaved, she could still see the darkish tint of his beard. He'd obviously showered, too, but the tousled state of his hair said he'd barely taken the time to run a comb over it afterward. If she looked at it for very long, she might not be able to resist running her fingers through it. Again, she wondered just how old he was. There was more silver streaking that dark brown mop than she'd realized. The fine scarring on his forehead and around his eyes obscured his age even further.

Thick tendons in his neck stood out in stark relief as he peered over his left shoulder before changing lanes. She would bite him there, given the chance.

The wayward urge startled her even as it made her smile.

Barrett glanced at her and she brazened her way through the short staring contest, knowing he'd have to look back at the road sooner or later. When he did, she continued her perusal. His lips twitched, but he didn't smile. He had great lips, soft and full and kissable—even if they *were* attached to a filthy mouth. Her heart bumped at the thought and she felt a tingle in a place she really shouldn't.

Here it was, another opportunity to be honest with herself. Yes, Barrett had been dead-on in his assessment of her reaction to his dirty talk. Hearing him use the F-word in relation to her made her hot enough to start forest fires. And wet enough to put them out.

Bad Jillian.

Knowing that Barrett was fully aware of her visual tour intensified the tingle. He wanted her to look at him, and now she really wanted to look. She wanted to know how it felt to allow herself to become aroused by just looking at a man. The potential had been there since the moment she laid eyes on him. It was, in fact, what had driven her to the M&M bowl. Barrett's physique was everything she'd ever unconsciously wished for in a man, so tall and broad that she felt dainty and feminine by comparison. For the first time ever.

What she hadn't anticipated was the realization of her own vulnerability, of her weakness in the face of his strength. God, he was strong. He could do anything he wanted with her, to her, literally any damn thing, and there wasn't much she could do about it.

Uh-oh. Tingle was becoming burn. How in the hell could she be turned on by a realization that ought to scare the living crap out of her? She studied the large hand grasping the steering wheel. His restraining hand, the hand he used to hold her in place while his other hand played her. Tortured her. Made her scream with want, and then with satisfaction.

Speaking of which... Barrett's right hand moved down to rest on his thigh and he shifted in his seat, pulling his left knee up and splaying the right one out. The position put that bulge behind his fly on prominent display. For her.

She could practically hear him now: *Look at my cock and love it. Beg for it.*

Suck it.

He'd made her do that. The loser she'd slept with way back when—what was his name again?—had begged her to do it to him, and she'd tried, truly she had, but it just grossed her out. He urinated out of that thing, for crying out loud.

So did Barrett. But that hadn't stopped her from doing as he'd ordered, hadn't stopped her from being thrilled out of her mind by his musky taste, by the velvety feel of that broad head filling her mouth, hadn't stopped her from licking her lips and swallowing what it spurted there. And feeling empowered by it.

Now, if that wasn't a paradoxical concept. How could she be empowered by his domination, by her own submission? She was going to have to think about that one. Maybe she should experiment, do it to him again, only on her terms instead of his, if she could figure out how to manage such a thing. Jillian felt the upward curving of her lips again and couldn't seem to quash it. She had the germ of a plan now and felt better for it.

"I'd give a lot more than a penny for your thoughts right about now," Barrett rumbled.

Jillian met his sidelong look easily now.

"I was just wondering how old you are."

"Sure you were."

"Mmm." What would he make of her smile?

"Okay, we'll play it your way. How old do you think I am?"

"Oh, no. Guessing someone's age is tricky business even under the best of circumstances."

"You don't consider these the best of circumstances?"

"Keep your eyes on the road, Mr. George. And I'm reserving judgment on that."

"Ah, playing it close to the chest, are you?"

"I thought that was supposed to be 'close to the vest'."

"Chest, vest, breast—it's all the same thing." He slid another look at her.

"Not really. You have a chest. I have breasts."

"You do, indeed."

"And I never wear vests. They make my breasts look like cantaloupes." She heard his sudden intake of air and froze. Okay, maybe that was just a tad too much bravado.

"Miss Fox," Barrett said mildly.

"Yes?"

"If your cock-teasing makes me miss kickoff, you're going to be on the M end of some serious S and M when we get to Kansas City."

Jillian winced. She didn't know if she was quite ready for that yet.

"Got it."

"Nice job, though."

A giggle escaped. "Thank you."

"I'm thirty-three. Any other burning questions?" She gathered from his tone that the prospect didn't thrill him.

"Just one more."

He sighed. "Well, spit it out, then."

"What's in the cooler?"

* * * * *

Shit. He really liked her.

"Just a few odds and ends. You didn't have lunch, did you?"

"Ha! You barely gave me enough notice to shower and get ready." Jillian sounded offended, and damned if he didn't like that, too.

"Well then, help yourself. I'll take a sandwich and a pop, while you're in there."

She unbuckled and twisted around to look for the cooler. He'd put it on the seat behind his so it would be easier for her to reach. She got onto her knees and stretched between their seats to rummage around for food and drinks. Her hip bumping his shoulder gave him some ideas that were dangerous, given their present speed.

"Oh, you put diet in, too. Thank you," she said over her shoulder. "What is this stuff?"

"Well, let's see—I think there's a couple of roast beef sandwiches and a couple of tuna sandwiches in the foil, and some relish-type stuff in the covered bowl." She'd put one knee up on the console and was still, by God, teasing him with that rounded hip, now just inches from his face. Just for fun, he trailed his fingers up the inside of her bare thigh. She twitched like he'd touched her with a live wire.

"Hey, if I'm a cock-tease, what does that make you?"

"I'm not teasing." His hand slid up the baggy leg of her shorts, advancing into panty territory without hesitation. He had to admit, loose shorts had their place in the grand scheme of things.

"Barrett!"

She started to jerk back down to her seat and he clamped his hand around the inside of her thigh, right in that sensitive crease, holding her against the side of his chest. He could smell her again, hot and spicy.

"Stay there."

"This isn't exactly comfortable. I thought you were hungry." She tried to sound exasperated, but he heard the catch in her voice. The little minx had gotten herself more worked up than she'd gotten him, which was hard to do. He'd just sat there and enjoyed her visual explorations, unreasonably pleased that she was finally acknowledging her erotic interest in him.

"Not as hungry as you, apparently," he said in a silky voice, slipping two fingers beneath the edge of her underwear. "I could swear I fucked you senseless no more than four hours ago, but here you are, dripping wet again."

She said nothing, just breathed hard as he continued to tease her, drawing his fingers back and forth along the edge of her slippery cleft.

"Is there anything I can do for you, Jill?"

"You know there is," she breathed roughly. "The real question is, can you do it without running us into the ditch?"

* * * * *

Where the hell was a camera when you needed one?

Barrett grinned as he downed a quarter of his sandwich in a single bite, glancing in the rearview mirror at the semi he'd just passed. The look on her face when he'd stuck the two fingers he'd wedged into her, and then the thumb he'd used on her clit, into his mouth and sucked them off, one by one... He could tell she still hadn't made up her mind if she was scandalized or fascinated.

You know there is. Man, those had been about the last words he expected to hear from her. He'd figured he would have to wrestle her into submission again, but she had surprised him by pulling the crotch of her panties aside to facilitate his efforts. That was the only moment he'd even come close to putting them in the ditch, and it would have been worth it.

His eyes returned to the mirror and he lifted his head to see the back seat. Jillian was there right now, with her hand down the open front of her shorts, trying to clean herself up with the moist towelette some considerate restaurant employee had packed in the picnic lunch. She'd dropped one over his shoulder, presumably for him to clean up the fingers he'd used on her, but he hadn't used it yet. Wouldn't for a while. He wanted to enjoy those fragrant reminders of her every time he took a bite of his lunch.

"Eyes on the road, George."

He was still grinning. Maybe he'd have to turn up the heat again tonight.

Chapter Ten

Pro football games had just rocketed to the top of her list of favorite ways to spend a Saturday afternoon.

"I didn't realize how much I'd missed this," Jillian said with a breathless laugh. They were down ten to seven at the end of the first quarter, but she wasn't worried. Barrett had informed her on the drive up that the Chiefs had a terrific record at home, one of the best in the league. Arrowhead Stadium was packed, and if it weren't for the fact that Barrett's season ticket seats were situated in the shaded end of the stadium, they'd be roasting alive in the late afternoon heat. Fortunately, quality refreshments were abundant, if expensive, and she'd already downed two bottles of water and another diet soda to keep hydrated. Barrett had chased his water with a beer.

"I have to say, you hadn't really struck me as a football fan," he said. "I take it you and the gridiron have a history?"

"Are you kidding? At OU?"

"Well, it's hardly a required subject."

"That's what you think. Actually, I was in the marching band all five years."

"Ah, the Pride of Oklahoma. Impressive. It's too bad you were there in the middle of their slump. Did you make it to any bowl games?"

"The John Hancock and the Copper Bowl."

"Beats staying home, I guess. Five years, huh? Did you work on a graduate degree or something?"

"No, I just couldn't make up my mind whether to follow my brain or my heart. I graduated just a few hours short of a second major in music education."

"Brain won, huh?"

"It pays better." She rethought the glib response almost instantly. "Well, if you really want the truth, I finally realized I wasn't music teacher material any more than I was performer material—I never seemed to get over the stage fright and it was just more stress than I cared to deal with for the rest of my life. College was enough."

"What instrument did you play?"

"Quite a few of them, actually, but oboe is my favorite. I generally played clarinet in marching band, though one semester I did play the alto sax."

Barrett looked at her hands. "You play the piano, too."

"Not much any more." He must have peeked into her middle bedroom-slash-office, where she kept a small upright. Actually, she still played quite often—just not for anyone but herself.

"Why not?"

"Busy. Did you ever play an instrument?" Anything to divert his attention.

"Just this one," he grinned, sliding his hand over his fly.

"No surprise there. I suppose you were a sports star."

"Maybe."

"Football?"

"Of course."

"Fighting Irish, huh? Let me guess—linebacker?"

He cocked his head at her. "Very good, Miss Fox."

Pleased with herself, she thought hard. "Let's see here. If you're three years older than me, that puts you at Notre Dame when I was in high school. Good Lord, I watched you play football, Barrett. Went to a few bowl games yourself, didn't you?"

"A couple," he drawled. "You're just full of surprises. I probably saw you march, too, but I mostly had eyes for the twirlers and flag girls back then." His gaze skimmed down her body. "Don't know what I was thinking."

She couldn't help smiling. "I suppose you played baseball, too."

"Nah, never cared for it. I wrestled from second grade through high school, though. Bet you didn't see me take State my junior and senior years."

Ooh, Barrett wrestling. There was something she'd pay good money to see. She'd attended a few wrestling matches with the high school pep band, but hadn't found anything sexy about them. Quite the opposite, in fact. If she'd known Barrett then, it might have been another story altogether.

"Sorry, wrong state. And I probably wouldn't have seen you anyway—my brother only watched football and baseball."

"You've got a brother, too, huh? Younger or older?"

"Um, a year younger. So why didn't you go pro?"

He paused but let the change of subject pass without comment. "I did, actually," he finally said. "With the Steelers, but I had a major knee blow-out during training camp."

"I'm sorry."

"I'm not. Football is a hazardous sport, especially for guys my size." He slid her another one of those sidelong glances. "If I'd kept going, this body would probably be in pretty bad shape by now."

Jillian gave him a little inspection of her own before saying deliberately, "Well, we couldn't have that, now, could we?"

Barrett grinned, apparently pleased with her response to his prompt, but said nothing as they turned their attention back to the football field. The second quarter started with a bang when KC returned a punt more than ninety yards for a touchdown. Barrett shot out of his seat like he was spring-loaded and Jillian followed suit with a smile, letting his deep shouts shimmer down her bones. What would it be like to make him yell like that for her?

Bad Jillian, bad, bad! Down, girl!

She was the first to sit, still smiling when he settled back into his hard plastic seat. She was happy to be sitting on her foam finger, even though Barrett's suggestive look at that long red Number One sprouting from beneath her thighs had made her face heat up again. His arm settled behind her shoulders, along the top of her seat.

"What, were you ogling my ass or something?" Barrett narrowed his eyes at her. "I'm not sure I like that look."

"Well, I wasn't going to bring up the skid mark, but since you asked…"

The wisecrack tripped off her tongue with startling ease and Jillian was pleased when the two guys in front of them snickered into their beers. Barrett surprised her by whooping with laughter, squeezing her shoulder tightly.

"Truce," he finally gasped as he shoved his beer into her hand and slid a thumb and forefinger under his glasses to wipe his eyes. A tremendous cheer went up from the crowd. "Aw, shit, Jillian, you made me miss the extra point!" he groaned.

"Serves you right."

He pulled her even closer and murmured in her ear, "I'll serve you right later, little girl. Paybacks can be a real bitch."

"Talk is cheap."

Barrett leaned in as if to answer and pushed his tongue against the shell of her ear, swirling it delicately along the rim. Jillian sucked in air on a shiver when it made a quick but hot foray into the canal.

"You're so right," he said smugly, rescuing his beer from her suddenly nerveless fingers.

"Maybe you two ought to get a room, bro."

"Maybe you ought to get lost, Dusty." Barrett grinned up at the lanky young man who stood beside him in the aisle.

"Maybe you ought to introduce me to your girlfriend." Without waiting, he leaned over and took her hand in his, blue eyes shining with mischief. "Hi, I'm Dustin George. What's a nice girl like you doing with a bonehead like this?"

"Maybe you ought to turn her loose before I loosen a few of your teeth."

"Maybe you ought to think twice about roughing me up with Mom and Dad up there watching." Dustin maintained his grip on her hand with a flirtatious stare.

Barrett heaved a noisy sigh. "Shit."

"Ha! This round goes to the younger, better-looking brother." Apparently they'd played this game before. "It would be impolite of me to let go of her hand before you introduce us, Barrett."

"I'm Jillian Fox," Jillian jumped in with a smile, sensing genuine aggravation rising in Barrett.

"Jillian, meet the bane of my existence."

* * * * *

"You can let her go now, Dustin." Barrett said the words with mock-menace that felt uncomfortably close to real menace. Jillian looked charmed by his little brother. She'd never looked charmed for him. She'd looked anxious, humorous, aroused and well-fucked, but never charmed. What the hell else did he expect, though? He hadn't been and still wasn't out to charm her. He was out to enjoy her for a few nights. Period. Which hadn't required charming, not from the instant their hands had first touched in Summerhall F.

So what if she was charmed by his brother's golden looks and candid smile? Charmed, Dustin could have. It was dark, not golden, that turned Jill into a river of savory cream on his fingers.

"Nice to meet you, Jillian Fox. You know, if you wanted some civilized company, you could join us up in the box." Dustin was still yanking his chain, but at least he'd taken his hand off her. "Oh, and you, too, bro."

Knowing it would be rude to avoid greeting the rest of the family, Barrett agreed, "We'll be up at half-time, okay? Now beat it so I can pay attention to the game."

Dustin eyed Jillian's makeshift cushion. "If he gets out of line, just wave that finger in the air and I'll be down to straighten him out for you."

"You mean this finger, Dusty?" Ostensibly scratching the side of his nose, Barrett flipped his little brother off.

"See what I have to put up with?" Dustin grinned at Jillian before heading back up the steps.

The Seahawks had made a field goal while Dustin was pestering them and now the Chiefs were on the offensive again.

"Football is a family affair, I take it," Jillian commented, her tone tentative.

"Only when I can't avoid them."

She looked surprised. "Don't you enjoy your family?"

Something made him answer her, eyes on the action, more honestly than he intended. "I don't really fit in."

He could feel Jillian's stare. "Well, there's something we have in common. I don't fit into mine, either. At least yours seems fairly normal."

That got his attention. "Something tells me you're the normal branch of your family tree."

"And you're not."

"Not by a long shot."

"I take it your father remarried?"

He nodded, eyes back on the game. "When Dusty was four. That's why he calls her Mom."

"What do you call her?"

"Sheila."

He was ready for the conversation to be over. This was why he should have left Jillian in Tulsa. They were learning more about each other than either of them needed to know. And what was the point? Unless she turned up pregnant, he didn't intend to see her again after his time in Tulsa was over.

Shit, she'd better not be pregnant. It didn't even bear thinking about, after all the years he'd spent taking every precaution against such a thing.

A memory rose unbidden, of Dustin as an infant, red-faced and screaming on the hall floor outside their parents' bedroom—

Barrett slammed the door on that image. No way would he ever chance subjecting a child of his to that kind of trauma. On the other hand, there was no way he would ever abandon a child of his either. He wasn't exactly sure what he'd do for it yet—set up some kind of trust fund, maybe arrange visitation with his family. Dad and Sheila would be all over any grandchild, legitimate or not, and he really couldn't see keeping them apart just because he wasn't cut out to be a father. They'd no doubt be a whole hell of a lot better influence.

In any case, he was sticking to Jillian like a sand burr until he knew for sure whether or not she was knocked up. A fairly simple task since they worked together—and now slept together. Which was what had gotten him into this mess in the first place. If he was in a mess.

His tangled thoughts were giving him a migraine.

Fortunately, Jillian seemed to have run out of questions. She'd also returned her attention to the game, and Barrett felt a sense of relief that was out of proportion to the situation. He made a conscious effort to relax—he'd gotten way too tense since Dustin showed up. Maybe he was over-tired. After all, he'd come like a geyser three—no, damn it to hell, four times in the last twenty-four hours, and driven from Tulsa to Kansas City for the game.

He wondered, not for the first time today, where to go afterward. If she'd been anyone else, he'd have taken her to one of the Mahoney executive apartments. But there were two problems with that plan—she was a Mahoney employee and she was damn loud. Hard to be discreet when she couldn't come without a scream that could break glass.

That left another hotel or home. He wasn't thrilled with either option. He'd never taken a woman to the house that had been his grandmother's before she moved to the retirement community, had no intention of ever taking one there. But he wasn't prepared to get down and dirty with Jill, potentially the mother of his unborn child, in the impersonal surroundings of even the most luxurious hotel suite.

Goddamn it. He liked her way too much.

* * * * *

Barrett had seemed kind of distracted for the rest of the game, even more so after they'd done their duty and greeted Anthony and Sheila George.

They were heading north on a surface road now, through the suburb of Independence, and Jillian had no idea where they would wind up. It was starting to get dark by the time they'd emerged from the traffic snarls at the sports complex, and since Barrett wasn't volunteering any information, it seemed best to just go where he took her. He was looking a little dangerous again, and she didn't think the shadowy light from the dash was entirely responsible.

Jillian couldn't get a handle on the Georges' family dynamic at all. Dustin seemed warm and caring, very open, dropping a kiss on Sheila's cheek as easily as if he'd been born to her—which was only natural since she must have raised him for nearly twenty years. Anthony and Sheila appeared to be just as warm, but they'd carefully avoided asking any personal questions of her and Barrett. He, meanwhile, had acted unusually reserved, leaving the introductions to his irrepressible brother, who'd also brought a woman to the game.

Barrett had looked startled when Dustin introduced Amber Larsen as his fiancée.

"The hell you say," he'd exclaimed, looking his brother up and down as he gave the petite, smiling brunette a short hug. "Don't you have to grow up to get married?"

"If I grow any more up, I'll be as humongous as you and she might not have me."

"In that case, you'd better hurry," Barrett slapped his brother on the back, adding with feeling, "You're a braver man than I'll ever be."

Anthony George looked at Jillian then, as if he were gauging her reaction to his son's words, and heat rose in her cheeks. Years of practice made her smile vapidly, but didn't quell the prickle of unease that slithered through her at Barrett's blunt sentiment. Awareness of their unprotected activities the night before was never far from the surface.

Although he'd shown no overt signs of it, Jillian knew that the silver-haired man was concerned about Barrett. He'd barely taken his eyes off his eldest son, watching him as if he were a ticking time bomb, a feeling she could heartily relate to. When Barrett said nothing beyond "Dad, Sheila," to either of them, Anthony had looked away briefly and something made her watch him until he felt her gaze and returned it. His wry smile had caught at her heart.

Then Barrett had taken her wrist and pulled her from the private box before anyone tried to invite them to stay. Steering her back to their section without further conversation, he'd chewed a couple of Rolaids and then slouched in his seat, not touching her except for the occasional brush of an elbow or leg. If she didn't know better, she'd swear he missed most of the last half of the game. When the Chiefs made that critical turnover in the fourth quarter, he'd just said, "Well, fuck." It had been hard not to smile.

Now she wasn't sure she wanted to know what was bothering him. She had the distinct impression his darkening mood had less to do with the lost game than with her, although it was hard to be objective about something like that.

When he turned off the major thoroughfare into a very comfortable-looking older neighborhood, Jillian looked around with subdued interest. She wouldn't have expected him to live someplace like this. He seemed more the apartment type, or maybe a condo. In Tulsa, he occupied the corporate suite and, judging by his charge tickets, dined in the hotel restaurant more often than not.

He turned into the driveway of a lovely house, an English-looking red brick with white trim and dark green shutters and ivy climbing the chimney. An old-fashioned gas lamp on the lawn shed a very Thomas Kincaid-ish light on the front porch and the mullioned bay window to its left. When the wide, fan-paned garage door opened, Barrett parked right in the middle of the well-lit space and switched off the engine. He sat unmoving for a couple of minutes, just looking at her, and Jillian had the urgent sensation she needed to figure out what was going on with him and quick.

"Are you feeling okay?

His clipped "Fine" said otherwise.

Crap. All the brooding sexual intensity of last night, but none of the humor. Her heart bumped. Jillian started to glance away and then thought better of it, locking her gaze with his. She wasn't going to let him intimidate her tonight. She hoped.

Whatever he saw in her eyes made fire flare in his. He opened the door, climbing out without another word, and she followed him to the back of the Suburban—for nothing, as it turned out. Barrett took both their overnight bags in one hand and shut the window with a resounding click.

"I'll deal with the cooler in the morning."

Trailing behind him into the house as the garage door closed, she tried to distract herself from the pulse-pounding prospect of what might happen in his bedroom. She made a careful inspection of his home and what she saw surprised her. The night light over the stove revealed a quaint, comfortable kitchen. He might have lived in the house for many years, could even have grown up here. There was a lamp burning in the living room, which must be on a timer when he was away, and though the furniture in here was relatively new, large and sturdy to suit its owner, the rest of the furnishings appeared quite old.

When Barrett disappeared into a long hallway, she wandered over to an ornate oval table in the corner. Unless she was mistaken, it was rosewood. Probably a valuable antique. The writing desk nearby looked to be antique, as well. Funny, she would never have pegged him for a collector. Adorning the cream-colored walls were several paintings that she examined with interest. She didn't recognize the artists, but the works themselves were lovely, mostly impressionistic landscapes. There were no photographs anywhere, that she could see. None of Barrett's family, or of the man himself.

"This was my grandmother's house."

Jillian jumped. Barrett had come up from behind without her noticing. "She moved to a retirement village not too far from here a couple of years ago and sold it to me, lock, stock and barrel, except for what she took with her." His tone did little to steady her nerves. He obviously had something on his mind besides the history of his house.

The air conditioner kicked on with a click and a whoosh, making Jillian stiffen further. The house was already chilly... *I like to get sweaty as much as the next guy, but I try to avoid heatstroke.*

That finger was tapping again.

"You've played games with other men?" His tone was too quiet.

"So what if I have?"

Her little foray into defiance drove the tension level in the room through the roof and her heart thudded deliciously in her chest.

"Come here, Jill, so I can punish you for that." The barely audible command almost made her whimper, and she was torn between obeying and running. Figuring that obeying would get her what she wanted faster, she moved to stand in front of him, not quite within reach, presenting her profile so that she could keep an eye on him without facing him.

"Bend over and grab your ankles."

Uh…this was probably a good time to show some real penitence. She hadn't forgotten that single, smarting slap to her behind and was none too sure about asking for more.

"Barrett, I'm sorry—you know I've never played games with any man but you." She kept her eyes on the wall.

"So, these games that you like would be…fantasies?"

"Yes."

"And you don't have any fantasies where I spank your ass 'til it's beet-red with my handprints while I fuck you from behind?"

Heat gushed into her panties as she twitched uncontrollably and it took her a moment to pull herself together before she could answer.

"As divine as that sounds," she said unsteadily, "I had something else in mind for tonight."

Barrett actually chuckled. "I like that answer enough that you get to play whatever game you want—unless it's not fun for me, too."

Well, damn. Well...maybe. Her game was a double-edged sword and she could be skewered as easily as he. He might go for it.

She turned and looked him in the eye. He appeared slightly too relaxed.

"Truth or Dare."

"Works for me. Truth or dare, Jill?"

"Why do you get to go first?"

"Because I'm bigger than you. Truth or dare?"

Since there was nowhere else to sit, she sank onto the foot of the bed. "Truth."

"Why haven't you ever learned to masturbate?"

Jillian was glad she was sitting down. Of course he would go for the jugular. She looked at the fingers twisting in her lap. "I, um...I tried a few times, but obviously...never got it figured out. Truth or dare, Barrett?"

"Hey, now—there's got to be more to it than that."

"What do you want from me?" she cried. "I tried and I couldn't do it."

"I want specifics, Jill. How did you try?" She could feel his eyes on her, willing her to look at him, but she couldn't. Not yet.

She swallowed before saying in a low voice, "With my hand."

"And what did you do with that lovely hand?"

"I rubbed..."

"Your clit?"

"Yes, you jerk," she whispered as the word slammed her there.

"Did you push your fingers inside your pussy?"

"No!"

"Why not?"

"Because that's not who I am," she admitted angrily, looking up.

Barrett met her stare and corrected, "You mean, that's not who you were."

Jillian looked away, startled to realize he was right. Touching herself had always seemed like the first step down the slippery slope toward some kind of perverted addiction. The only times she'd attempted it were after she'd failed to come with Evan and been so wound up she was unable to sleep after he left, and then she had been too consumed with shame to explore further than her clitoris, which he'd usually rubbed raw already.

After everything Barrett had done to her body last night, playing a little touchy-feely with herself seemed positively tame. She might even be able to produce an orgasm now, if the need arose, but she didn't want to do it in front of an audience.

If she chose Dare tonight, Barrett would make her do it for him.

"Truth or Dare, Barrett?" she asked roughly.

"Dare," he said without hesitation.

Damn it. Double damn it. There was probably nothing she could think of that would faze him. It occurred to her too late he would never choose Truth.

"I dare you to stand up, right here in front me, for ten—no, wait, make that fifteen minutes and don't move, not even a finger, while I touch you however I want to."

"Am I disqualified if my cock moves on its own?"

Jillian hid a smile. "I suppose involuntary responses can be excused."

Barrett rose to his feet and came to stand directly in front of her, glancing at the clock on the dresser. "You have fifteen minutes." He stared down at her with a veiled expression.

"And no retribution when time's up," she added. "The game continues."

"You're wasting your seconds. Don't think I won't be keeping track."

Jillian hopped off the bed and walked behind him, getting right down to business by pulling his shirt out of his jeans as quickly as she could. Darn it, why hadn't she gone for broke and said thirty minutes, or even an hour? When she tried to lift the shirt off him, his heavy arms refused to budge. She didn't protest because he was following her instructions to the letter, even if it was just to spite her. She left the shirt bunched in his armpits and reached around his waist to work on his belt, knowing he wouldn't be any more cooperative about his pants and shoes. So be it. Dragging his jeans and boxers down his legs and leaving them crumpled around his calves, Jillian stood back to inspect him.

God, he was a magnificent man. She reached up under his shirt until she touched the thick hair at his nape, then skimmed a fingertip as lightly as she could down his spine, loving the hiss of his gasp, the shiver he couldn't suppress, the gooseflesh that rose on his arms and legs. She didn't stop at the small of his back either, but continued on down, increasing the pressure when she reached the intriguing cleft between his round, muscular buttocks.

"Didn't you say something earlier about paybacks being a bitch?" she murmured, eyes wide at her own audacity. Like she would ever...

"I never dish out what I'm not prepared to take," he intoned with rich intent, and Jillian paused. Good Lord, he would actually let her...

"Chicken, Jill?"

"Did I say you could talk?"

"You didn't say I couldn't."

Damn. She would have to learn to be more specific.

"I'm not chicken. And I'm not your proctologist." His huff of laughter made her smile. "And I'm here to please myself, not you."

She continued downward and slipped between his thighs to weigh his testicles in her palm. They drew up immediately, but he didn't make a sound. Standing so close, she was unable to resist pressing her lips to the corded muscles of his back once. And again. Her tongue slipped out to taste his flesh, finding it hot and slightly salty with the afternoon's sweat.

"You have eleven minutes." To her dismay, Barrett sounded completely unaffected. She needed to make him as crazy as he'd made her since the moment they met.

Jillian reached up and pulled off his glasses, folding them and setting them on the highboy. But when she tried to pull his face down to her, he remained ramrod-straight, so she kicked off her Reeboks and scrambled up to stand on the mattress. She'd intended to kiss him, but the location of his face in relation to her chest gave her a better idea. Without a second thought, she pulled her tee shirt over her head and unhooked her bra, letting them both fall to the mattress. His avid green eyes and roughened breathing pleased her immensely, so she went ahead and pressed her lips to his forehead in a leisurely fashion, trailing kisses over his brow and down the bridge of his nose. Barrett's eyes finally closed when she kissed him there, just touching the very edges of her lips to his lids and lashes. She kissed down his cheek, bypassing his mouth to lightly bite his chin.

"Eight minutes."

Fine. She placed her hands around his neck and leaned forward, enveloping Barrett's face with her breasts. He breathed deeply and his eyes were closed again, but he still didn't move, so she ran her hands through his hair and down across his shoulders, brushing the deep curve of her cleavage back and forth over his face. When he remained motionless, she pulled back and pressed one stiff nipple against his lips, and when that failed to elicit a response, she used her thumb to pull his lower lip down, inserting herself against his teeth and allowing his lips to close around her, pushing herself as close as she could get without smothering him.

He was breathing hard now, so she pulled away and leaned down to whisper in his ear, "I'm very impressed with your self-control, Barrett."

"Five minutes, Jill."

That might not be long enough for what she'd like to do, but she gave it her best shot. Skinning down her shorts and panties and lacing her arms tight around his neck, Jillian grasped two handfuls of his tee shirt and climbed aboard. Barrett didn't stagger at all, absorbing her weight with his incredible back and leg muscles while she impaled herself on his erection. Air hissed out of him again and his stomach muscles jumped against her wetness as she slid down with a loud groan, her socked feet locked behind his waist. Jillian tightened her thighs, halting her downward progress about halfway onto him. As she squeezed with her internal muscles, she kissed him, forcing her tongue between his teeth, plundering his mouth the way he'd done hers.

She'd just let go of a long suck on his bottom lip when she felt his hands grasp her wrists and pull them free of his neck. He lowered her to the bed and Jillian fully expected him to follow her down. Instead, he jerked her ankles apart and pulled out, staring down at her with fire in his eyes while he ripped off his shirt. He must have toed out of his shoes, because he stepped out of his pants at the same time.

"Time's up." He said it with such a wealth of satisfaction that she shivered in anticipation. Which made it all the more bewildering when he settled naked into the recliner after scraping off his socks and putting his glasses back on. His hugely erect penis glistened with her secretions and he made no move to cover it as he relaxed into the plush upholstery, chest and belly heaving, hands once again laid upon the armrests.

"Truth or dare, Jill?"

This could not be happening. Barrett wouldn't leave them both literally hanging out to dry. Would he?

Jillian sat up, arranging herself in a more dignified position, hands casually draped across her aching sex. She should say truth. Dare was a bad, bad choice. But she needed, oh yes, she *needed* desperately enough to dare just about anything.

"If I take a dare, will you promise to give me a truth?"

"That's not how the game works, Jill. You take a dare at your own risk." Barrett's look was impassive. "But I'll make a deal with you. You give me an extra truth while you're working on my dare, and if you follow it through to the end, I'll answer any question you ask."

Well, that was better than nothing.

"Okay. Dare."

Uh-oh. His smile, thoroughly male and downright wicked, made her stomach drop like she'd just encountered cataclysmic wind shear. "Very good, Jill. I dare you to lie back on the pillows and spread your legs..."

* * * * *

"One down, one to go," he told her with husky satisfaction. "You're doing great, Jill. Rest for a few minutes, and then we'll continue." She lay just as he'd instructed, back against the pillows, knees up, feet spread wide on the pale blue sheet. The growing wet spot beneath her ass was enough to make his cock try to rocket across the room without him.

Jillian's face was scarlet. It was kind of endearing to realize how much more familiar he'd been with her body than she ever had. He'd helped her to arouse herself, murmuring words of erotic encouragement, bending her to his will. His demand that she suck her own large nipples had met with the most resistance, but she'd done it, and she'd done it 'til her pussy was slick and clenching visibly. After stimulation like that, she hadn't needed more than a minute of plunging her two middle fingers into her vagina, her palm slapping against her clit, to come hard. Watching her face contort as she arched off the bed had just about done him in, though he was disappointed she hadn't made any noise.

"Would you like something to drink?"

She shook her head, not looking at him. "Can we just get this over with?"

"Now that's hardly the right attitude, Jillian. You should love your body and look forward to playing with it. I certainly do," he added. Rising from the chair, he crouched and opened the overnight bag he'd tossed in the corner. Reaching inside, he pulled out a black paper sack.

Jillian eyed him warily as he sat on the edge of the bed. Eyeing her in return, he laid the bag's contents out on the nightstand with deliberate care, making sure she got a good look at each of the items.

He was very pleased when her eyes squeezed shut and her breathing shallowed out to almost nothing.

* * * * *

"It looks like you're plenty wet, but in my book, there's no such thing as too much lube."

Jillian had lain there with her eyes closed forever, tortured by the sound of plastic ripping and batteries thudding onto the carpet. He'd had to go to the kitchen for a screwdriver and it had taken every ounce of her self-control not to jump off the bed and get dressed.

His comment made it impossible not to look.

The dildo was smaller than the ones Cherry had given her, and much less intimidating. And *purple*, for crying out loud! She could hardly keep a straight face as he iced it with a tube of clear lubricant.

"I told you I'd only let you use that on me if I got to use it on you first."

"I'm not going to use it on you." He held it out to her with a look that dared her to object. "You are."

Like a mindless robot, she took it, unable to tear her gaze away from him. Dark excitement brewed in his eyes, making her stomach flip with urgent desire. What kind of supernatural power did this man hold over her that he could make her do these things—and enjoy them?

"Push it into your pussy—nice and slow." When she tried to close her eyes, he stopped her. "Watch it go in, Jill."

With heat blazing in her face, she steeled herself to complete her dare. The sensation of pushing her fingers into herself had been strange enough—her interior was nothing like she'd expected, had felt so much better than she'd expected—but this... The cool, hard fullness was making her walls quiver.

"All the way in, Jill," he ordered. She complied, gasping as her fingers came up against her drenched flesh. Then he reached between her legs and touched the dildo. The vibration that commenced just about sent her through the roof.

"Oh God!"

"You're doing great, Jill," Barrett praised, his voice half a register lower now. "How does that feel?" He chuckled at her broken cry. "I'll take that as a *good*. Now pull it all the way out and tease your clit for a while."

"Barrett!"

"Do it, Jillian."

Her moans echoed in the bright, chilly room as she did what he told her, circling her now-prominent clitoris repeatedly.

"Okay, now I want that truth."

"Now!?"

"Now. What hot little snapshot developed in your head when I suggested a three-way with Bay?"

Jillian started and stared at him. No *way* could she tell him that!

He grinned at her. "I told you never to play poker with me, Jill. Now answer the question."

She closed her eyes and whimpered.

"Talk."

"You and him," she finally groaned.

"By ourselves?" he goaded.

"No. Me, too." Oh God. The scene flooding her brain was inspired by the nasty-channel movie she'd laughed over with a few other women after a party at Cherry's apartment. One particular series of close-ups had filled her with outright shock and a secret something else she hadn't cared to examine too closely. She could not tell him that. Her head tossed on the pillow. She couldn't.

"It's just a fantasy, honey. Tell me."

She tossed her head again, shaking with arousal.

"Are you familiar with the term *double penetration*, Jill?"

"Yes!" She gasped and then groaned. She was so close to coming, it was terrifying. "Ah! Oh God, Barrett, please don't make me do that with him!"

"Fantasies are just that, Jillian—fantasies. They don't all have to be fulfilled."

She couldn't open her eyes, but she had to know.

"Have you ever done that?" she asked raggedly.

"Mmmm. It's not your turn, but I guess I could reward you for your progress. Yes, Miss Fox, I have."

"With Bay?"

"Once."

She had to open her mouth to get enough air. God, where was all the air?

"I've also had my share of ménages with two or more women. That's what happens to college football players who win bowl games." Jillian groaned helplessly. Was there no bottom to this man's well of depravity? "Now I want one more detail. Who was going up your ass?"

"I don't know," she choked out.

"Hmm." His weight shifted on the bed and she opened her eyes enough to find him kneeling in front of her, stroking himself, his eyes glued to her weeping sex, his face ruddy with arousal. Almost absently, he murmured, "I'd love to fuck your ass, Jill. It's even tighter than your pussy. I don't know if you could take both of us yet, you're so tight, but I want you to think about it while you fuck yourself for me."

"Barrett, stop!"

"Oh, you'd love it, wouldn't you?" he pushed. "Why don't you wrap your fist around that dildo and ram it into your hungry little cunt, close your eyes and imagine it's Bay fucking you while I find a way up your ass."

"Oh my God!"

"It scares you that you want that, doesn't it?" The words scraped out of his throat like rocks on a washboard as he leaned over her, working his cock hard with his fist. "Because now you know all you have to do is say the word and you'll have two well-hung men shoving their cocks between your legs, fucking you every way there is and making you love every minute of it."

Jillian finally had to close her eyes, moaning frantically as he pulled her hips down the bed and knelt in the wide vee of her thighs. Tossing her head at the intense heat washing through her, the incredible tension coiling in her belly, she surged upward, keening, plunging the dildo into her vagina again and again, the edge of her hand slamming against her clitoris with every pass. Barrett's harsh panting sharpened her focus and she whimpered when his fingers passed below hers. They glided through the wet crease between her buttocks and drove deep into her ass without the slightest hesitation. The pain of his penetration paled in comparison to the rough, full-throttle thrill of it, and Jillian exploded into a thousand screaming pieces while he pumped her relentlessly.

By the time she gathered her scattered wits, Barrett had withdrawn his fingers and was pulling her flat on the mattress. He captured her damp hands and held them out wide as he stretched himself onto her semen-slicked torso, pressing her into the bed, kissing her with more passion than she'd ever thought to experience. His tongue demanded a response from hers, plunging deep and swirling until she was completely lost to the moment. The dildo still buzzed inside her, and Barrett's pubic bone grinding against hers triggered one more brief orgasm that shimmied through her like a dream.

* * * * *

"Okay, you've earned your truth," he said, pulling her into his chest as water doused them from six different directions.

She looked at him from under spiked lashes.

"I've earned more than one."

"Agreed. What do you want to know?"

"What's going on with you and your dad? Things seemed really strained between you."

He had to hand it to her—instead of asking about his face, as he'd expected, Jillian had homed in on his personal ground zero like a heat-seeking missile. It was time for a diversion. Unfortunately, sex wasn't an option. In the last twenty-four hours, he'd pretty well wrung out his dick and unless he was mistaken, Jillian was hovering somewhere around the double-digit mark on the Big O scoreboard. Why the hell wasn't she in a coma?

It was times like this that being a low-down liar, instead of a low-down pervert, would come in very handy. He couldn't talk about this, had never been able to talk about it with anyone, but he was honor-bound to give her some semblance of the truth, no matter how difficult it was. In light of how completely she'd opened herself to him, he owed her that much. At the very least. But his heart picked up speed and his muscles tensed just thinking about it.

The irony made him smile grimly. All the years of probing attempted by his father and grandparents and a dozen counselors had only served to reinforce his iron control. And yet Jillian, a woman who was supposed to mean nothing to him beyond a great weekend lay, had nudged him to the brink of panic with one shrewdly-chosen gambit in a harmless little sex game.

"My mother committed suicide."

His words hung in the air.

Holy shit. Just like that, he'd said it. For the first time ever. And his pulse was slowing even as he thought about it. What the hell…? Somehow he'd expected to pass this moment in a haze of screaming pain, breaking the furniture and generally acting insane.

Jillian gaped at him and he turned away reflexively, reaching for the shampoo bottle and squirting a puddle of into his palm. What had just happened here? Why wasn't he having some kind of psychotic break?

He felt her slender hand on his jaw, applying pressure until he turned his head toward her. Standing on her tip-toes, she pulled his head down and pressed a gentle kiss to his lips. "That really sucks, Barrett. I'm sorry I made you dredge it up."

Barrett urged her back under the spray and worked the shampoo through the water-darkened mass of corkscrew curls. He couldn't seem to think of anything to say, lost as he was in the puzzle of his own sudden and inexplicable acceptance.

"Do you want to talk about it?"

"I don't know," he said honestly, stroking his fingers down over her silky shoulders. "Maybe not now."

He needed to let this simmer for a while, figure out what was happening. Taking his time, he soaped her all the way down to her pink-polished toenails, drinking in her moans and sighs with deep satisfaction. It was beyond him how such a tactile woman could have gone so long without having an orgasm. Oh the other hand, he was certainly reaping the benefits of her drought-breaking flood of sensuality.

Once he got her rinsed, she insisted on having her turn at the wheel. She skipped the shampoo and took the bar of soap straight to the point, and hell if she didn't start something he didn't think was possible yet. Barrett braced his feet apart, groaning as his cock rose to full-blown attention. When her curious fingers smoothed the lather behind his scrotum, he finally had to push her away and rinse himself—it was either that or blow come all over her belly again, and he already had more...*involved* activities in mind for the next round.

"Do you mind if I ask you another question?" Jillian's index finger drew a circle around his navel and took a lazy path up his chest while he washed his hair.

"I guess not."

"Why were you living with your grandmother?"

Now she asked. He stuck his head under the spray and rinsed, then sluiced the water from his eyes with his hands before answering.

"She took care of me after a meth lab exploded in my face."

The finger froze and she blinked repeatedly, her eyes fixed on his.

"I take it you weren't cooking the meth?" she asked without moving.

"Hardly." Barrett shut off the water and opened the shower door. Steam billowed around him as he stepped onto the plush mat. He handed her a towel before grabbing one for himself. "I was working a drug task force for the sheriff's department at the time and peeked through the right window at the wrong time."

Jillian's breathing started to sound a little hitchy. "Barrett," she whispered. "You could have died."

"Only the good die young is more than just a catchy tune, Jill. The way I'm headed, I'll make it to a hundred, easy." He grinned as he rubbed the towel over his head, but she wasn't having any of that.

"You came close, though, didn't you?"

He reached for his glasses, but she pushed them away and pulled his head down to examine the telltale scars. Feeling the slight tremor in her fingers, he turned firmly and finished drying off. He could joke about horse shoes and hand grenades. He could tell her that at least there was one less drug dealer walking the earth now. He could even say the explosion had been a blessing in disguise, taking him out of another dangerous line of work only slightly the worse for wear. Pat, easy answers had always worked for him before.

What came out of his mouth instead was, "Yes, Jillian, I almost died, and at the time, it would have been fine with me."

"I'm glad you didn't," she said. "I hate to think what I might have missed."

"You'd have figured it out sooner or later," he dismissed. "Most women do."

"I'm not most women. And you're not most men."

* * * * *

His eyes caught hers, initiating a new staring showdown. Without the glasses, he seemed half as intimidating. And twice as attractive.

"Truth or dare, Jill."

"Truth," she said tentatively.

"Are you in love with me?"

The tingle of a blush began to work its way up, but she didn't look away as she sucked in a shaky breath.

"In truth—I don't know."

"It might not be a very good idea," he said quietly.

"For whom?"

That made him look away, jaw working.

"For either of us."

"What if it's too late?"

He reached for the glasses again. "Jill, I'd really, *seriously* prefer not to hurt you." He didn't look at her as he switched off the light and walked back into the bedroom.

Jillian sighed. Oh yeah, it was way, *way* too late. In her mind's eye, she saw her fingers letting go of that string she'd clutched so tightly, for so long, and her heart bobbing away like a helium balloon on a stormy breeze. Some things were just beyond her control, and oddly enough, now that her heart was no longer hers, the imperative to keep it safe had evaporated.

But it was time to pull back a little bit and regroup—she needed some time to think. Or not think.

Following him to the bed, she waited until he'd settled against the headboard before straddling his thighs. His hands slid over her hips as she leaned over and laid her lips briefly against his.

"I know you would. And thank you," she added with a cheeky grin.

"I'll probably regret asking, but for what?"

Jillian tossed her damp hair over her shoulder. Reaching for his hands, she urged them up over her breasts, moaning at his gripping response.

"For daring me to learn how to take care of myself after you leave."

"Oh. No problem."

Chapter Twelve

Circling the drain.

That's what he was doing, circling the damn drain, and love was the force that was sucking him down. Jillian was in love with him. He could feel it pouring off her even when she was asleep, her nose and forehead touching his shoulder, her hand wrapped softly around his bicep. And all he could do was stand back and let it happen.

The emotional responses churning inside him in the predawn gloom were powerful and frightening. He hadn't slept at all yet and his head was starting to pound like a son of a bitch, but he couldn't bring himself to break the skin-to-skin contact long enough to take some of his migraine medicine. Hell, he needed to eat even more than he needed the medicine, but he wasn't ready to move…

He should have known. The minute he forged inside her without a condom, he should have realized that the woman had shifted some critical weight inside him, knocked him dangerously out of balance. It wasn't his inner deviant who'd staged the jailbreak—it was his flash-frozen heart, shriveled, hungry and desperate to claim possession of Jillian Fox.

He wouldn't be doing her a favor by letting this go any further, but he might not have any choice now. Loving him had never been easy for anyone. It was probably going to be a real nightmare for Jillian.

She didn't stir when he finally rose from the bed and tucked a blanket around her. He pulled on his jeans and shuffled to the bathroom. It was probably too late to head off a full-blown migraine, but it didn't hurt to try. One glance in the mirror made him cringe. Shit, he looked even worse than he felt, if that was possible.

He stared at himself in the bright light.

"My mother committed suicide," he whispered aloud. Yeah, the pain was still there. But where was the anger?

Why had she done it? He'd never really wanted to know before. As a child, the why had been the one thing he'd never wanted to hear spoken. He'd thought it was his fault. Why else would a mother leave her son forever? They'd told him it was postpartum depression, but he'd known better.

In the kitchen, he ran himself a quart-sized tumbler of ice water in the light from the range hood and downed it along with his pills and several more antacid tablets. After putting a pot of coffee on to perk, he scarfed down two peanut butter sandwiches and some dried apricots, figuring that ought to hold him 'til breakfast. Then he picked up the phone and punched in the number before he could change his mind. His father was always up well before the sun.

"Hello, Dad."

After a short silence, his dad said, "Barrett?"

"Yeah, it's me. Sorry to call so early, but I need a favor…"

* * * * *

"And just where are you going?" Jillian asked, wide-eyed. They'd pulled into the circular drive of a huge colonial house and she couldn't have been more surprised when Barrett said it was his father's. Until he climbed back into the Suburban after he let her out.

"I need to go see my Gran."

She stared at him, hands resting in the open passenger window, and he stared back. It would have been nice if he'd given her a little warning. They'd just spent a surprisingly relaxing hour grazing on the breakfast buffet at a nearby waffle house — it wasn't like he hadn't had time.

But he must have had reason.

"Okay."

"I'll be back after lunch."

After lunch! Good Lord, she hoped someone was expecting her.

Jillian turned to the house after he'd driven away. It was still early for a Sunday, barely nine o'clock. Not a very polite hour to come calling unannounced. The front door opened and Anthony George stepped onto the porch, dressed for golf. He smiled and held out his hand.

"Good morning, Jillian. Please come in. Sheila's waiting for us in the sun room."

Jillian smiled back uncertainly and moved toward him. "Well, I'm glad you were expecting me, Mr. George. I certainly wasn't," she added under her breath. He laughed and took her hand, folding it through his arm as they headed toward the back of the house.

"Now why doesn't that surprise me?" he asked. "And please call me Anthony."

"I guess it shouldn't. I'm finding that Barrett rarely does anything the way most people would."

"You can say that again," Anthony said with a shake of his head.

They found Sheila George on the enclosed porch. She was also dressed for golf, in lime-green shorts and a sleeveless sweater.

"I hope I'm not keeping you from your game," Jillian said as she settled into the patio chair Anthony held out for her.

"Not at all. Our tee time isn't until two," Sheila assured her. "Would you care for coffee or tea, or perhaps some juice?"

"Coffee would be fine, thank you."

"Actually, Jillian," Anthony said, leaning back and stretching his legs under the glass-topped table in a posture reminiscent of Barrett's, "we would be on our way to church right now if my son hadn't called at the crack of dawn. This is the first time in twenty years that Barrett's asked me for anything, and I would have cancelled an appointment with the Almighty Himself to oblige him."

Jillian met his gaze. "And why did Barrett call you at the crack of dawn?" *While she was dead to the world in his bed, dreaming warm, disturbing dreams of him.*

"He asked me to tell you everything I thought you should know about his mother's suicide. And about him." Jillian struggled to maintain a neutral expression as her heart started to knock. "He told me to answer your questions as honestly as I could."

"Did he tell you why?"

The man actually smiled. "No, but I have my ideas."

Jillian couldn't bring herself to smile back. "Are you going to share them with me?"

"First, tell me, Jillian—are you in love with my son?"

She trembled before she answered. *Here we go...* "Is it so obvious?"

Anthony closed his eyes and continued to smile while his wife grabbed his hand and squeezed it tight. When he opened them again, they were bright with unshed tears. "Thank God. For Barrett's sake, anyway. As disloyal as it sounds, I think I should offer *you* my condolences. I doubt he's going to make it easy for you."

"Easy has never been my thing," Jillian said quietly.

"You two are well-matched, then. Maybe you won't scare off as easily as he thinks."

Well that didn't sound good.

"That might be what he's thinking, Jillian, but the fact that he brought you to me instead of just dumping you tells me..." Anthony ran his hands through his silver hair. "You'll have to decide for yourself after you've heard the details."

"I'm ready," she told him, bracing herself.

"Before I start, let me just say thank you, Jillian. I have a feeling you're about to be the best thing that ever happened to my son."

Jillian was unable to stand the suspense any longer. "So what happened?"

Twenty minutes later, she was having trouble keeping it together. Her hand shook as she took a sip of her cold coffee and she really, really needed to find a hidey-hole and have a good cry. Lord, she'd known Barrett had issues, but this was beyond anything she could have imagined.

"I'm so sorry," she said softly. "For all of you."

"I'm the one who's sorry," Anthony said. "It's a shocking story and I'd give a lot to never have to tell it again. But I'm not sorry that Barrett finally wants to share this part of his life with someone. I'd almost given up hope he ever would."

Sheila set a plate of apple-cinnamon muffins and a fresh pot of coffee on the table.

"He's never talked about it to anyone, that I know of, and worse yet, he's never listened. God only knows what's gone on in his head all these years."

Although she was still full from the breakfast buffet, Jillian accepted a muffin and picked it apart with nervous fingers.

"You know, I didn't think anything could hurt more finding Karen that way, but when Barrett started having sex at such a young age…" He sighed heavily. "I thought at first that he was looking for love and affection, trying to fill the void his mother's death had left in his life. He quickly disabused me of that notion."

She was afraid to know, but she asked anyway. "How old was he?"

"Barely thirteen."

Jillian gasped. "He was a baby!"

"Not in any way that showed. I came home from work early one day and caught him with a neighbor's sixteen-year-old daughter. It obviously wasn't her first time and she'd probably initiated it—he was six feet tall already and a good-looking kid." Anthony shook his head pensively. "He wasn't the least bit repentant when I tried to talk to him about it, and later that week, I heard from a couple of parents that he'd bragged to his friends about *nailing* her. After I heard that, I swear to God, I had nightmares of him becoming some kind of rapist."

Sheila laid a hand on his arm. "But he didn't."

"No, he didn't," Anthony sighed, taking her hand and rubbing his fingers over her knuckles. "He just became—distant. Loveless. I took him to see a number of different counselors, and when none of them could even make a dent in his Goddamn armor plating, I began to worry that he'd become suicidal, too. I watched over him as much as he'd let me until he moved out three weeks after graduation. After that, I had to just turn him over to God."

"It's been like pulling teeth to get him back here," Sheila said. "He's only come home a handful of times in the last few years, all of them for large parties. Barrett avoids small family gatherings altogether. He hasn't been here for Christmas since he moved out."

"It didn't happen here, did it?"

"God, no," Anthony said. "None of us could have stood that. We stayed with my parents for a few weeks and then moved into a house not too far from them. We moved in here after Sheila and I were married because it was larger and in the same school district."

"I don't think Barrett ever forgave his father for marrying me." Regret darkened her expression.

"Barrett never said so, but Sheila might be right. It wasn't too long afterward that I caught him with the Wickerman girl." He smiled at his wife with wry affection. "But love rarely chooses an opportune time, and if you try to put it off, you chance losing it. I wasn't willing to chance losing Sheila." Then he caught Jillian's gaze. "Did you have a question?"

Jillian bit her lip. "I'm trying to think how to ask this. Did you know that it was postpartum psychosis? I mean, were there warning signs?"

"There were, but I didn't know enough to pick up on them. Karen had always been subject to extreme highs and lows—I think they call it bipolar now—and I knew she was terribly melancholy after Dustin's birth. I just had no idea it could get so bad. That was back before depression was routinely diagnosed and treated. There was a lot more stigma attached to mental illness in those days, and when her doctor suggested Karen might need hospitalization, she got so hysterical, I just..."

Anthony rose and stood at the window, his throat working. "The weight of guilt just about killed me in those first few weeks. I could barely function. If my folks hadn't been there to take control of things..." He shook his head. "When an informal investigation revealed that Karen's mother had also committed suicide, I was blindsided. She'd never said anything—I don't know if she even knew. Her father died in a car accident before she was born and she was raised by an aunt and uncle. They might not have told her something like that."

"I'm so sorry that you all had to go through that kind of heartache," Jillian said. "Is it possible that Barrett didn't understand...?"

"I'm sure he didn't. Maybe he has some intellectual understanding today, but then again, maybe not. I just don't know. As I said, we've never talked about it. I've spent hundreds, maybe thousands of hours putting myself in his place, trying to understand what was going on in his mind, and the things that occurred to me were terrifying."

Jillian had no doubt of that. Just the thought of trying to get inside Barrett's head now made her break out in a cold sweat. She'd known there had to be something ugly running around in there, but Jesus... Under that iron-willed wall of muscle was a ten-year-old boy screaming in agony—angry, guilty and no doubt terrified of loving and being loved.

As if he'd read her mind, Anthony said, "Much as I'd hate to help him scare you off, Jillian, I feel it only fair to tell you that Barrett has a reputation for never seeing the same woman twice. It's entirely possible he's had hundreds of one-night-stands in the last twenty years. *Many* hundreds."

The intensity of his expression carried a definite warning: *Make Barrett use a condom until you're sure he's clean.*

Though that horse had already left the barn, Jillian nodded numbly. She'd known he had worlds of experience beyond hers, but hearing it boiled down to raw numbers wasn't pleasant.

"I knew you were different right away, Jillian," Anthony assured her, taking her hand as he returned to the table. "Except for your, uh, build," he said apologetically, "you're about as far from his type as a woman can get."

"And what is Barrett's type?" And did she really want to know?

"Oh, I'm sure you know them. Brassy, self-assured ball-busters—if you'll pardon the expression—who know the score and stick to the rules. From what I can tell, he steers clear of any woman he could hurt or be hurt by, and conversely, love or be loved by."

"Except for me."

"Except for you," he agreed. "And I'm trying not to get too excited, but I think you could help him finally get past this." Jillian shivered as she looked into his eyes, a slightly darker green than his son's. He had a lot more faith in her abilities than she did. "But I need to make sure that you understand something before you take one more step in Barrett's direction."

Jillian waited.

"He's been stuffing some heavy-duty emotions for over twenty years, and anger is definitely one of them."

"I understand."

"He wouldn't hurt you deliberately, but there's probably going to be some collateral damage when he finally lets it all out."

Jillian's heart pounded, but she said with confidence, "He won't hurt me."

* * * * *

Great. They were looking at pictures of him. He'd asked for it, he supposed, bringing her here. The two of them were in the dining room, going through one of the two dozen photo albums and scrapbooks piled on the table.

What was his dad thinking right now?

"I'm glad we didn't meet up when you were in full gear," Jillian said without looking up. "With all the pads and the black under your eyes, you look downright scary."

"More scary than now?"

She peered at him from under her lashes. "Way more."

Well. Guess he had his answer.

"Though you do look like hell," she tacked on, rising. "Are you feeling okay?"

"Headache." Jillian moved to put her hand on his forehead and he just stood there and let her. Her palm was cool. In fact, she looked cool all over in her white cotton blouse and peachy capris. Sort of like sherbet. Tasty and sweet.

"Did you take anything?"

"Yeah, but it's not helping much."

"How was Mom?" Anthony asked.

Barrett couldn't help grinning. "Full of it, as usual. To hear her tell it, bingo orgies and Viagra fountains are a way of life there."

"The ladies at the club say she always shares the best gossip," Anthony chuckled.

"Are you ready to go, Jill? There's supposed to be a cold front coming through later and the weather map shows us in the red for severe weather all the way home."

"I will be as soon as you give me the keys." She held her hand out. He wasn't about to argue with her—his eyeballs felt like someone was trying to gouge them out with rusty nails.

"They're in the ignition."

Barrett waited as his father approached them.

Sheila hurried in, carrying a paper sack. "Here, I made a little care package for the road," she said, handing it to Jillian with a hug. "I'm so glad we got to meet you."

She turned to Barrett, slipping an arm around his waist before he realized what she was up to and giving him a quick squeeze. "Thank you for bringing her by, Barrett." She stepped away and busied herself with the books on the table while he watched her. He didn't think Sheila had tried to give him a hug since high school.

"No problem," he murmured. He cast a wary glance at his father. A hug from him might be more than he was ready for.

He stuck out his hand. "Thanks, Dad."

Fortunately, he just shook it and replied, "You're welcome, son." He wasn't so restrained with Jillian. His bear hug practically lifted her off the floor and he whispered something in her ear that made her nod.

It was time to get her out of here.

* * * * *

"Are you hungry?"

Jillian watched as Barrett made another quick security check of her house, even though it was still daylight. He'd dozed most of the way back from Kansas City, but it didn't look like it had helped much. His mouth was drawn tight and his forehead was creased.

"Not right now." She followed as he tugged on the sliding door and then headed for her bedroom. It hadn't escaped her notice that he'd carried his bag in right along with hers. He dropped them both into the chair and slanted the blinds until the room was bathed in shadows. Setting his glasses on the nightstand, he slumped down on the edge of her bed, rubbing his eyes with a deep sigh.

"Can you take something more for your headache?"

"Mmm...there's a prescription bottle in my bag, if you're interested in getting it for me."

Jillian left him there and went to the kitchen for ice water. When she returned, he drained the glass after swallowing his pill.

"Thank you."

Feeling bold because of his marginally weakened condition, she went to her dresser and selected a CD, popping it into the player and setting the volume moderately low. Rich cello filled the room as she programmed the unit to play continuously before returning to the bedside. Barrett watched her in the dim light. Dark clouds were just moving in when they hit the northeast corner of town and now thunder was starting to rumble in the distance.

When the timorous moan of bagpipes joined the strings, he asked, "Celtic music?"

"It's relaxing." It only took a small shove with both hands to make him collapse into a supine position, arms over his head. Going down on one knee, she pulled off first one sneaker, then the other.

"Holy cow, what size shoe do you wear?"

"Sixteen."

She grinned as she pulled off his white crew socks and tucked them into the shoes. "You live up to your monogram in every way, don't you?"

"I try," he murmured. "Is there anything Dad didn't tell you?"

"If he didn't tell me, how would I know?"

"Good point."

After she'd pushed his shoes under the edge of the bed, leaving just the heels peeping out beneath the ruffled skirt, she rose up and leaned over him. It seemed like the most natural thing in the world to reach for his belt buckle and undo it with a couple of yanks of the leather.

Wooden flutes echoed softly as she popped his snap and pulled down the zipper of his jeans. Knowing there was no way to finish undressing him without his help, she tugged on a handful of his tee shirt and he sat up immediately. When he would have whipped the shirt over his head, she stilled his hands and urged them up. Taking her time, making sure her nails trailed over his ribs, she pulled the hem of the shirt up and took it off him, satisfied to hear his sharply indrawn breath. He waited until she'd given the ends of his belt a tug before standing, his green eyes shadowed and heavy as he watched her with plenty of interest. Poor guy, he really was tired.

She took his boxers down with his jeans and he stepped out of them.

Well, his eyes were tired anyway.

Jillian nudged him out of the way and pulled the spread down 'til it fell to the floor at the foot of the bed, glad she'd taken the time to replace the sheets before leaving the day before. The top sheet followed the spread, though she left it tucked in instead of tossing it across the room like he'd done.

The light, sweet call of a penny whistle made her smile as she swept her arm over the bed in a pointed gesture. Unusually passive, Barrett lay down with his head on the pillow, hands folded behind his head. At her shove, he scooted toward the middle. She turned one lamp on low and tilted the shade so that the light didn't hit his eyes.

Jillian didn't have the least bit of difficulty undressing in front of him tonight. Whether that was because of their previous intimacy, or his incapacity, or what she'd learned about him, or simply the music, she couldn't say. She kicked off her sandals and tossed her shirt and capris in the chair on top of his clothes. In the interests of furthering her own agenda, she left her bra and panties on.

Watching his eyes, she approached the bed from the bottom and crawled up between his bare feet, smoothing her hands up his calves as she went. The sprinkling of dark hair rasped pleasantly against her palms. He didn't move a muscle, except to breathe, leaving her to spread his heavy, tanned legs apart with her hands and knees. She settled back on her heels and looked her fill. When she'd seen Barrett nude before, she was too distracted by his eye-popping hardware to pay attention to the more subtle details of his body.

His torso was lightly browned, except where shorts or swim trunks would have covered him, and lightly freckled as well. The tan on his arms and neck was darker, the freckling denser, though the undersides of his arms were vulnerably pale. His armpit hair was thick, as was the wedge of chest hair that arrowed down and widened again to surround his groin. Twin moles that could have been vampire bites just above his left hipbone drew her finger. She let it trail down the shadowed valley between his thigh and scrotum, thrilled when that ruddy skin drew up in response.

The wail of a lonely soprano saxophone sent a chill up her spine before a female voice began singing in Gaelic, surely a prayer. Running her palms up his thighs felt like a prayer, and it was answered by the heavy weight of his testicles, the rippled musculature of his abdomen, the pinkish discs of his nipples as they rose to her fingertips.

Rising, she reached up with the intention of pulling off her scrunchie and brushing her hair across him, but he stopped her.

"Leave it." She'd never heard his voice so mellow. "I want to see your face."

Letting her lashes drape over her eyes, she crawled up his body and lay over him, her legs between his. She rested her forearms on his shoulders and held his jaw in her palms as she kissed him. Delicate, hungry, she tasted his mouth, slipping her tongue between his open lips and running it along the edges of his teeth. His uneven breathing told her he was far from unaffected, as did the fully erect penis sandwiched between their bellies, but he remained still and passive, eyes barely open. Stroking the tip of her tongue over the lush surface of his felt like the most erotic thing she'd ever done, and she did it over and over, prodding until he responded with a long suckling pull that had her moaning.

Pulling back, she skidded her body down his, pleased when he groaned. He jerked once when her teeth found his nipple and blew out a couple of hard breaths. Jillian smiled, wondering if she'd nearly made him come. When he had himself under control, she gave his other nipple the same treatment, but this time he was prepared and gave no sign he even noticed her teeth.

Not so when her tongue dipped into his navel, bare millimeters from the head of his anxious penis. His stomach jumped at her light touch and he groaned again, tensing. Sliding further down between his legs, she rested her ribs against his scarred knee and trickled the fingernails of one hand over his sac. His knee jerked up this time, putting his goods out of her reach.

"Jesus, Jillian, that tickles!"

"Sorry," she grinned.

"I can tell," he muttered. He reached down and scratched the offended spot before relaxing again.

"I never thought it would be so exciting to see a man touch himself," she confessed.

"That's a two-way street, honey."

Done with talking, Jillian braced herself on her hands and slid her tongue up his erection, taking his head into her mouth without hesitation, humming her pleasure at his musky flavor. The sounds that rumbled from his throat were sweeter than any music she'd ever heard. She took her time, laving him with her tongue, drawing him deep and letting him slide out. The tightening of his testicles was endlessly fascinating, and she squeezed him with her palm, delighting at the change in texture.

Eventually he told her in a tight voice, "I'm about to come."

It sounded like the warning took real effort, so she rewarded him for his thoughtfulness by sucking him as deep as she could and sliding her tongue repeatedly along that sensitive ridge. He came with a roar, arching up into her as his fingers tangled in her hair, holding her there while he jerked repeatedly. Tears pricked her eyes at the incredible joy his satisfaction gave her. The tug against her scalp as his fingers curled more tightly into her hair made two of them drip onto his belly.

God, she loved him.

When he relaxed his hold on her hair, Jillian settled by his hip with her face against his belly, her hand brushing up and down his thigh in languid strokes.

When he mumbled, "Your turn," she didn't budge.

"I've had way more than my share of turns in the last couple of days. You need to go to sleep."

"You swallowed all my come," he murmured. "Did you enjoy it?"

"I did." Darn it. She still wasn't sure she wanted to be the type who enjoyed something so earthy, but with Barrett, she just couldn't seem to help herself. "You're turning me to the dark side."

"Oral sex is hardly the dark side, Jill."

Lightning and thunder cracked simultaneously, plunging the room into silent darkness.

"You were saying?"

He chuckled, massaging her scalp. "Believe me, it's not."

"Yeah, well, that's easy for you to say. You've lived there long enough to be comfortable with it."

He didn't have anything to say to that, so she continued to lie there and stroke his thigh, listening to the thunderstorm and the odd sounds his stomach was making.

"Why did she do it, Jill?"

The light flickered back on and Jillian sighed as she laid her chin on his belly, looking up at him. "Basically, sweetheart, she just had more pain than she had resources to cope with it. Do you know anything at all about what happened?"

When Barrett shook his head, she explained bipolar disorder and postpartum depression in great detail. It wasn't hard—she'd done plenty of homework about mental illness over the years. Then she went on to relate all that his father had told her, placing special emphasis on Anthony's feelings of guilt.

"He's lived in fear you might ultimately choose the path your mother did," Jillian said quietly. "It would have killed him, Barrett."

"I would never do that," he said thickly.

"No, you wouldn't. You developed coping mechanisms that your mother never had." She debated for a moment before continuing, "Just like I developed coping mechanisms mine never had."

Barrett's eyes opened. He didn't ask, but she answered the question she saw there.

"My mother has been trying to kill herself for years."

"I take it she hasn't succeeded?"

"Almost." She smiled sadly. "She overdosed on prescription painkillers almost a year ago and has been semicomatose ever since. The doctors don't expect her to live much longer."

* * * * *

Barrett rolled away from her without a word and bounded out of the bed. He made it through the bathroom door just in time to puke up what little was left in his stomach. Sinking to his knees on the pink tile, he hovered over the bowl, clutching the porcelain as dry heaves continued to rack him.

"Oh, Barrett."

"Go away," he gasped.

"Forget it. If I can handle what erupts from your penis, I can certainly handle what erupts from your mouth."

Barrett couldn't help a weak grin at her frankness. Her imagery wasn't bad, either. It beat the hell out of what had filled his head moments before. When she'd said what she did about her mother, he'd found himself standing in front of his parents' bedroom door again, knocking until he had to switch hands because his knuckles were beginning to hurt. Fear had made his stomach had cramp then, too.

He heard water running in the sink. An instant later, Jillian laid a damp cloth laid over his neck and slid her cool hand onto his forehead.

"I'm so sorry. I shouldn't have laid that on you when you were feeling bad. You have a migraine, don't you? And an ulcer, too, I'll bet. God, I knew I shouldn't have forced myself on you like that."

A short laugh huffed out of him. Shouldn't that have been his line once or twice in the last forty-eight hours?

"Let's be clear on one thing here, Jill." He sighed, watching his breath ripple the water's murky surface while she smoothed his hair back from his face. "You never have to apologize for a great blow job."

* * * * *

When he'd brushed his teeth, Jillian shooed him back to bed and disappeared. She returned with a tall, icy glass of Sprite. It seemed she was either unaware of or unconcerned about her attire, or rather her lack of it. After pulling the covers up to his waist, she'd perched on the edge of the bed in her bra and panties and was now watching him with obvious concern.

"I'm fine," he said, sipping the soda. "Much better, in fact."

"Are you seeing a doctor about your ulcer?"

"It's not an ulcer, Jillian. I've had a touchy stomach all my life."

Her brows shot up. "That's not normal, Barrett. You need to see a doctor."

"Yes, dear."

She rolled her eyes at the sarcasm. "Why do I even bother?"

"Good question." After a couple more swallows, he put the soda down on the coaster she'd set out for him. "I'm sorry about your mom."

"Me, too. I don't remember her ever being truly happy. She traded one addiction for another her whole life, trying to feel good about herself. Drugs, alcohol…" She looked away. "Men. Every time the latest guy picked up and left, she sank a little lower. That's what triggered her final breakdown. Darrell left her after three years for a much younger, prettier woman and he wasn't nice about it. Mom swallowed a bunch of pills with her booze. I don't think she really meant to kill herself. She just wanted to make him come back."

"Watching her live like that couldn't have been fun for you," Barrett said, laying a hand on her thigh and squeezing.

She met his gaze again. "More than it was for her. I developed my own coping mechanisms, remember?"

"Orgasm avoidance? Chocolate binges?"

"Well, that came later." After years of hiding in her room, reading and listening to music and fantasizing that she was a long-lost member of the Brady Bunch who would soon be returned to her wonderful, stable home. She narrowed her eyes. "You're very quick, Mr. George. Now tell me how you made me come when no one else could."

"That's easy," he said, running a finger along the scalloped edge of her bra. "I wanted it bad enough to dare just about anything." He dipped in to brush her nipple and it hardened immediately. "Why don't you come up here and let me play with your tits for a while?"

"That's so not going to happen," she scolded. "You're sick, Barrett." Then she blinked. "Are all men as fixated on breasts as you? I always thought it was just the losers."

"Trust me, Jill—any man worthy of the title wants tits like yours in his hands at all times."

She hesitated for a moment before confessing, "Evan didn't." In fact, his utter lack of interest in them was one of the things that had really appealed to her about him. At first.

"Evan being one of the pricks who couldn't give you an orgasm?"

"Actually, he would be the only one."

"You've only been with one other guy?" Barrett sat up straight enough to pull the scrunchie out of her hair and shot it across the room like a rubber band, snickering when it landed in the open laundry hamper. "Bet that'll smell good tomorrow."

Jillian wrinkled her nose and shook her head, enjoying the feel of her hair against her bare shoulders.

"Yes, Evan was the only other one before you."

"How old were you?"

"It was my last year in college. He was a junior and we were in the marching band together."

"So what the fuck was his problem?"

She had to say it. "I think the fuck was his problem."

"Now you're headed for the dark side," Barrett said with a grin. "Say it for me again, Jill."

Jillian smacked him on the chest. "Nothing doing."

"I could make you."

"Yes, you could—but you won't."

Whatever he saw in her face made him say, "You're right, I won't. Not tonight, anyway." He twirled a strand of her hair around his finger. "I don't want to know about the prick, Jillian—I'm just grateful he didn't know his ass from a hole in the ground. You're a beautiful woman and his loss was definitely my gain. I don't think I've ever been the first to make a woman come before."

Jillian's heart swelled painfully when he called her beautiful.

"So you never tried again, huh?" he asked.

"Well, if your first time out was as crappy as mine, you'd have taken your time, too. I told you I liked safe guys."

"Hey, I shot my wad in my shorts the first time, but I got right back in the saddle—so to speak."

He was grinning, but Jillian didn't even want to go there right now. She rolled her eyes and said, "You are such a man."

"Thank you."

"I wasn't trying to flatter you, you nitwit."

"That's the best kind of flattery. Come on, Jill," he coaxed. "Sit on my face for a little while."

Everything from her neck down contracted, but she refused to be ruled by her hormones. "Why don't you just let me take care of you?"

"You already took care of me. Now I want to take care of you." He was looking stubborn—exhausted, but stubborn.

"Okay, Barrett, let's do a little math here. How long have we been sleeping together?"

"Almost forty-eight hours."

"Right. And in that time, how many times have you come?"

"Seven," he said at once.

"And how many times have I come?"

"About a dozen." God, he didn't even have to stop and count.

"Well, it's good to know you're keeping such close track," she said dryly. "So, what this means is that one or the other of us has had an orgasm every two or three hours, twenty-four hours a day, for the last two days. I don't know about you, but my body isn't used to that kind of pace. It needs a little time to recuperate."

Barrett didn't look like he agreed with her reasoning.

"Okay, how about a compromise," she improvised quickly.

"What kind of compromise?" The bullheaded man was trying unsuccessfully to suppress a yawn even as he argued with her.

"You go to sleep now, and when you wake up, no matter what time it is, I'll…do it. I promise."

"You'll…?" he prompted, eyebrows raised in inquiry, and she frowned at him.

"You're going to make me say it, aren't you?"

"Just to make sure we're on the same page, yes, I am."

Sighing, Jillian promised through her blush, "Fine. Whenever you wake up, Mr. Domination Freak, I'll sit on your face. Are you happy now?"

"No. But you've got a deal."

Chapter Thirteen

A tickle across the back of her neck made Jillian scrunch her shoulders and groan. She tried to roll to her back but something blocked her butt halfway over. Twisting her torso the rest of the way, she yawned, blinking in the dim light from the hall. Barrett sat on the edge of the bed, dressed in the same jeans and tee shirt he'd worn the day before.

"What time is it?"

"Ten after five."

A hot hand smoothed over the breast exposed by twisted sheets, capturing her nipple in the vee between his fingers.

"Why are you dressed?" she moaned, closing her eyes and drawing her arm up over her head.

"I'm going to head in and see if I can catch any funny business going on at the Tower."

"Barrett, do you ever sleep?"

"I slept."

"Three hours!"

"Three plus four equals seven, Jillian. I conked out for quite a while before you sat on my face, remember?"

She rolled away from him with a groan, hating the feel of blood rushing into her cheeks and ears. Would she ever get used to his bluntness?

His chuckle sounded an instant before a slap stung her rump. "Come on, Jill. Loving my tongue in your cunt isn't anything to be embarrassed about."

"Would you stop!" she screeched into her pillow.

"Probably not until you stop reacting like this. It's way too much fun to make you squirm."

"Go to work."

Another swat landed on her butt before his weight lifted from the edge of the bed.

"Wait." She rolled to her back and sat up, making a conscious effort not to clutch at the sheet as it drooped to her waist. "How's your head?"

He tweaked a nipple as he leaned down to claim her lips in a hard, brief kiss. The man had zero impulse control. "Perfect. You were just what the doctor ordered."

"Good." She tried to hold it in, but an admonishment burst from her anyway. "You need to take better care of yourself, Barrett."

"Yes, ma'am," he said mechanically. "I'll get right on that, ma'am."

Flopping back against the pillow, dragging the sheet up as she went, she just sighed, watching as he pulled his sneakers from under the bed and sat in the chair to put them on. It was on the tip of her tongue to tell him she was going to be late getting to the office, but if she did that, he'd want to know why. And then he'd probably insist on going along to the hospital, however much he really wasn't up for it. She didn't want that. He had enough emotional baggage of his own to handle without shouldering any more of hers.

"Take the Suburban in," he said, dropping his keys on the dresser as he headed for the door with his overnight bag on his shoulder. "I'll be a lot less conspicuous in your loaner."

Well, crap. What if he needed something out of his SUV before she got to work?

Jillian propped up on her elbow and opened her mouth to call him back, but hesitated, torn. And then it was too late—his long legs had carried him into the garage faster than she could make up her mind. She flopped back down with a sigh, hoping he wasn't going to be too annoyed.

After the rumble of the garage door died away, she rolled to her side and hugged his pillow, savoring the salty masculine scent that clung to it. How he could sleep with it all wadded up like he did, she'd never know. Jillian liked her pillow fluffy and cool, and she often flipped it once or twice in the night, especially in the summer, just to keep it "breathing right," as her mother had always said.

Knowing she'd have plenty of time to think about her mother later in the morning, she squeezed her eyes tight and focused on Barrett's scent once more, shuddering at the memory of his raw late-night pillaging of her body. He'd wakened her by flipping on the bedside lamp, and without so much as a word, dragged her upward, dazed and confused, until her knees were beside his ears. His big, long tongue had rocked her world while she clung to the headboard, and his bigger, longer fingers had slithered around in the embarrassing flood of her response, painting her all the way back to her tailbone.

Just the thought of where he probably intended to put one of those fingers had set her off like a Roman candle, but that hadn't gotten her out of it. She was still in the throes of that first orgasm when he pushed her to her back and knelt over her ribs, his massive back to her as he pushed her left knee out and pinned it to the bed. First with one finger, and then two, he worked his way into her bottom, then proceeded to ream her until she was scratching at his hips and begging him for release. In response, he worked her clit with his thumb, and when she screamed with the force of the contractions that pulled her shoulders up off the mattress, he sank it deep into her vagina. The two-pronged intensity of his thrusts turned her cries to choked, guttural groans.

When he'd wrung every last spasm from her, he turned. Trapping her upper arms under his shins, he slid a palm under her limp neck, pulled her head up, and shoved his already pulsing penis into her mouth, grunting, "Suck it out, Jill."

God, she'd thought he would never stop coming. She couldn't swallow it all, and by the time he pulled out, semen was seeping down both sides of her chin.

"Shit!" Her hand flew to her face and she groaned, throwing the sheet back and stumbling to the bathroom. It wasn't as bad as she expected, but it was bad enough. Where her chin wasn't sticky, it was flaky. Whatever happened to the woman who couldn't go to sleep without washing her face and brushing her teeth?

Her unwilling grin turned to a frown when she pushed back the white lace shower curtain and saw the water beaded on the tile. Barrett must have slept less than he claimed if he'd showered. Pushing the shower head toward the wall, she turned on the water and let it heat up while she used the toilet. She hadn't intended to get up this early, but no way could she go back to sleep now.

The hot spray hitting her back made her groan, and she rolled her shoulders slowly, letting the water do its magic on the kinks between her shoulder blades before stepping back to douse her head. She just stood there and let it pour over her face like a waterfall, breathing through her mouth. The scent of semen grew stronger as the crust on her skin was rehydrated, but she was reluctant to reach for the soap. Instead, she licked her lips as she stood there, capturing the last musky hint of Barrett with her tongue.

Without warning, a sob ricocheted off the pink ceramic and hot tears spurted from between her closed eyelids, joining the rivers of water streaming down her cheeks.

"Oh God! What's wrong with me?"

Jillian scrubbed shaking hands over her face as the storm struck, tearing her open, setting free the raging emotions she'd managed to stuff since yesterday. She howled as the fear and pain blasted through her, and when the shaking intensified, she half-crouched and propped her hands on her thighs. Her stomach heaved and her harsh sobs turned to unproductive retching under the relentless pounding of the shower.

Once the sick flood of feeling had passed, she leaned against the wall, resting her temple against the chilly tile and sighing deeply, over and over, while the rest of the intolerable tension washed out of her. By the time she stepped out of the tub, the water had cooled and her legs felt like rubber bands.

She dried off slowly, dragging the towel over her face as the tears continued to slide from beneath her lashes. This wasn't going to end well. As much as she wanted it not to be true, as much as she now longed for a rosy, cozy, happily-ever-after with Barrett, there wasn't a snowball's chance in hell she was going to get it.

She threaded the towel over the brass rack and stumbled naked back to bed, hair still dripping, back dotted with chilling moisture. The thermostat was set right where he'd left it but she couldn't bring herself to change it. Instead, she wrapped herself in the quilt and huddled in a ball on the mattress while the tears slipped from the corners of her eyes, dripping off the bridge of her nose and landing with muffled plops on the sheet. Her heartbeat was slow and dull in the waxing dawn.

She was gonna hurt so bad when this was over.

It doesn't have to be that way!

Sure it does. Love always ends that way.

The insidious whisper of hope refused to be silenced. *When did you become such a fatalist? Such a coward?*

I'm a realist. Let's face it — the chances of this leading to anything but heartbreak are slim to none.

So why was she barreling ahead with the affair like it was going somewhere? She was rushing headlong toward the train wreck to end all train wrecks and had no intention of heading it off. This was going to be the most awful, most painful thing that ever happened to her, but she couldn't make herself hit the brakes. It was a compulsion, something she needed to experience.

Just like her mother.

The thought nearly touched off a wave of fresh sobs, but she choked them back and sat up, wiping her eyes.

Pulling herself together, Jillian padded back to the bathroom and took a real shower. Dressing in the bright, pink-hued sunlight slanting through the blinds, she did her best to empty her mind as thoroughly as she'd just emptied her heart. She wasn't looking forward to the coming visit.

* * * * *

Well, that was a total waste of morning wood.

Barrett drained the dregs from the coffee cup and crumpled it in his fist, shoving it, along with the three breakfast sandwich wrappers and a four-inch strip he'd peeled off the antacid roll, into the brown bag before opening the door and climbing out of the mid-sized sedan. The most incriminating thing he'd seen in the last two hours was one of the housekeepers parking in the guest lot, and since she was limping a bit, he really couldn't see busting her chops for parking closer to the building.

Yawning, and then wincing as his jaw cracked, he headed for the front door. The sky was cloudless, and the air still and relatively cool, but the drive-time news had told him what he'd already figured — the so-called cold front was already just a dream and today was going to be another long, hot bitch of a day.

Traffic in the lobby was fairly light, not too surprising considering the hour, though it sounded like Mirabella was having a busy morning. After a quick detour through his apartment for a change of clothes, he headed to his office. Penny wasn't at her desk yet, so he started the coffee pot, which was loaded and ready to go, then unlocked his office door and opened it just enough to poke his head in.

Someone had been in here — the wadded-up tissue he'd tossed behind the door when he left on Friday was out of place, almost touching the baseboard. Housekeeping was under strict orders to leave his office alone, which meant somebody was snooping.

There was a big, oily fingerprint on his mouse, too, but he wasn't worried. He'd hijacked administrative access to the system from Chuck Geary for the moment—there was plenty to keep him busy in guest and conference services—and it would take an encryption expert weeks to crack the new passwords he'd assigned.

He was pleasantly surprised to find the four background checks he'd ordered in his email and got down to reviewing them first thing, barely grunting when Penny brought him a cup of coffee. Three of the four employees had undisclosed felony convictions, reaffirming his faith in his instincts. And "falsify" didn't begin to cover what that dirtball Patton had done to his application—if the guy could spell, he'd probably be an ideal candidate for writing fairy tales.

Why the hell Alderton hadn't spotted him for a phony was a mystery. Or was it?

He picked up the phone. When Jillian didn't answer her extension, he called Penny.

"Do you know where Jillian is?"

"She's not in yet. She probably won't get here before nine-thirty."

"Why not?"

The plump, fifty-something Penny appeared in the doorway, coffee pot in hand. Her canary-yellow pantsuit just about blinded him.

"Jillian visits her mother on Monday mornings," she said, stepping up to refill his cup. "She likes to get it out of the way first thing so she doesn't spend the whole week dreading it. Her mother must be getting worse. Usually she's just kind of withdrawn afterward, but last week she didn't even make it in."

"Yeah, I remember." He frowned as she turned away. "Thanks, Penny."

Barrett sat there tapping his pen on the desk for a long moment, jaw clenched, trying to figure out why he was annoyed. So Jillian hadn't told him she'd be late, that she was going to the nursing home to see her mother. Big deal. Maybe she'd forgotten—he'd disturbed her sleep to feed her a pretty intense midnight snack, and after a pretty fucking intense weekend, at that. He was feeling the strain of it himself and he was used to dealing with both pressure-cooker situations and marathon sex. Jillian wasn't. Add to that the fact that she probably needed a lot more sleep than he did...

But no—something told him she'd been fully aware of her plans this morning and had deliberately chosen to shut him out. The idea irked the hell out of him, after the way he'd put all his shit out there for her viewing pleasure. She didn't trust him. After all that, she didn't trust him one damn bit.

Then again, why should she? It wasn't as if he were anything like her, soothing and sweet and patient. Just the opposite, in fact.

It was still annoying. He'd given the woman her first orgasm, for crying out loud. A whole shitload of orgasms. She'd trusted him enough for that, hadn't she?

Get over yourself, bonehead! Jesus, it wasn't like he really wanted to go see the pathetic remnants of Jillian's mother. It made him twitchy just thinking about it, and the realization had a rueful grin pulling up the corner of his mouth. If she'd asked him to go along, he would probably have come up with some lame excuse and run for the hills.

Which didn't make him any happier that she hadn't given him the opportunity.

Barrett shifted in his chair with a grunt. It seemed Miss Jillian Fox still had a few lessons to learn.

* * * * *

She'd aged ten years since last week.

Jillian stood at her bedside, staring down with a vague sense of unreality. Even having watched the years of substance abuse grind away most of her mother's former beauty, her gauntness was a shock. Her skin had thinned to shiny parchment, emphasizing the gnarled ropes of her veins. Short, straight hair, once pure mahogany, had gone a yellowish white and her lips were sunk against gums from which the last few decayed teeth had long ago been pulled to accommodate dentures. Even with the aid of oxygen, every short breath pushing up her fragile breastbone was labored and harsh.

She was fifty-six years old, but she looked eighty or more.

Jillian looked at that wizened right hand for a long time before sliding her fingers carefully underneath and picking it up. She covered it with her other hand and chafed it lightly, disturbed by its coolness.

"Hi, Mom."

The words rang in the tile-floored room. Because the second bed was unoccupied for the moment, that side of the room was bare of decorations and other personal items that would have helped muffle her voice.

It had been a while since she'd really talked to her mother. A long while.

"I'm in love, Mom." Jillian closed her eyes, sucking in a shaky breath at the terrifying thrill of saying it out loud. She'd never come to her mother with her problems, never talked about boys or dating with her, but now the words bubbled straight from the seething cauldron of her heart, and it felt good. Right, somehow.

"Yeah, I know—you never thought you'd hear those words from me, did you? But I am. Totally, helplessly...hopelessly in love with a man who's going to leave town in a couple of weeks and never look back."

Saying that didn't feel so good, but there it was.

"His name is Barrett and he's just..." Tears choked her and it took everything in her to fight them back. "Mom, why in the world do I look at him and see *beautiful*? Barrett is big and crude and arrogant, and oh my God, he's so intensely sexual, he scares the wits out of me. He's everything I never thought I wanted in a man...and yet he's so incredibly vulnerable." Her laugh held no humor. "He'd deny it with his dying breath, but he is. So vulnerable that he'll never risk loving a woman after what his mother did."

She gave her mother's fingers a companionable squeeze. For once, she had a glimmer of understanding, felt a certain kinship with her that had nothing to do with blood. How it must have hurt to love the wrong man and lose him, not just once, but over and over again, to never find that happily-ever-after that she'd always searched for so frantically. The losing part hadn't even happened to Jillian once yet, but she could feel the inevitable weight of it bearing down on her.

"Is it worth it?" she asked, tears tightening her throat again. "Is love worth the pain?"

But she already knew the answer. She wouldn't trade a single moment of the pleasure, the vividness, the pure, unadulterated life she'd experienced this weekend with Barrett, for all the security she'd had before she met him. No matter how badly it wound up hurting, love like this was more than worth it.

Bending down, she kissed her mother's papery cheek. "I love you, too, Mom."

* * * * *

She was back at her desk by nine-thirty.

Walking past Barrett's office had been an exercise in breathlessness. Penny had no doubt told him where she'd gone and Jillian had no idea how he'd react to the news. Relief at his absence had almost made her dizzy.

Her respite from stress was short-lived.

Finding an odd bank envelope in the morning mail, Jillian sliced into it with her letter opener and was dismayed to discover an overdraft notice for the operating account. Four checks had been paid, with service charges applied to two of them.

"Oh, great."

She picked up the phone at once, propping it under her ear and dialing while she pulled out the check register.

The news from the other end of the line just about brought back her dry heaves. Disconnecting the call with fingers that shook, she dialed Penny's extension.

"Penny, where's Barrett?" she asked without preamble.

"He just walked…" After a brief pause, she heard Penny say in the background, "It's Jillian." Then she came back on he line and said, "He's on his way to your office."

She hadn't replaced the receiver yet when he strode through the door. One look at her face had him frowning. "What's wrong?"

Jillian handed him the notice. "This just came in the mail, so I called the bank to find out what was going on. I thought maybe one of the transfers I made last week had gotten posted to the wrong account or something."

"But…" He cocked a brow.

Swallowing down bile, she said, "But apparently Mr. Alderton wrote a check to Cash for four thousand dollars out of the account before he left."

Barrett blinked a couple of times before holding his hand out. She gave him the check register.

"He took the last check from this book, which is why I didn't notice it, and since I always try to keep a thousand-dollar cushion in the account, checks are just now starting to bounce. Barrett," she said hoarsely, "Heather says I countersigned the check. The memo says 'Employee Bonuses'."

He pulled his cell phone out of his pocket and started dialing. "Did you sign it?"

"Of course not!" she gasped.

"Then don't worry—forgery is pretty easy to prove."

Whoever he was calling hadn't answered yet when her phone rang and he moved away to stand by the door.

Picking up, she said, "Jillian Fox."

"Hi, Jillian, this is Heather. I have a feeling this is going to be some upsetting news, but Mr. Alderton came in ten days ago and cashed in two CD's totaling eighteen thousand dollars."

Jillian's stomach clenched.

"Oh my God!"

"He apparently had the paperwork for rolling the money into a different type of account at another bank, so it didn't raise any suspicions, and it happened before you canceled his signature card."

"Is that all, I hope?" Like that wasn't bad enough!

"I haven't found anything else, but I'll fax over interim statements on all your accounts. God, I'm so sorry you're having to deal with all this, Jillian."

"Thanks, Heather."

She hung up the phone with numb fingers. All that money gone—on her watch!

"What's the damage?" Barrett had sat on the edge of her desk after finishing his call.

"Twenty-two thousand total, that we know of. God, what a mess!"

"Hey, it's going to be okay." Glancing at the open door, he grinned. "If the police weren't on their way, I'd give you some mouth-to-mouth to get you over the shock."

"How can you make jokes at a time like this?"

"Who's joking?"

Jillian jumped to her feet. "Barrett, this is serious! I could lose my job over something like this!"

"Chill, Jill," he ordered, pointing at her seat. "If you weren't involved in the theft, you're probably not going to lose your job. And now that we've got some concrete evidence of Alderton's criminal conduct, the police will finally lend a hand in tracking the bastard down."

Probably not going lose her job. She sank back into her chair with a groan and let her head fall onto the desk.

"God, what a crappy day!"

Barrett's fingers slid down her jaw and under her chin, pulling her face up. His green eyes glinted with laughter. And lust. "Which will just make tonight that much better."

* * * * *

Rising from the tepid water, Jillian pulled the plug with a sigh and stepped out of the tub. She didn't feel like a million bucks, but she was as clean as she'd ever been in her life.

After arriving at her house with a bucket of fried chicken, four sides, and a pile of biscuits, Barrett had practically force-fed her and then sent her to take a long, hot bath. Since she'd already had two showers today, a bath had seemed kind of silly and self-indulgent, but she'd soaked for almost an hour anyway, letting the water, silky and fragrant from the bath beads, melt away some of her tension.

The music had helped, too. Barrett had put in one of her favorite CD's, a home compilation of classical pieces that usually made her sigh with both satisfaction and longing. Tonight, it had helped relax her muscles but wasn't enough to completely dispel her anxiety.

Already short on sleep and emotionally wrung out, she'd spent the rest of the day meeting with investigators, filing reports with the bank and corporate headquarters, verifying balances at other banks, recounting the safe, working on payroll… She'd barely had a moment to breathe, much less have lunch, and she hadn't seen Barrett at all after the police left at noon. Considering she'd skipped breakfast, as well, she should have been ravenous, but she'd barely choked down half of what he gave her and it had sat like a ball of lead in her belly until the hot water started working its magic on her.

Leaving her clothes on the bathroom floor, she wrapped herself in the towel and walked into her bedroom. Barrett was sitting in the chair wearing only his slacks, and something about his expression made her hard-won tranquility dissipate just the tiniest bit. She was getting to know that look all too well.

"Interesting music."

She smiled. "Is that code for *It sucks out loud*?"

"Oh, no. I like it," he said, standing and holding out his hand. "Very much."

Jillian went to him without hesitation, anxious for the comfort of his arms. He didn't disappoint her. Drawing her close, he kissed her with exquisite tenderness, his lips soft and searching on hers, his tongue inquisitive but gentle as it played in her mouth.

By the time he lifted his head, she was lost in the rich taste of him, in the feel of his hot, muscled body. She offered no resistance when he parted the edges of the towel and let it fall away from her. He took her hand and led her to the bed. When he spread the towel over the middle, she looked at him.

"Lie down on your stomach."

His voice was soft, but it was clearly a command, and Jillian's stomach curled at the heat in his eyes. She hesitated only a moment before obeying.

It wasn't long before she heard the rasp of his zipper, the rustle of fabric as his pants slid down his legs. Her heart kicked when his weight came down on the edge of the bed, but then his warm hands slid over her back and she realized they were oily. She groaned as he brushed aside her hair and went to work on the muscles of her neck and shoulders.

Hours could have passed while he massaged the rest of the tension from her body. He left no part of her untouched—

shoulders and back, arms and hands, legs and feet... She'd never had her feet massaged before. God, what had she been thinking to refuse all those pedicures with Cherry?

"Get up on your hands and knees."

Jillian's brow wrinkled in puzzlement, but she obeyed once more and was both thrilled and unnerved when he moved behind her. His body curved over hers and his hands slid from her back to her belly, still massaging the oil into her skin. She groaned when one moved up to her breasts, embarrassed that her nipples were already tight with arousal. When the other slid down between her thighs, she gasped. She was damp from the sheer enjoyment of his talented hands, and that dampness quickly advanced to wet, and then dripping, when he massaged her clitoris. His breath was hot and quick on the back of her neck and his penis bumped between her legs and against her bottom, inciting all kinds of desperate wiggling. If he wanted to do her from behind, she was ready.

He leaned around her and Jillian opened her eyes in time to see him grab a bottle of oil off the nightstand. The next thing she knew, it was dripping into a puddle in the small of her back and trailing down into the crease between her buttocks.

Uh-oh. She was still a little sore from last night.

"So how was your visit with your mother?"

She heard the bottle land back on the nightstand and then his hands were sliding the oil over the cheeks of her bottom. He'd used a ton of it, she could feel rivulets sliding down her thighs and into the towel.

"Um...Barrett, are you mad at me?"

"No." His thumbs slid down into her cleft and dipped ever so slightly into her vagina before moving back upward. He kept the pressure on, pushing her cheeks slightly apart. "Should I be?"

"I don't know."

Those thumbs never stopped moving, but they were focused now on her bottom, going up and down, around and around. When one pushed against her anus, she jerked.

"Barrett…"

"Do you trust me, Jill?"

She blinked, her heart suddenly racing.

"Jillian?"

"Yes, I trust you."

"Good." His thumb thrust into her and she whimpered, arching her back. When the other thumb approached, she tensed.

"Don't do that," he told her. "Relax."

"But—"

"Relax."

She tried, and though it took real effort, she succeeded somewhat. He took immediate advantage, pushing his other thumb in beside the first, inciting a squeal at the stinging pressure.

A whole squadron of butterflies scrambled in her stomach. Barrett wasn't just going to do her from behind—he was going to do her behind.

Say no! Tell him you're not that kind of girl!

"This music is perfect for fucking," he murmured, sliding his palms over the slippery skin of her cheeks as his thumbs pulsed a slow, steady rhythm in her aching bottom. "I never realized classical music was so carnal."

"It's not!" she groaned. "It's romantic!"

"What it makes me want to do to you is anything but romantic, Jill."

She held her breath as the stinging increased. "That hurts!" she gasped.

"Not as much as it would if I fucked your ass without stretching it first."

"Barrett...ah, please!" She could feel it now, his thumbs twisting, pulling in opposite directions, opening her up for whatever he wanted to do with her. Instinct made her try to crawl forward, but his fingers clamped around her hips, holding her in place.

"I think you need this, honey."

She stilled. "I do?"

"Mmm-hmm. After the day you've had, you need to give me control."

"Why? You'll take it whether I give it to you or not."

"You're right." His thumbs left her as his hands slid up her back until they reached her shoulder blades. Jillian resisted his downward pressure for only an instant before allowing her arms to collapse. He continued to press until her face turned to the side and her shoulders were flush against the towel, leaving her bottom high in the air. "But by the same token, you'll give it to me whether I try to take it or not. You want to be expanded in every way, and since the moment we met, you've known I can do that for you."

Hot fingers skidded down her arms from her shoulders to her wrists, pulling them into the small of her back. "Do you trust me?"

"I already told you—yes!" she cried raggedly, fascinated and horrified at the idea he wanted her bound. She hadn't had time to change her mind when he looped something soft and stretchy around her wrists and knotted it securely.

"No condom."

"Okay." Far from bothering her, the idea raised goose flesh on her arms. "Can I ask why?"

There was a moment of silence as the tracks switched and Jillian heard the disconcerting sound of flesh on wet flesh. He was right behind her, stroking himself while he looked at her butt.

"Because I want to pump my come into your ass and then prop you up and watch it run out of you."

Lightning seized her lungs. "Barrett!" she squeaked, jerking against the fabric binding her arms.

And then his hands were gripping her hips again, pulling her back against the thick head of his penis. "This is gonna hurt a little, Jill."

Her scream was piercing in the cold air, but it wasn't the pain of his breaching that caused it. Instead, an intense orgasm gripped her, and with every spasm, Barrett groaned harshly, thrusting deeper and deeper into her rectum. In the midst of it all, Jillian had the oddest sensation that her body was eating his, contraction by contraction, swallowing him one sublime bite at a time.

When she'd swallowed all of him she could, they both took a moment to breathe. Barrett laid his body over her back, careful not to crush her arms, and licked the skin behind her ear.

"You're just one kinky little surprise after another, aren't you, Miss Fox?" He shifted, smashing even deeper into her, and Jillian moaned. "Is there anything you won't let me do to you?"

"Don't hurt me," she gasped.

He surprised her by murmuring, "I'll do my best." And then he started to move and her thoughts scattered like leaves in a gale.

Chapter Fourteen
ଛ

Barrett kicked his shoes off under Jillian's desk as he munched on a frosted peanut butter bar and waited for her laptop to boot up. The wait wasn't long—her home computer was newer and snazzier than the ones at the Tower. Popping the last bite into his mouth, he brushed his hands together and logged into his email account.

Bay's message made him grin into his glass of milk. *Date with Yva cancelled and man, is she torqued. This had better be worth it.* The ancient ladder-back chair in front of Jillian's desk creaked ominously as he leaned over the laptop's keyboard. If she had any idea what he was arranging on it, she'd probably put a password on the system and padlock her office.

But it was her own fault. After a week of him in her bed—and it had been one hell of a good week—she still hadn't learned when to hold and when to fold.

She was going to learn tonight.

You have no idea, he typed in. *Pick me up at Jillian's house, 8:15. Concert starts at 8:30, but I'd rather miss a little than chance her seeing us before her solo.*

"Um, I'm leaving, Barrett." The tentative announcement drew his gaze away from the monitor. Jillian had changed into the tailored slacks and ruffled white blouse that served as a uniform for her orchestra and was hovering in the doorway, looking worried. With good reason. He'd made it very clear that her refusal to let him attend her concert tonight was going to cost her. "Do you want another peanut butter bar?"

"Nah, I'm good. You know, there's still time to change your mind."

"Oh, Barrett!" she cried, clutching the doorframe. "Honestly, knowing you were there would totally destroy my focus, and I just can't afford that tonight."

She'd explained, several times, that she had a long, complicated solo—one of the hazards of being the ensemble's only oboe player—and would require absolute concentration to do it justice. He'd grudgingly given in to her pleas, although he had no intention of missing the concert. So far, he'd never heard her play a note—if she'd practiced at all, she'd done it when he wasn't around, and he was around most of the time.

The fact that she was willing to share that part of herself with hundreds of strangers but not with him bugged the shit out of him.

"Will Cherry be there?"

"No, she's in Dallas for some kind of conference."

He nodded. "What time will you be done?"

"Probably around ten. Rehearsal is from six to eight, and then the concert begins at eight-thirty." When he didn't reply, she asked, "So you'll be here when I get back?"

"Yes, Miss Fox, I certainly will." Even while it warmed him, the relief on her sweet face almost made him laugh. If she had any inkling of his plans for the evening, relief would be the last thing she'd feel. "You wanna go out for a bite afterward?"

"Sure, if you're feeling up to it."

"Oh, I'll be up to it all right." Now she looked suspicious, so he went for the diversion. "Hey, I forgot to ask—did Alderton ever mention someone named Marshall?"

Her brow furrowed. "Not that I remember. Why?"

"There were a couple more hang-ups on his direct line today, so I finally wised up and answered with hello instead of my name. The guy on the other end said 'This is Marshall—where the hell is my money?' When I tried to get some information out of him, he slammed the phone down in my ear."

"Oh, jeez—Mr. Alderton must have had some serious problems if the money he stole wasn't enough to pay that man off."

"Yeah, I'd say so." In fact, it wouldn't be a huge surprise if the guy turned up in the morgue, but Barrett didn't want to freak her out by saying so. She'd barely recovered from all the nail-biting she'd done before the authorities confirmed that her signature on that check was a forgery, and he didn't want to set her back now. The unfortunate teller who'd assisted Alderton hadn't thought to check the signature card, a mistake that was going to cost someone a lot of dough. "Keep your eyes open at the Tower, Jill. I don't like the way this thing is shaping up."

"I will," she promised. "Well, I'd better head out."

He gave her one more chance. "Sure you won't change your mind?"

"I'm sure." She bit her lip. Smart girl—she knew she'd bought herself a shitload of trouble.

"I'll see you later, then. Enjoy yourself, Jill." *While you can.* She shuddered visibly, as though she'd heard his silent threat. *Smart girl, indeed.*

After she'd gone, he continued the reply to Bay. *We need someplace with lots of mirrors…*

* * * * *

Bowing to thunderous applause, Jillian let her head hang momentarily, feeling the tight muscles in her neck stretch and ease. Thank God that was over. She loved being part of the volunteer orchestra, needed the creative outlet it provided, but the solos she could do without.

The house lights came up while she straightened and she barely suppressed a yawn as she slid her music back into its folder. Despite the repairs to the HVAC system, it was warmer than usual in the auditorium tonight and the stage lights only made it worse. After sweating against the metal folding chair for the last four hours, her slacks were stuck to her butt, so she made a discreet attempt to pull them loose before turning her back on the dwindling crowd.

Folding up her chair, she hooked it over her forearm and grabbed her music stand, leaving her other hand free to carry her oboe. In the hall, she deposited the chair on the rack and then followed the line of chattering musicians into the rehearsal room. Heading right for her seat, she disassembled her oboe, carefully wiping down each piece with the chamois before packing it into the case. She made a mental note to stop by the music store for new reeds in the morning and snapped the lid shut.

"Great job, Jillian."

She smiled up at the lanky clarinet player. "Thanks, Tom. You, too."

"Uh-huh. Third chair has some pretty spectacular parts."

"Every voice is important," she chided.

"I know—I'm just envious of your talent," he grinned. "Walk you to your car?"

"That would be great, thank you."

Dropping their folders into the box beside the door, they drifted into the crowd that meandered down the long, narrow hallway, discussing the high and low points of the concert. His insistence that her solo was the high point made her blush. The low point, no contest, was the baby in the audience who'd screamed through the first half of the program.

"Why would anyone even bring a baby to a concert?" Tom asked as he caught the outer door and held it open for her.

"New mothers probably need a night out more than most people." She pulled her keys out of her pocket. "I guess if you can't find a babysitter, you either stay home or take the baby along."

"If I get a vote, it's *stay home*."

"Easy for you to say," she grinned. "You'll never have to worry about being a new mother."

The grin faded as her words hovered in the air like a prophecy of doom and the illusion that her life was getting back to halfway normal melted into the night. Her period was due sometime in the next few days, and for the first time ever, she would be thrilled when it started. She was crazy about Barrett, but the absolute last thing she wanted was for him to feel obligated to stay with her.

They reached Tom's pickup first and Jillian stopped in front of the gleaming grill guard. "I'll be fine from here. My car's just over…"

Seeing Barrett's muscular frame leaning against her driver's door made her pulse skitter. Seeing the man at his side froze the sultry evening air in her throat.

How could she have believed for even an instant that her life was anything resembling normal?

"Do you know those men, Jillian?" Tom sounded concerned.

Nodding, she managed to croak, "Yes." When he made no move to get into his truck, she looked at him. "Really, everything's fine. The big one's my…" A nervous giggle nearly burst from her. "Boyfriend." Like Barrett had ever been any woman's *boy*friend.

Apparently reassured, Tom said goodnight and climbed into the truck, waiting until she'd made her way across the crowded lot before nosing into the exit lane. She waved him off before steeling herself to face Barrett.

"That was incredible, Jill." He was still in his work clothes, hands in his pockets, and for a second, déjà vu tilted her world. He watched her with knowing eyes, his lips curved into a wicked grin. "I feel like one of Pavlov's dogs—I'll never hear the oboe again without getting a hard-on."

"It's unanimous, then," Bay murmured. Jillian didn't know him well enough to read his expression, especially in the dark, but the husky timber of his voice spoke volumes. She suddenly felt very isolated in the sea of vehicles crawling out of the parking lot.

"Barrett, no." Her voice was shaky with panic. Or something that felt like panic. Did panic make other women's panties wet?

"We just want to take you to dinner."

"It's late."

"I happen to be on excellent terms with the owner of a very nice restaurant."

"Barrett!"

"Just dinner, Jill."

Her joints were weak, buzzing with tension.

"Just dinner," she repeated. "Nothing more."

"That's what I said."

And dinner was what she got. A lovely salad, crusty warm bread, herbed lime chicken... Another treat of fine cuisine that left the table almost untouched—except for the Australian Cabernet, which she consumed with alacrity. Having the balcony all to themselves, Barrett and Bay kicked back while they ate and talked about everything from common acquaintances to sports to home improvement. As the evening waned, the restaurant grew progressively quieter, and when their server moved to top off her wine—the bottle looked to be a little more than half empty—Barrett covered the stem glass with his fingers.

"You didn't eat much. I want you clear-headed." His crooked smile made her heart thunder.

Bay nodded and the server, a young man whose diamond-studded ears and neat pony tail looked surprisingly right with the crisp black and white uniform, cleared the bottle right along with the dinner dishes. After serving her coffee and a decadent wedge of tropical chocolate torte, which she hadn't ordered but certainly appreciated, he departed without serving any to the men. It was a little weird to eat it in front of them, though still engrossed in their conversation, neither seemed to notice her discomfort. She tried to immerse herself in the light, intricate chamber music that floated overhead, in the clinking of dishes and the indistinct chatter of the restaurant's staff as they cleaned up below, and had just flattened the last rich bite between her tongue and palate when a new music track started to play.

Jillian stilled, blinking rapidly, saliva welling in her mouth as the chocolate hovered there. She didn't dare look up from her plate. The men talked on while she concentrated on breathing.

Maybe it was a coincidence. *Pachelbel's Canon* was a popular piece, after all.

Relaxing a little, she glanced at Barrett, who was apparently oblivious, and swallowed the pasty mouthful. She chased it with a long sip of her coffee, cursing the slight tremble in her hands. She'd deliberately blanked her mind all evening, refusing to let it wander into the dangerous territory being with these two men evoked, but the music was threatening to undo all her hard work. This was the first piece on her collection of personal favorites. At the time she made it, the mood had seemed…hopeful. Wistful. Yearning. It was Barrett who'd made the more accurate assessment, calling it Music to Fuck By.

She sputtered into her coffee when the next piece started and Bay patted her on the back.

"Are you all right?"

Barrett chuckled. "This one always makes me laugh, too."

Jillian wanted to look daggers at him, but couldn't. Painful heat flooded her face. She wasn't laughing, damn it!

Bay leaned into her peripheral vision, resting his elbows on the table. "Why?"

"It's called *Air on the G String*."

Bay's huff of laughter was short. "I'll bet that's the only piece of classical music you can put a name to."

"*Au contraire.*" This time Jillian nearly did laugh—any self-respecting Frenchman would call Barrett out for his grating accent. "I know all the songs on this CD."

"Okay, what was the first one?"

"*Pachelbel's Canon in D Major.*"

"What's the next one?"

Jillian swallowed hard, more heat surging into her neck and ears. *Please, Barrett...*

He waited until the next piece started before saying, "*Marcello's Adagio.*"

Silence gathered as she stared at her empty plate, her heart pounding in tandem with the music as she waited for the other shoe to drop. When it did, she was unprepared for its effect on her. "But I like to call it 'Prelude to an Ass-fucking'."

Jillian squeezed her eyes shut as goose bumps raced over her skin. She could hear the men shifting in their seats, but nobody said anything. The music rippled over her, mellifluous, pregnant with intent, and she shuddered as images began to solidify in her mind and moisture to pool between her thighs. He'd conditioned her to this, she realized suddenly, though it didn't help to know it. He'd only done it twice, massaged her to Pachelbel and Bach, prepared her to Marcello...

Sodomized her to Albinoni.

Helpless against the brutal twist of desire in her gut, she wrapped her arms over her abdomen and whimpered as memories overwhelmed her. Everything was getting too hot now—her hands and feet, her nipples, her crotch... Her clitoris tingled like it had been touched, stroked over and over.

You know all you have to do is say the word and you'll have two well-hung men shoving their cocks between your legs.

The opening strains of Tomaso Albinoni's *Adagio* trickled down the back of her neck, haunting, deliberate...foreboding.

"I had her ass cherry to this one." The lilting violins teased her, building behind Barrett's barely audible confession and then falling back to a contemplative pulse that echoed between her legs. Jillian rocked on her seat, head bent, too far gone to care what Barrett revealed about her. "She came so hard, I wasn't sure I'd get my dick back in one piece."

Say the word and you'll have two well-hung men shoving their cocks between your legs.

"Jill needs a hard, dark edge to really let loose."

"I've got a hard, dark edge for her."

It sounded like a promise and a threat, and she groaned, rocking harder, tears of need hovering just under her lashes.

"Spread your legs, baby. Wider. Oh, that's it, now do it."

Barrett's command was thick with arousal and Jillian's lips trembled as she obeyed, resting her forearms on the table and rotating her hips in time with the music. She was panting now, whimpering as the violins soared once more.

"Christ, she's gonna come, isn't she?"

Her stomach muscles spasmed hard and Jillian opened her eyes, on the razor's edge. She looked back and forth between the flushed, still faces watching her so intently. Jerking straight up, smashing her clitoris against the seat, she bleated an unconscious plea and gave in to the ripples of release.

But they weren't enough, oh God, not nearly enough.

She dropped her head between her forearms, gasping, groaning at the fierce craving clawing at her belly. Barrett's hand slid over her nape, under the neckline of her blouse, and his fingernails scraped delicately at her skin, provoking a hard shudder.

"She needs cock."

* * * * *

Jaw set, nostrils flaring, Bay stared at him.

"How in the *hell* did you find her—and where can I get one?"

"Luck of the draw, man," Barrett muttered, still reeling from the sight of Jillian's response to their seduction. Jesus, she was already deep into the ménage and it hadn't even started yet.

They'd fix that.

His fingers trailed a lingering caress over her neck as he withdrew from her blouse and got to his feet. Bay stood, too, moving behind her chair, ready to pull it out.

"Stand up, Jill."

A long, muffled whimper rose from her lowered head, but she didn't move. Barrett took her upper arm in a light hold and tugged. "You've got to stand up."

"Why?" she moaned.

"Because we need to be sure that you want this."

"I want it!"

"Then stand up, Jillian. Now."

Her head jerked up and she glared at him, red flags—annoyance or desire?—flying in her cheeks. "Sometimes I hate you, Barrett," she snarled. Shrugging off his hand, she put her palms on the table and pushed herself up until she was standing—sagging against the tabletop, but standing.

"I know it." He grinned darkly. "Now take your clothes off."

Her eyes clashed with his, crackling with definite annoyance, their blue irises barely discernable rims around her expanded pupils. But instead of dressing him down, she straightened defiantly.

"Make me."

Bay growled and Barrett had to squeeze his eyes shut against the fresh spurt of excitement. Oh, she was asking for it, and by God, she was going to get it. Once his cock stopped twitching and the constriction of his throat eased, he opened his eyes. "You wanna rethink that position?"

"Time out." Bay's eyes roamed up and down Jillian's back, stripping her, devouring her, before they rose to his. "What's her safe word?"

Barrett's mind went blank. Shit, he should have thought of that. Being forced to comply was a big part of the head game for Jill, and while he thought he was probably familiar enough with her by now to know how far was too far, Bay wasn't.

"Think of one," Bay ordered. "I'll be right back."

* * * * *

Oh, crap—she was in big trouble.

"Do you know about safe words, Jill?"

She nodded. Her heart thumped in her chest, but she held her ground, breathing loudly. Barrett was watching her like he expected her to run.

Not until he knows your safe word...

"Chiefs," she whispered.

"That's your safe word?" He raised one brow. "Chiefs?"

She gave another jerky nod. When he reached out for her with one hand, she took a quick step back, knocking her chair over, and Barrett's eyes narrowed.

"You know when to use it?"

"When I want—" Jillian sucked in a breath with difficulty, "everything to stop."

"Mmm..." His eyes didn't leave hers as he casually flipped the clasp and pulled off his watch, laying it on the table. "Been holding out on me, haven't you, Jill?"

She opened her mouth to deny it and jumped when he shouted, "Bay!"

"Yeah?" He sounded like he was right below them in the main dining room.

"Chiefs."

A shout of laughter rang out. "Wonder who thought of that one."

"She did, actually." Barrett grinned at her then. "Got any cuffs lying around?"

The words had barely registered before she was granted a reprieve.

"Sorry—not on the menu tonight."

"Too bad. We'll have to think of something else to do with her, then."

"That shouldn't be a problem," came the arid reply.

Handel's *Passacaglia* came to an abrupt end and silence echoed in the restaurant as the chandelier went dark, leaving Barrett spotlighted under one of the recessed ceiling fixtures on the balcony. The top of his head gleamed like a silvered halo, a striking contrast to the slightly demonic shadows falling over his face. When he adjusted his stance, Jillian's heartbeat kicked up another notch—he was toeing off his shoes. His hands went to his belt buckle and the supple leather swishing through his belt loops made her stomach fall into her pelvis like a bowling ball.

"Barrett..." She put her shaking hands up in front of her like she was trying to soothe some savage beast. *Where's an oboe when you need it?*

The rude, metallic screech of a guitar just about sent her through the roof and the driving rhythm that followed told her the time for seduction was officially over. Swallowing a scream, she ran like hell, narrowly dodging Barrett's outstretched arm and tearing down the darkened staircase.

"Here she comes!"

The shout sounded behind her a split-second before she plowed into the shadowy figure at the foot of the stairs. They both grunted at the impact, but Bay held his ground, locking his arms around hers, trapping them at her sides. Instinct made her struggle, but she was helpless against his strength. His faint sandalwood scent pierced her with shards of both curiosity and aching desire.

"Going somewhere?" he breathed against her neck. The puff of hot air over her super-sensitized flesh made her shriek with unexpected laughter, and she felt answering rumbles from his chest as he propelled her backwards up the stairs. "Someone's ticklish," he said unnecessarily.

"And in some very interesting places," Barrett added from directly behind her.

She made the fatal mistake of relaxing just a little and Bay released her, letting her fall backward onto Barrett's hard chest. It had barely registered that he was sitting on the stairs when the two men began their offensive. Barrett's hands skidded roughly over her torso while Bay made short work of her belt and zipper, then shoved her slacks and underwear around her ankles and forced her knees wide. He buried his head between them, driving his tongue straight into her streaming folds with long, hard strokes.

"Oh my God!"

The hail of buttons hitting the wall barely registered over the intensely sexual rhythm rocking the building. After Barrett ripped her blouse open, he yanked up the cups of her bra, and Jillian writhed uncontrollably as he filled his hands with her naked breasts, rubbing none too gently, his palms hot against her nipples. His mouth was a restless marauder at her ear, biting and sucking at the lobe, and his tongue reaming the canal made her squeeze her eyes shut, blocking out the dim arched ceiling of the stairwell.

Determined lips latched onto her clit and then Jillian felt the thickness of fingers—oh, too many fingers!—plunging into her vagina. She went crazy under the raw bombardment, reaching for something, anything to hold on to. A new music track started and the sound of a woman keening in sensual abandon echoed around them. She was joined by a rough-voiced man singing some very raunchy lyrics.

"What kind of music is this?" she screeched. "Who are those people?" Oh God, it was getting so hard to breathe...

"Meet Nine Inch Nails, baby," Barrett gasped in her ear. "Tunes for a nasty fuck."

Jillian tried to grab Bay's head, make him ease off the intensity, but his hair was so short, she couldn't get a grip.

"Ow! Turn her over before she snatches me bald," he growled, pulling back.

Together they flipped her over 'til she lay belly-to-belly with Barrett and then strong hands under her ribs lifted her upward. Her own hands fumbled up one carpeted tread after another while her flats, pants, and underwear slid off her feet.

Then she felt hair and hard plastic frames brushing the insides of her thighs, hot breath on her wet nether lips.

"Barrett!"

His fingers skimmed down over her hips, pulling her onto his waiting mouth. When more fingertips spread her labia wide, Jillian pushed straight up on her arms.

"Oh Jesus!" The cry was wrenched from her as one tongue shoved into her vagina, over and over, while the other lapped at her over-stimulated clitoris. It was too much—too much! When her thighs trembled in the face of the firestorm, she started screaming and couldn't stop, her hoarse cries mingling in eerie counterpoint to the breathless, broken moans from the audio system. Her back arched like a cat's as she ground herself onto Barrett's mouth, coming in great, hot spasms in the dark anonymity of the stairwell.

Before she could wind down, the tongue inside her slid out and upward, making a bold sweep over her anus before circling it repeatedly.

Jillian panicked when it went for the bull's-eye. "No! Chiefs!"

Her safe word rang in the pause between tracks and both men froze.

"What happened?" Barrett sounded drugged.

Jillian swallowed in an agony of uncertainty, breathing frantically. "I, uh... He shouldn't..."

"Rim job."

"Ah." Barrett snorted, and the snort rolled into a chuckle.

"It's not funny!" Jillian tried to kick loose, but they held her fast. "That isn't sanitary."

The chuckle blossomed into full-fledged laughter from both men.

"She's too damn cute."

"Yes, she is." Barrett continued to chuckle against her dripping crotch. "We haven't done that yet."

Yet.

"And you call yourself a gentleman?"

"Hardly."

"I should hope not."

"Do you guys mind?" Jillian renewed her struggles. "This is embarrassing."

"Bay has a big-time ass fetish, Jill. Let him rim you." He paused before adding, "He's good at it."

"He'd know, too."

"And just how would..." *Oh. My. God.* As visuals went, this one was absolutely breathtaking.

"It was an accident." The words were defensive, but in a very casual way.

"More of a challenge," Bay corrected, humor evident in his tone.

I'll try anything once.

"We were wrestling at the lake, one of those *I'll show you whose is bigger* contests after a little too much beer—"

"Mine was."

"Bullshit! I just wasn't used to protecting my back. Besides, you were older—"

"He loved it."

"Get off me, you asshole." Barrett was laughing again, bucking behind her, and some instinct made Jillian drop her butt onto his chest. The situation was taking an unexpected but intriguing detour.

"Bay, you...you swing both ways?" She twisted, trying to get a look at him, but only the muted gold of his crown was visible in the darkness. Maybe that was just as well.

"Only on special occasions."

She turned to gaze down at Barrett's dark head between her knees and ran her fingers into his hair. The dim light from upstairs reflected off his glasses, obscuring his eyes, but his lips were still curved up in a smile.

"Did you do anything else to him?" she wondered aloud.

"I tried for his cherry, but he was pretty determined to keep it."

Barrett snorted. "Still am. He may be bent that way, Jill, but I'm straight as my dick, no matter what happened at the lake."

Jillian blinked, trying to get her head around what they'd just revealed. Barrett hadn't denied enjoying what Bay had done to him, and Bay acted far from disgusted. The two obviously shared some mysterious male bond that transcended the sketchy boundaries of sexual orientation. In fact, they seemed to love each other, though she'd bet only Bay would own up to such feelings. That they'd chosen to share their closeness with her filled Jillian's heart to overflowing.

Recalling the slithery warmth between her buttocks did the same to her pussy.

Darn it, she couldn't let him do that to her. Absolutely not.

Fingers of heat crawled through her belly. *Yes, let him!*

Oh, no. Not that.

The fingers contracted hungrily, squeezing a moan out of her. *He wants it, and — be honest! — so do you.*

She shuddered. "Can I take my safe word back?"

* * * * *

Barrett shook with the force of his need as he pulled out of her, a thorny tangle of emotions bouncing off his innards like the Pinball of Torture.

He should have known that, even in this, nothing would go quite like he expected. With Jill, nothing ever did. Spread before him on the floor of the ladies' lounge, her luscious ass in the air, her shoulders and the left side of her face pressed against the carpet, she was open to him in every way there was. Whatever he suggested, she did, and whatever he wanted, she gave. After she'd knelt at their feet and sucked them both off, one right after the other, he'd made her hold her own cheeks apart, her sighs and tears and moans bubbling out unchecked as he prepared her with the lube on his fingers and then worked his cock all the way into her tight little hole. She was still holding them apart, more than ready for what was about to come her way.

Sinking back on his heels, he stroked her hips with sticky palms, inciting more moans. He hadn't let her come since that first one on the stairs, though she'd begged for it over and over. As shy as she'd been about having her ass eaten, she'd gotten into it in a big way and they'd barely managed to pull her back from the edge. But he wanted her desperate for both of them, wanted to see her come completely unglued when they trapped her between them and crammed her full of cock. Jesus, she was beautiful when she came, so damn beautiful it hurt like a son-of-a-bitch, and he was dying to see what this did to her.

Bay watched them from the couch, buck-naked and wringing his cock in a loose fist. Barrett started to grin at him and then stilled at his expression. The hot lust he'd expected to see was definitely there, but in place of the cool-eyed grin that usually tempered it curved a warm, genuine smile that hit Barrett like a sledgehammer. Heart pounding, he looked away. When in the hell had his world turned so upside-down?

He knew the answer to that before he'd even finished the thought.

"Barrett." Responding reluctantly to the command in Bay's voice, Barrett looked him in the eye once more. The smile had only grown warmer. "'Bout time, man."

Barrett blinked, clenching his teeth as he ruthlessly squashed the panic mushrooming in his chest. The burning in his belly wasn't as easy to douse, but there was no way in hell he was taking a Rolaids break right now. Jillian would be all over him, and not in a fun way.

Striving for balance, he stripped off the condom without much care, since he hadn't come yet, reaching over and dropping it into the trash can before gesturing for another one. "You gonna sit there and be a wallflower all night?"

Bay's smile finally morphed to a lascivious grin as he tossed over the foil packet and tore open a second one for himself. "Hell no—I came to dance."

Though he'd lost some of his rock-hard erection to that sickening sweep of emotion, Barrett lay down on his back beside Jillian and pulled her chest over his. She lifted her head with a whimper and stared down at him, her eyes smudged, unfocused.

"Fuck me, Barrett. Please."

Well, that took care of one problem. He groaned as blood surged back into his dick, making it jerk against her belly.

"You heard the lady." Hairy thighs nudged his knees apart and then Bay was in place, helping Jillian get seated. She was just pushing against his chest, trying to lever herself up, when Barrett grabbed her ass and drove upward into her cunt. Hands still on her hips, Bay shoved her down at the same time and her scream rent the air as Barrett's cock hit the end of her channel. Unnerved, he paused.

"God yes! Like that!"

A whine choked him and he tried to draw back, desperate to ram into her again and again 'til he lost what was left of his mind, but Bay was still holding her down.

"Hey, chill out a minute! This might be my only chance at you two and I intend to enjoy it."

Barrett closed his eyes and swallowed, counting his harsh breaths until they slowed. *Real smooth, dude — you just about finished her DP fantasy before it even started.* Jillian moved restlessly over him, rubbing her face against his shoulder and her hands down his sides, mumbling words he couldn't understand.

His eyes snapped open when Bay nudged his thighs even further apart. There was movement against the underside of his cock—fingers in Jill's ass?—and three groans bounced off the mirrored walls, one of them his.

"Shit, I thought you opened her."

"I told you she's not really broken in yet."

Stiffening in his arms, Jillian sucked in a deep, shaky breath. "Barrett!" Her thighs squeezed his hips and she started to climb him. "Barrett!"

He kept a firm grip on her ass, holding her in place, opening her further to Bay's thick cock. "Don't panic, Jill. You know how to breathe and push—you just did it for me. Let him in."

"I don't know," she moaned. Her tangled curls whipped his chin as she tossed her head back and forth. "I don't know, I don't know…"

"Jillian, do you remember your safe word?"

"I don't know, I don't know!"

"Tell me your safe word, Jill—now."

"No! I'm not—oh, *shit*!"

Her cunt strangling his dick told him Bay had worked his way in, and *Oh, shit!* didn't begin to cover Barrett's reaction. "Fuck, I'm gonna blow!"

"The hell you are! Put a cork in it." Bay didn't sound any too steady himself. "Jillian, you doin' okay, sweetheart?"

Clamping down hard on the fierce blaze in his balls, Barrett let go of her ass and took her face in his palms, forcing it up. Her exaggerated grimace worried him. "Answer him, Jill."

"Give me a minute," she said through clenched teeth.

"Do you know your safe word?"

"Yes!"

"Are you going to say it?"

"NO!"

Oh yeah. "Then open your eyes and look at us."

She braced her hands on his chest and pushed up on shaky arms. After blinking a few times, she finally focused enough to turn her head and Barrett followed suit. They both watched in the mirror as Bay slid his hands around her waist, cupping her stubble-reddened tits and pulling her up and back. She groaned harshly when he drove his cock the rest of the way home and held there, his balls snugged tight against Barrett's. Tears streaked down her cheeks as she leaned her head back on his shoulder and stared at their erotic reflection.

Barrett slid his hands up her thighs. "You're doing great, babe. The hard part's over."

Bay rocked suggestively. "Speak for yourself."

"Oh God, look at me," Jillian cried. "I'm a slut!"

Squeezing her hips, Barrett said, "Only for me, Jill."

She looked down at him then, relief and humor tempering the dismay in her eyes. "I guess I can live with that."

* * * * *

The minute Bay dragged his cock backward, she lost it. Fire tore along every nerve ending in her stinging bottom, touching off a terrifying chain reaction of explosions that turned her inside out. She fought to escape the fierceness of it and his arms squeezed tight, restraining her as he rammed back in to the hilt and held there. Once the throbbing had eased and her sobs had tapered off, he lifted her slightly and then Barrett was arching upward with a ragged shout, pounding her pussy with sharp, deep strokes of his cock that set her off again.

He came after the fourth, grunting in time with his spurts inside her. Jillian opened her eyes at the last moment, saw his face scrunched tight with passion, and felt her heart shatter with love. She almost said it. *I love you, Barrett.*

"Jesus, you two need to work on your self-control," Bay huffed in her ear. "I've barely gotten started here."

"Don't worry." Gasping for air as he grinned, Barrett thrust again, forcing another shriek from Jillian. "This hard-on isn't going anywhere for a while."

* * * * *

She was never going to come again. There was no way she could—they'd wrung more orgasms out of her than one human being could possibly achieve in one night and now there was nothing left. For the moment, anyway. With Barrett, nothing was as impossible as it seemed.

Bay pulled out of her bottom, which was slick with the lube but raw from excessive use, groaning as he dragged a kiss up her damp, limp backbone.

"Too fucking amazing." He kissed her ear. "Call me—"

"One-time deal," Barrett rumbled.

"I figured. In that case…" Bay cupped her chin and turned her head for a long, wet, tongue-filled kiss, which was nice, but now that the moment had passed… Well, he was no Barrett. Breaking off with a smacking sound, he told her in a low tone, "Call me if you ever need me."

"She won't be calling," Barrett said sourly, though his look was humorous. Bay just grinned as he pulled on his briefs and slacks and then went off in search of the rest of his clothing.

After the door closed, Barrett stroked her hair away from her ear and nuzzled it with his mouth. "Let this be a lesson to you, Jill."

Puzzled by the sudden darkness in his tone, she pulled back to look at him. He wasn't smiling.

"I won't let you hide from me."

Tapping her last reserves of energy, she reached up and threaded her hands into his hair. "Then don't you hide from me."

They stared at each other for a long moment, passing all kinds of coded information that might take a lifetime to figure out. Then he kissed her like he couldn't get deep enough into her mouth while she hugged him like she couldn't get deep enough into his heart.

Chapter Fifteen

"You're never going to believe this," Barrett said to her when she walked in with checks for him to sign almost a week later.

"Well...?" She set the stack in front of him and sank into one of his chairs.

"They found Alderton in Vegas."

Jillian stared at him. "What was he doing there?"

"Warming a bunk in the county jail."

"What!"

He kicked back in his chair and grinned. "Yeah. Seems he tried to stick up the local bank."

"Oh my God! Why would he do that?"

"Well, for one thing, he was in debt up to his fucking eyeballs. He compounded the problem by trying to hit it big on the blackjack tables and lost all the cash he withdrew from City Federal."

"Hasn't the man ever heard of Chapter Thirteen?"

"Loan sharks and dope dealers generally aren't very responsive to bankruptcy filings."

"Good Lord, Barrett. I never even had a clue."

"Don't worry about it. Especially in cases like his, it takes one to know one."

"He was probably the one stealing cash from the registers, too."

"No doubt. I'm thinking this is all connected with those calls on his direct line last week, but it's bigger than just taking cash. And unless my gut is wrong, quite a bit nastier. There's something screwy going on at the front desk, too, so I've ordered a complete audit of every department." He gave her a very direct look. "Is it going to be a problem for you to have internal auditors tearing through everything?"

"Not at all," she assured him. "I'm just glad you're getting to the bottom of it. So... what does this mean for you?"

Jillian held her breath. They'd settled into something of a routine in the past two weeks, a very homey routine that made her nervous. They rarely made plans more than an hour in advance. Their nights together, every night together, just happened. She was already getting entirely too used to hearing Cops and ESPN blaring through the sliding door while she watered and picked tomatoes from her little garden, to seeing his mammoth shoes parked in the corner of her bedroom and his overnight bag in her chair and his beer in her refrigerator, to shopping and cooking for two instead of one. It was starting to scare her, because they'd never had another intimate conversation since the night they came back from Kansas City.

Well, except for that brief exchange after her concert last weekend—after he and Bay had fulfilled her darkest, most private fantasy. Just thinking of it was enough to give her chills. She'd never forget the sight of her naked body, looking delicate and pale, sandwiched between their long, tanned ones. Or the incredible heat of it, the mind-boggling thickness. The smells and tastes of sweat and semen and her own lavish arousal. The harsh shouts and groans, the frank masculine praise and shrill feminine screams that had split the night...

"...and we'll watch while you and Cherry eat each other."

Jillian landed in the present with a thump, breathless from the trip down memory lane. "Excuse me?"

Barrett's knowing grin inspired a blush. "Just seeing if you were listening. I was saying, I'm not sure how far in advance I can plan, at this point. I imagine corporate will fire off Alderton's pink slip with all due haste and light a fire under human resources to get the new management team in place."

"So you won't be leaving for Kansas City today or anything?"

His look said she should be so lucky.

"No, I'll be home tonight. We can talk about it then."

Home. Jillian steeled herself against the gooey feeling that gave her and tried not to let her hopes soar too high. He hadn't given her any concrete reason to think he truly cared about her or that he wanted to continue seeing her after his job here was done. If anything, he was acting edgy, anxious to be done with the Mahoney Tower Tulsa.

Her stomach fluttered uncomfortably. They'd both heaved a big sigh of relief when she spotted a little on Sunday night, which generally meant her period would start the next morning. Barrett had acted put out, though she knew he was really amused at her squeamish refusal to have intercourse for the next week. He'd made a show of grudgingly allowing her to switch to plan B for his sexual gratification and then set out to expand her horizons even further. God, if her career ever hit the skids, she could probably make a spectacular living selling all the skills he'd taught her.

But nothing had happened the next morning, or the next, or the next…

Her period was now almost a week late and counting.

* * * * *

They didn't talk about anything that night, as it turned out. Orders from corporate had Barrett catching a late afternoon flight to interview Alderton and get whatever information he could from local officials. He called from Vegas Friday night and told Jillian not report to work until he got back.

"The auditors will be there tomorrow and it'll be just as well if you're out of their way."

"Thanks," she said dryly.

"You know what I mean," he said in a severe tone. "Jillian, I'm not kidding—there's been some bad stuff going down at the Tower and I want you to stay the hell away from there."

"I've got it, Barrett. Jillian—work—no way. Okay?"

"Good. Thank you." There was a slice of dead air before he asked, "How are you?"

She swallowed. Maybe it wouldn't hurt to tell him. "Lonely."

"Yeah."

"When are you coming back?" she finally had the courage to ask.

"I'm not sure. I'll probably have to stop in KC to powwow with the bigwigs. Monday night at the earliest, I would think."

Jillian couldn't think of anything good to say to that. She missed him way, way too much. She had a three- or four-day weekend coming and she'd probably spend most of it crying.

"Hey, Jill," he said softly.

"What?" God, did she just sniffle into the phone?

"Have you ever had phone sex?"

Despite her weepy mood, she snorted into the receiver. "Not unless you count a rash of heavy breathing calls I got in college."

He chuckled in her ear. "It only counts as phone sex if both parties come."

"Is that so? I must not have gotten the memo on phone sex etiquette."

"Check your email later—I'll spell out the rules in graphic detail."

Her lips curved. "I can't wait."

"So is it a date?"

"Is what a date?"

"Phone sex? Tomorrow night at, say, nine?"

Disappointment speared her. "What's wrong with now?"

"I'm supposed to meet with one of the investigators in about twenty minutes."

"At this time of the night?"

"Vegas is a this-time-of-night kind of city."

"Well, twenty minutes is—"

"Not enough," Barrett said firmly. "You can't rush good phone sex."

"Okay, then—I'll be waiting by the phone tomorrow night at nine." She was brimming with anticipation at the prospect, but his mention of the investigators had reminded her of something. "Hey, Barrett?"

"Yeah?"

"Did I ever tell you that my brother Tyler is in prison for drug trafficking and grand theft?"

"Why no, Jillian, you never did." He sounded a little startled, but not upset. "Are you serious?"

"As a heart attack. I just thought you should know."

"Duly noted. He had a little trouble with coping mechanisms too, huh?"

"Exactly. And that doesn't bother you?"

"No. Is it supposed to?"

"I don't know. Some people..." She sighed. "Well, you know how it is. People tend to paint family members with the same brush."

"Jill, you're obviously a Rembrandt in a family of caricatures."

Tears pricked her eyes even as she laughed. The man certainly had a way with words. Reluctant to get too mushy, she turned the tables.

"So it wouldn't bother you, then, to find out that my twin sister is a porn star."

"You've got to be kidding."

She snickered. "Actually, yes I am. Sorry—you were so blasé about my felonious brother, I just couldn't resist."

"Well, you're going to pay for that one, little girl," he told her. "I was already picturing you dressed up like a slutty Catholic schoolgirl and striking an obscene pose." He paused before asking seductively, "Have you ever thought about making movies, Jill?"

* * * * *

Twenty-four hours later, pregnancy fears tucked into the deepest, dustiest corner of her brain, she lay sprawled on her bed, naked as the day she was born, completely over the top with love and lust and power.

"So, did you do anything fun today?"

Jillian could hardly answer around her breathless expectation. After Barrett had made her beg him not to buy a video camera, she'd felt it necessary to teach him a lesson.

"Yes, I did."

"Are you going to tell me about it or should we just get right down to business?" His lazy drawl didn't do much to disguise his agitated breathing. Barrett was already as excited as she was.

And he was about to be a lot more excited.

"I was a naughty girl today," she told him in a husky tone.

Nothing but breathing came over the line for ten seconds.

"Oh yeah?"

"Mmm-hmm."

"Go on," he invited.

"Mmm..." She stroked her bare mons very lightly with her fingertips and shivered. Cherry had practically jumped up and down with excitement when she asked her where to go for a Brazilian wax. She'd arranged a rush appointment with her own waxer and waited in the lobby while Jillian got the embarrassing works. It had hurt, but not as badly as she'd expected, and the redness was almost gone already.

She moaned, deliberately inciting him. "You weren't too attached to spitting hairs, were you, Barrett?"

He drew in a sharp breath. "Jillian, what did you do?"

Smiling, she slid her fingertips between her already wet labia and breathed into the line, "I had my pussy waxed and I'm playing with it now."

His harsh groan came over the line loud and clear, thrilling her out of her mind.

"Oh, Goddamn it, Jill!" he gasped. "Fuck! Fuck!"

Jillian jerked her hand away and sat up straight, her heart pounding.

"What? I'm sorry, I'm sorry! Tell me what's wrong!"

"You made me come already," he wheezed. "Dammit. That was supposed to last for at least an hour."

She collapsed in a fit of belly laughs. "You shouldn't have been handling the merchandise so soon," she razzed. "Besides, just think how much you'll save on your phone bill now."

"I wasn't! And screw the phone bill. We're not done here, not by a long shot."

"Mmm-hmm. You just couldn't wait for me, could you, Barrett?"

"Oh, just you wait, Miss Fox. This wouldn't have happened if you hadn't made that preemptive strike. Jesus, I can't believe you waxed while I'm out of town," he groused. "And said pussy out loud, too. You'd better not show yours to anybody else before I see it."

"Darn—there go my plans for naked aerobics in the park tomorrow morning."

"Just keep pushing," he growled. "Hey, Jill..."

"Yes?"

"Do you have a picture phone?"

"Barrett! No, I don't—and I'm not buying one, either, so you can just forget about that."

"Web-cam? I've got my laptop and a high-speed connection."

"Nada."

"Digital camera?"

Jillian bit her lip, going hot all over. She couldn't do that. Could she?

"You do, don't you? Oh, man," he groaned. "Come on, Jill. This is me, begging you, and I've never begged for anything in my life."

"Do I have to show my face?"

Dead air met her ear.

"I'd like it better if you did, but I guess you wouldn't have to," he finally said in a grudging tone.

"But will you still respect me in the morning?" she simpered into the phone, grinning.

"As much as I ever have."

"Ha! That's it, forget it!"

"I was kidding, Jillian!" he shouted. "I respect you more than anyone on the face of the planet, living or dead!"

"In that case…"

"Oh, yeah," he moaned. "And Jill…"

"Now what?"

"Use the dildo for me."

"Greedy," she accused, hot all over again.

"Only for you, Jill."

Chapter Sixteen

ೞ

"Miss Fox, good morning!" Amanda exclaimed, eyes wide. "Sorry—I didn't recognize you."

Jillian gave her a limp smile. She'd done the unthinkable and shown up at the hotel in sweats and a ratty tee shirt, with her hair in a haphazard pony tail. In short, she looked like shit.

"Yeah, I'm not feeling all that great today."

Now there was an understatement. She'd taken a home pregnancy test a couple of hours ago and was still reeling from the sight of those two pink lines.

The humiliation of it had struck her first, enveloping her in a total-body blush so painful, it brought tears to her eyes. What a hypocrite she'd turned out to be, and how arrogant to have believed she was above this. Thirty years old and knocked up by the second man she'd ever slept with—talk about foolish! At least her mother had planned her "unplanned" pregnancies and carried them out with ruthless determination. Jillian had just gotten caught.

Caught. It was an excruciating sensation for a woman who'd always done the "right" thing, who'd never been called down by a teacher for talking, much less been sent to the principal's office. She'd never cheated on an exam, or lied to get out of jury duty, or driven drunk. Hell, she'd never even gotten a speeding ticket.

But she'd managed to accidentally create another person, a living, flesh-and-blood human being.

The realization had allowed awe to set in, and close on its heels, breathtaking joy. She and Barrett had made a baby. Instead of killing or maiming some innocent bystander, like driving drunk would have, their momentary lapse of sanity had resulted in new life. Their passion, however fleeting it turned out to be, had created proof of its own existence, a son or daughter who would love her and always be there for her.

Shame had consumed her then. How selfish was that? She was actually *happy* about this. For God's sake, she was either going to raise a child alone, depriving it of the father it deserved, or she was going to trap a man into marriage—both circumstances she'd sworn all her life to avoid. And yet tears of joy trembled on her lashes.

She was so damn selfish. And stupid and thrilled and terrified—

"Miss Fox, are you okay?"

Amanda's question yanked Jillian's head out of the roiling mist of conflict.

"I'm fine," she said, looking around self-consciously. "Where's Darwin?"

Amanda grabbed the two-way radio from under the counter and paged him.

"I'm in her office," Darwin's voice crackled.

Waving her thanks, she headed up the wide staircase to the mezzanine level. Darwin had called a half-hour ago and said the auditors were having trouble finding some key files. When she opened her mouth to say they'd have to figure it out for themselves, he'd told her importantly, "Mr. George said I was to stay with you at all times."

Jillian rolled her eyes. Supercop, Darwin wasn't, but you had to give the poor guy points for trying. She had a feeling he wasn't going to be part of the new GM's management team.

She walked through her office door and stopped, looking around with a frown.

"Darwin?"

A nasty-smelling hand settled over her mouth as the door slammed shut behind her and Jillian began to flail wildly—until she felt something cold against her throat.

"Don't make one sound, bitch, or it'll be your last," Darwin said in her ear. God, the rest of him smelled just as gross—cigarette smoke, whiskey, and the acrid scent of unwashed body just about turned her stomach inside-out. "I don't have to cut you, if you don't make me. I just need money to get out of town, so just open the safe and I'll let you go."

"And I'm supposed to believe you because…?"

"Because you don't have any choice, you fucking bitch." He pushed her forward. "You just had to go and call corporate, didn't you? I could have been out of here…"

He steered her behind her desk and shoved her down in front of the safe, keeping the knife blade against her neck. "Open it. Now."

Jillian raised a shaking hand to the combination lock. "What in the hell has been going on here?"

"What do you think would be going on in a hotel, you stupid cunt?" he sneered, breathing hard. "We had a sweet little prostitution setup until that ass-wipe got himself in too deep with the wrong guys. You can bet he's not going to live to go to trial. Hurry it up!"

"I'm trying!"

"Well, try harder. And then you got that fucking bulldog down here, digging into everything… It didn't take him long to get your sweet ass in the sack, did it?" His mouth was right next to her ear again and Jillian shuddered in fear. Damn it, why wasn't the safe opening? She spun the dial to the right a few times and tried again. "I should have waited a little longer before I knocked on the window that night. I could have watched while he screwed you right there on the front seat."

When Darwin's free hand slid into the back of her sweat pants, she jerked hard, making the point of the blade pinch painfully against her throat. "No!"

"Why not, bitch? You put out for him."

His fingers curled into the crease between her buttocks and Jillian came up swinging. Her elbow connected with a sickening crunch and Darwin bellowed with pain as she jumped to her feet, whirling around to face him, panting with fear and anger. He'd stumbled back a couple of steps and was swearing as he cupped his hand over his nose. Blood spurted down the front of his shirt and Jillian felt a stab of vicious satisfaction.

"He smells a lot better than you," she spat.

Wiping his bloody hand on his jeans, Darwin advanced on her, the knuckles of his other hand white around the knife handle. He had her backed into the corner and the only way out was over the top of her desk. God, that blade looked evil, long and thin and way too sharp.

"You're going to be sorry you did that, money lady," he snarled.

Jillian opened her mouth to scream.

"Not as sorry as you're going to be, you little prick," came a deadly voice from the doorway.

"Barrett!" Jillian cried without taking her eyes off the knife.

Darwin lunged for her and she instinctively backed her butt onto the top of the safe. Leaning on her hands, she kicked both feet out in front of her, screaming at the top of her lungs. She felt the blade slide into her inner calf and kicked harder, hysterical now.

Barrett had him off her instantly and then it was Darwin who was screaming as he slammed into the wall. The knife bounced across the carpet.

"Goddamn son of a bitch!" Barrett bellowed as he plucked him up and threw him onto the floor. "You cut her, you fucking prick!"

Darwin never stopped screaming as Barrett fell on him, punching him savagely, over and over. "Fucking prick!"

Jillian scrambled over her desk and grabbed the knife. She opened the bottom file drawer just enough to drop the horrible thing inside and then sagged against the bank of file cabinets.

For an endless moment, she sat there watching, frozen in horror, as Barrett laid into the smaller man with everything he had. He was out of control now, howling with fury, his face purple.

"Barrett, stop!" She was on her feet, yanking on the back of his shirt with both hands. "You got the bad guy, now stop!"

"You fucking little prick!" Barrett rammed a brutal fist down again, producing another scream of agony.

Jillian could hardly believe Darwin was still conscious. She wrapped her arms around Barrett's neck and pulled hard. "Oh God, Barrett, please stop!"

"He cut you, the fucking lowdown prick!" Voice hoarse, he shrugged her off and drew back to deliver another blow. Jillian threw herself against him, grabbing frantically for his arm.

"Barrett Isaiah George," she yelled, "Stop before you kill him!"

* * * * *

It was the smell of blood that finally popped the furious vacuum squeezing his head. Men's voices ricocheted off the inside of his skull, distorted and unintelligible, and he blinked repeatedly, trying to focus. Where was he?

The room was wall-to-wall with uniforms, and that oily metallic odor was closing in harder with every breath. Barrett swayed and felt several hands grab for him.

"Barrett, can you hear me?"

Someone was shaking him and he turned toward the voice. "Dad?"

"Barrett!"

Jillian.

Nausea exploded in his gut when he saw her lying on the floor. Her face was chalky, her eyes wide and bruised-looking.

She swatted at the firemen's hands and tried to get up, but they held her in place, trying to calm her down.

A pool of blood surrounded her. Was *coming* from her...

The rhythmic roaring in his ears grew louder and Barrett stumbled backward, shrugging off the hands that chased him. Blood was everywhere. He was too late again.

Someone called his name when he fell over a chair and banged his temple against the doorjamb, but he kept right on moving, desperate to escape the nightmare of terror descending on him. Falling into the hall, he pushed himself up and ran.

*****

Cherry beat the ambulance to the hospital and Jillian burst into tears at the sight of her, grabbing her hand and squeezing it tight as the paramedics rolled her into a trauma room.

"You've got to find Barrett!" she cried.

"Oh, honey, I will, but first you need to calm down and tell me what happened."

Jillian gave her the abridged version as her sobs and hiccups subsided, craning her head to talk around the nurses as they took her vital signs and started an IV.

"He looked so scared," she whispered.

"We'll find him," Cherry said firmly. "Does he have a cell phone?"

"The police tried it, but he didn't answer."

"Does he have any friends around here?"

"Bay!" Jillian's heart jumped with hope. "Call Chartreuse. Bay might know how to find him."

Cherry pulled out her cell phone. "I can't use this in here—I'll be back in a couple of minutes."

A tall, slender doctor came in while she was gone and it took Jillian a moment to realize it was Paul Danner. After a surprised greeting, he was all business, probing Jillian's leg until she bit her lip to keep from crying out. As she looked anywhere but at the grisly, throbbing gash on her calf, she couldn't help comparing him to Barrett. He was a good-looking man, in a washed-out sort of way, and his hands were soft, his touch gentle and totally non-threatening. In short, he was exactly the type of guy she'd always tried to date, until Barrett.

It was hard to remember why now.

"I'd like to have a surgeon look at this, Jillian," he told her as he laid the bandage back over her wound and covered her with the blanket. He picked up her chart and started making notes on it. "We'll get something on board for pain and then go from there."

"I think I'm pregnant," Jillian said thickly, her chin wobbling.

He paused in his scribbling and looked at her intently. His pale blue eyes were kind, concerned, and it was all she could do not to throw herself into his arms and beg him to tell her that everything would be okay.

"We'll do a pregnancy test before we administer anything," he promised. "Is there someone I can call for you?"

"My friend Cherry is—"

"Right here." She slipped through the door, shaking her head as she leaned against the jamb. "He left for LA last night and won't be back until next Thursday."

Laying her head back on the crunchy pillow, Jillian blinked hard to dam the flood of tears. "I need to call Barrett's dad."

Paul returned to his notes. "Just as soon as the surgeon's done with you," he said without looking up. Then he passed the chart off to a waiting nurse and took her hand in both of his. "Everything's going to be all right, Jillian. Dr. Strang will take great care of you."

Everything's going to be all right. The echo of her wish gave her a very weird jolt and she looked away as she tugged her hand free. God, whoever had coined the phrase "be careful what you wish for" had certainly known what they were talking about. She didn't really think he was any more interested in her than he'd been before, but the idea of getting chummy with any man but Barrett suddenly made her skin crawl.

"Thank you, Doctor," she said, closing her eyes.

The nurse took a couple of vials of blood and checked her IV, then walked out. After the door thudded, Cherry spoke up. "Nice brush-off."

Jillian's eyes flew open. "Was I too mean?"

"No, silly—I'm just glad to see you finally steering clear of guys who don't do anything for you."

"Well, I'm kind of involved right now," Jillian said quietly. Fear for Barrett spiked again.

"Yeah, pregnant is pretty involved."

"I wondered if you'd heard that." She smiled wryly. "Yeah, I'm pretty sure. My period's way overdue and I peed two pink lines on the stick."

Cherry nodded. "So, are you okay with it?"

"I don't know. Part of me is thrilled. All of me would be thrilled, if I thought..." She bit her lip to keep it from trembling.

Two nurses and an orderly walked in and started getting her gurney ready to roll.

"Keep looking for him, would you, Cher?"

* * * * *

Anthony George walked into her room the next morning, early enough that the surgeon hadn't even been by yet, and gathered her up in his arms.

"I'm so glad you called," he said against her hair, his voice fierce. "Have you heard anything from Barrett?"

Jillian gave a negative jerk of her head and then burst into tears. He held her while she cried, rocking her and murmuring words of comfort. Once upon a time, his fatherly embrace would have been all the solace she needed. But his weren't the arms she wanted around her now. His wasn't the chest she wanted to bury her face in. God, she needed to touch Barrett, to nuzzle the heated skin of his neck with her lips, to slide her palms around his naked ribs and squeeze him tight against her breasts and feel the thick, strong weight of him between her thighs. She needed him to fill her, to make her whole.

She needed to know he was all right.

Drawing back, she reached for a tissue and blew her nose while Barrett's father remained seated beside her on the bed.

"Sorry," she said with a watery smile. "I'm just so scared for him."

"He's pretty tough."

"Not as tough as he thinks."

"That may be true, but frankly, at this point I'm more worried about you."

Jillian smiled at his thoughtfulness. "I'll be fine. I just need to stay off my leg for a week or so, take it easy 'til the stitches come out."

He gave her a look and tapped on her sternum with a fingertip. "I meant in here." And then touched her forehead. "And here."

"They'll be fine, too, as soon as I know he's safe."

There was a knock at the door and her surgeon stuck his head in. "Just need to have a quick look at that incision."

Incision. The word almost made her smile. *Stab wound* would probably have sounded too shocking, especially in front of a visitor.

Anthony stood up. "I'll come back after I get settled in at the Tower, Jillian."

"Hi, I'm Dr. Strang." He reached out to shake hands. "Are you her ride home?"

"I don't know." Anthony looked at her. "Am I?"

"That would be great, if you're free. Cherry said she would take me, but I know she's got several showings today."

"I'm yours whenever you need me."

"She'll need you around eleven," Dr. Strang grinned.

"Guess I'll see you at eleven, then." After a quick peck on the cheek, Anthony left her.

The doctor unwrapped her leg and looked it over carefully for signs of infection, a real concern when a dirty knife was involved. Jillian shook her head at the long arc of stitches—thirty-eight on the outside alone.

"It could have been a lot worse," he said, wrapping her back up.

"Don't I know it."

There was another short knock, and then a nurse came in. "Oh, sorry, Doctor. I was just going to check her IV and get her vitals."

"I'm done here—have at." He looked at Jillian. "Keep it dry 'til the stitches come out. My nurse has already made your follow-up appointment, and I've left orders for painkillers and antibiotics that someone will need to pick up for you. But they'll explain all that when you're discharged."

He left while the nurse was fiddling with her IV line.

"I was going to say, 'Hi, I'm Meg and I'll be your nurse.'" She grinned, repeatedly punching a button on the IV pump. "But it sounds like all I'll be doing is getting this thing out of your hand and discharging you."

"Works for me."

Before Jillian could answer, there was another knock on her door.

Meg rolled her eyes. "Grand Central around here in the morning, isn't it?"

When no one entered, Jillian called, "Come in."

Barrett walked through the door.

"Oh my God! Barrett, are you okay?" Her eyes devoured him, anxiously cataloguing the taped glasses, the dark circles shadowing his eyes, and the unshaven jaw.

"Isn't that what I'm supposed to ask you?" His grin was strained as he glanced around the hospital room, taking in the numerous bouquets and the muted TV. He looked...nervous. His fingers, bruised and swollen, were clenching and unclenching at his sides like a gunfighter's.

"*Are* you okay?" Jillian nudged.

"I'll be out of here in just a minute," Meg told him, laying her fingertips on Jillian's pulse.

"That's okay." He eased one hand carefully into a pocket and drew out—

Jillian's breath caught and her heart skipped a beat. It was a jeweler's box. *He looked nervous...*

"Oh my God." She smiled through the tears pricking her eyes. A proposal was about the last thing she'd—

He tossed the box onto the bed. "Patton hadn't hocked these yet."

The tidal wave of joy was sucked back in a sickening rush, leaving fiery embarrassment its wake. *What an idiot!* Talk about jumping to conclusions.

It took everything she had, but Jillian kept the smile in place. "Wow." She blinked rapidly, reaching for the box. "So he was the one who..."

"Yeah." His gaze slid away from her. "I should have figured that one out a little sooner."

"I can't believe it. I was sure these were gone forever. Thank you, Barrett."

"No problem."

"So." She took a deep breath, trying to get herself back on an even keel. "You haven't told me how you're doing."

"I'm fine. In fact, I'm on my way to Boston."

The nurse hadn't let go of her wrist yet and Jillian wondered if she could feel the sudden, thick thudding of her heart.

"What's in Boston?" she asked warily.

He didn't look at her when he answered. "Another embezzler, probably, but that's not for public consumption."

"How long will you be…gone?"

"I'll probably be in Boston for several weeks." His eyes finally met hers again, and the blank look in them made her stomach drop sickly. "But you knew I'd be leaving, Jillian. Just as soon as this assignment was over."

She nodded several times, trying to calm the storm rising in her chest. Barrett wasn't just *not* proposing…he was dumping her. Meg's grip on her wrist tightened and her thumb moved gently over the back of her hand. Swallowing hard, Jillian mustered another tight smile. "So it's over."

Barrett nodded, too. "Yeah, it is." He looked at his watch. "Well, I need to get a move on. It's a long drive and I haven't packed yet."

"Okay. Well, thanks for coming by. And for bringing the—" A sob rose to her lips, but she bit it back. She couldn't, however, stop the tears that slipped down her cheeks.

A muscle jumped in Barrett's jaw. "I didn't want to hurt you, Jill."

Hurt didn't begin to cover the agony washing through her. A thousand words crowded into the back of her throat, all of them pathetic. *I love you, Barrett, please don't leave me, I'll do anything you want, be anything you need, just don't leave me, please don't...* She couldn't say them. She wouldn't.

"Then don't." Her voice was thick and unsteady, and oh, how she hated herself for letting even that much slip out. God, where was her pride? She was her mother all over again.

Barrett was still for a moment and childish hope had just begun to swell in her heart when he pulled his keys out of his pocket. With a hand on the door handle, he looked at her one last time. "I have to."

Chapter Seventeen

The brunette at the end of the bar was giving him a speculative look. Barrett gave it back, eyeing her svelte body, artfully packed into hip-hugging jeans and a too-tight tank, with frank appreciation. Brunette could be good. Maybe just what the doctor ordered. His ten-day blonde bender had begun to pall—hell, last night he hadn't even been able to get it up, and if that didn't scare the shit out of a guy, nothing would.

"Send Tank Top down there another of whatever she's drinking," he said. "I'll have a Beck's this time."

"You got it, sir." Being a canny businessman already, the baby-faced bartender didn't point out that his first beer was far from gone. But it was warm now and most of the label lay in shreds on the mahogany bar, two more signs that he wasn't settling in here like he should. He felt irritable and on edge from the time he woke each morning 'til the moment he tumbled into bed eighteen hours later, achy and exhausted. Hell, he was even nervous in his sleep—his dreams lately had been crazy to the point that he dreaded going to bed.

But going without sleep only made things worse. Getting rip-roaring drunk and passing out was a tempting idea, but he had a feeling he'd really go ape-shit if he tried that. He also had the creepy feeling that if he could see himself in a mirror right now, he'd look crazed—kind of like a ceramic pot with a defective glaze, only bump him the wrong way and he was liable to shatter into thousands of pieces that no meds or therapy could ever glue back together.

The unconscious bouncing of his left heel had started again. Bracing it hard against the stool's footrest, Barrett took a swallow from the fresh bottle and watched the brunette from the corner of his eye. *Come to Papa...*

It had been a relief to find that a good hard fuck still took the worst edge off his anxiety. He knew there were probably drugs that could do the same thing, but they came from shrinks—shrinks who wanted you to cry them a river in exchange for their John Hancock on that prescription tablet.

He wasn't in the mood to cry.

Tank Top picked up her drink and wandered over to take the empty seat beside him. "Thanks for the drink."

"You're very welcome." He turned in his seat and gave her a thorough once-over. No point in beating around the bush—so to speak.

The lady grinned. A good sign.

"Don't think I've seen you here before," she said, sipping casually. From this close, she looked quite a bit older—speaking of crazed—but that didn't bother Barrett. In fact, the older the better, within reason. He didn't need another shrinking violet.

"That's because I've never been here before." He stuck out a hand. "I'm Barrett."

"Nice to meet you, Barrett," she smiled, putting her fingers in his. "I'm Jill."

* * * * *

He sat in the Walgreen parking lot and took a hefty swig from the big blue bottle of antacid, which wasn't easy considering how hard he was shaking. Jesus, his stomach was killing him.

After Tank Top dropped her bombshell, every muscle in his body had locked up while acid surged in his craw. He'd somehow managed to contort his stiff arm far enough to fish a twenty out of his wallet and slap it onto the bar, and then gotten up and stumbled out without a word. He'd followed that up by hurling what little he'd had to eat and drink today into the dark gutter behind his Suburban.

Could his life get any more fucked up?

Twisting the lid onto the bottle, he shoved it in the console and turned on the ignition. Even at this hour, traffic was still pretty heavy. He cruised around the city aimlessly, rubbing his aching stomach, searching for... Shit, even he didn't know what he was looking for. He should go back to the hotel, but he needed something.

Laid. He needed to get laid, take the edge of this damn grinding in his gut, but after the way that last encounter had gone, he doubted he'd be able to manage any sort of finesse. Which left him one alternative. His jaw tightened as he turned toward a moderately seedy part of town he'd stumbled across a couple of nights ago, where the girls who walked the streets didn't require any finesse—just cold, hard cash.

That, he could manage.

It didn't take long to hook up. An angular, dark-haired chick in micro-shorts and fuck-me heels cocked out a hip as he crawled past. He stopped and rolled down the window, waiting for her to step up.

"You a cop?"

The hair was fake. Just like the tits.

"Do I look like a fucking cop?"

"Hell, no." Her frown deepened the creases in the pancake makeup on her forehead. "What you look like is trouble."

"If you're not interested..."

She opened the door. "I'm interested. Rough stuff'll cost you, though."

After he'd pulled away from the curb, he pulled several bills out of his wallet. "That ought to cover what I'm interested in."

"Probably," she agreed, tucking them into the tiny purse strung over her shoulder. She looked to be in her mid-twenties and smelled like cigarettes and cheap perfume, but she didn't appear to be a junkie. "So what's your name?"

"I don't have one, and neither do you." He looked straight ahead. "Do you have a room?"

"No, but you can get one around the corner." She pointed. "Take a right up here."

He paid cash for the night, ignoring the manager's grin. The motel room was a shit-hole and smelled like thousands of unwashed hookers and their unwashed johns had literally come and gone, but he wasn't there for the ambience.

The minute the door closed behind them, she pulled a condom out of her purse and unzipped his fly. Her eyes widened at the sight of him, but she didn't comment as she rolled the latex, thicker than he usually bought, over the hard spike of his cock. Made for some serious ass-fucking, no doubt. Maybe he'd give her that, too.

Just as he reached for her, she dropped to her knees on the stained shag carpet and took him in her mouth.

"Ah, a mind-reader," he murmured, twining one hand into her hair as he shoved deep. The wig shifted a little but stayed in place and Barrett closed his eyes, pushing into the welcoming cavern of her throat with long, easy strokes while she sucked him like the expert she was. "If you're this good at everything else, it's no wonder you can afford the tits."

He came in short order, breathing hard, gagging her with the force of his final few thrusts.

She didn't complain.

"You're a credit to your profession."

She shook her head, sitting back on her heels. Her makeup was thick enough to be more disguise than decoration. "This is a gig, not a profession. I'm going to be a lawyer."

A cruel joke came to mind, but he stifled it. Her dream probably wouldn't come to pass anyway—one prostitution conviction would see to that.

Moving to the sink, he slid the lipstick-smeared condom off. Something in his stomach went ping! at the sight, but he gritted his teeth and carried on. After swabbing himself down with a washcloth from the rack over the toilet, he tucked his cock back into his boxers. Leaving the fly of his jeans undone, he sat on the edge of the bed. Fire raged in his gut, making him wish he'd brought the bottle in.

The hooker sat beside him and crossed one slender leg over the other, bouncing it casually as she propped herself on her hands. "What's your pleasure, big man?"

"Oh, a little bit of this, a little bit of that." He scooted back and leaned against the headboard. "You strip? You've got the body for it."

"Nah, I'm shy."

He crooked a brow. "I hadn't noticed."

"I'm better at lap dances."

"Well, let's have a little demonstration, then."

She took her time, teasing him with the long, straight hair of her wig, dragging the surprisingly silky black strands over him as she undid the buttons on his shirt one by one. When his stomach gurgled unpleasantly, she paused. "Hungry?"

"Not for food."

Shrugging, she threw one long, bare leg over his knees and crawled sinuously upward, gyrating like a bona fide belly dancer. She settled her ass onto his lap and slithered her glittery top up and off. Maybe he was just fooling himself, but she looked genuinely aroused, her smile heated, her eyes dilated. *Nice.*

"You like having your pussy eaten?"

"Is that a trick question?"

He grinned, flipping open the front clasp of her bra and sliding his hands under the curves of her bulbous breasts. God, they were tight, with stretch marks running every which way. She must have been an A cup before the surgery. "Show it to me, then. I can't eat it in those shorts."

She moaned as he plucked at her nipples but backed away and climbed off the bed. Turning her back, she unzipped and wiggled her ass while she slid the skin-tight shorts slowly to her knees. She bent at the waist, giving him a shot of bare lips as she shoved them to her ankles, and then she was crawling back up his legs, an inviting smile curving her still-crimson lips. When she was close enough, Barrett reached around and grasped her hips, pulling her crotch up for his inspection.

Every drop of blood drained from his head. Her lips were shaved bare, but her mound was covered in tight coppery curls.

A fucking redhead.

"Hey!" She fell onto the floor with a shriek as he jumped from the bed. Raw, red pain slashed at his belly, as raw and red as the rage that boiled up in his neck.

"No, no, *no*! No fucking way! You're not supposed to be a redhead, you little bitch!" he yelled, charging around the motel room, looking for a way out, any way out. "I don't *fuck* redheads! I don't do fucking *redheads*!"

"Holy shit, take it easy, man," she squeaked, scuttling backwards on her butt, wearing nothing but the fuck-me shoes. "It's okay. You don't have to—here, I'll go shave it off."

Barrett grabbed his hair as lightning cracked through his skull. "No, no, no," he rambled. "I can't do this, I'm not going to do this. Jesus, Jillian, I'm so sick, so Goddamn sick, I can't deal with this..." He was losing it. Sobs were clawing at his chest and he didn't know if he could keep them down.

Get it out!

He grabbed the armchair by the window and smashed it into the wall, feeling the reverberation jar its way up his arms and into his shoulders. The damn thing creaked but hung together, so he did it again and again until it was nothing but kindling, a woman's screams echoing in his head the whole time. It should have helped, should have made him feel better, but the rage, oh God, the rage was still there, and the pain... Christ, the pain was enough to drive him to his knees, but he locked them, determined to fight through it. He pounded his forehead into the wall, absorbing the repeated blows with satisfaction, welcoming the sharp reminder that reality was still here, still within his grasp.

Hold onto it!

Acid churned in his stomach, forcing its way up once more. He tried to make it to the bathroom but got tangled in his jeans and fell onto the bed instead. The impact knocked his glasses somewhere and tears squirted from his eyes as a fiery blast of vomit hit the white sheets. *Red* — it was red, all red, and oh fuck, it hurt!

"Jesus, dude, what the hell is wrong with you?"

Voices were twisting with the thundering in his head, men stomping up the stairs, running, shouting...

"Charlie, you okay in there?"

"Monty, get in here!"

He curled into a ball and heaved again, sobbing as he puked up his insides. That metallic smell was back, thick and terrifying, and the look on her face was so damn lost and hurt... He'd made her look like that. "Oh Christ, I'm sorry, I'm so, so sorry! I love you so much, Jill, please don't leave me!"

"What the fuck happened in here?" a man's voice demanded. "Do you want me to call the cops?"

Barrett put his hands over his ears, screaming, "No! No policemen, no firemen! They can't bring her back!"

"Okay, it's okay!" someone crooned. Tender hands smoothed his head while he writhed in an agony of fear and regret and guilt, and more pain than any man could stand. Everything was red and black, black and red...

"...an ambulance, now!"

"Why?" he groaned. "Why did you leave me? Don't leave me, Jill!"

"Everything will be okay," a soft voice whispered. "I'm here. I won't leave you."

Shards of broken glass rolled up from his stomach, tore through his chest, poured out of his mouth, and by the time he heard the sirens, Barrett knew he was going to die.

* * * * *

Exhaustion weighed like an anchor on Jillian's back as she trudged across the parking lot toward her SUV. It didn't feel like autumn yet, no matter what the calendar said. The pavement still radiated heat, making her wish she'd just left her jacket in the office. Too bad it wasn't winter—she could go home, wrap herself up in a quilt, and hibernate all weekend. Instead, she had to clean out the garden, which she'd totally let go the last few weeks. It had been a relief to hear that Darwin and Mr. Alderton had both pled out, so at least she didn't have the ordeal of a trial to look forward to now.

And things were finally settling down at the hotel. As it turned out, the new GM had pretty much cleaned house. The police investigation revealed that a shocking number of employees had had some stake in Patton's little scheme, and even more had looked the other way out of fear of reprisal. If Anthony George hadn't wielded his considerable influence, she'd probably be looking for another job herself right now. As it was, she was thinking about it anyway—it was no fun being one of the last holdouts from a crappy era.

Cranking the AC and rolling the windows down, she entered the flow of rush-hour traffic with a sigh. She thought about stopping at the cemetery to see if her mother's grave stone had been set yet, but she just couldn't face another minute of the heat. That was one more thing to do tomorrow — along with the garden and the laundry and the grocery shopping. She was out of clean underwear and there was no food in the house, to speak of.

Not hungry, but knowing she needed to eat, Jillian pulled up to the Wendy's drive-thru and ordered a chicken sandwich and a salad. And added a Frosty at the last minute because she'd polished off the Ben and Jerry's after last night's crying jag. *No Ben and Jerry's...* That thought alone was enough to make her tear up. If she weren't so tired, she'd stop at the store for a few pints. No crying jag was complete without a chaser of quality chocolate- and nut-riddled ice cream.

The sun hadn't yet sunk to the horizon when she pulled into the garage and lowered the door behind her. Her cell phone rang and she dug it out of her purse as she turned off the ignition and opened the car door.

"Hey, Cherry." She climbed out and reached back in for the Wendy's bag and the Frosty.

"Hey, yourself. You got plans for tonight?"

"Besides a shower and bed? No."

"Feel up to some company?"

Jillian hesitated. She really should work harder to snap out of this funk, but...

"Not really."

"Oh, Jillian," Cherry sighed. "I wish there was something I could do for you."

"I'll be fine. I just need some time to work through it." She dropped her purse and supper on the counter, put the ice cream in the freezer, and then headed for the bedroom. A glance at the answering machine made her pause. There were four messages.

Ruthlessly plucking the bud of hope that insisted on blooming, she walked right on by. That machine had really gotten a workout since Barrett left. Getting stabbed and dumped and losing her mother on three consecutive days had caused an unexpected groundswell of emotional support. These days, she didn't have to spend a moment alone, if she didn't want to.

"So, I assume you haven't heard from him?"

"Nope." Stopping in the hall, she bumped the thermostat down a couple of degrees. The fan kicked on immediately.

"Have you decided whether or not to tell him?"

"Not yet." She had, but she wasn't ready to talk about it.

Cherry's sigh was louder this time. "Okay, I'll quit bugging you. But I do wish you'd let me come over."

"I really need to sleep, Cher. Maybe some other time."

"No maybe about it. We're going out to dinner this week."

Jillian agreed just to get her off the line, then turned off the phone and set it on the dresser. A long, cool shower helped wash away the day's grimy heat, and a pair of boxers and a camisole exposed enough of her damp skin to raise a satisfying batch of goose bumps. Pulling the quilt off her bed, she dragged it into the living room and dropped it on the couch. The trash can was overflowing with wadded up tissues, so she took it to the garage and emptied it into the big plastic garbage can to make room for more.

She popped a mug of water into the microwave and eyed that glowing red four on the answering machine until the timer went off. That was all she could take. Pushing the play button with a trembling finger, she listened to her messages while she fixed herself a cup of peppermint tea and nuked her sandwich.

"Jillian, this is Meg. Hey, I just wanted to let you know that Dr. D's going to give it one last shot." She grimaced. "Sorry—I tried to head him off, but some guys just don't know hopeless unless it smacks them in the face like a dead carp. You're probably going to have to dial up the bitch factor or he might not get the message. Maybe we can catch a movie this weekend or something. I'll call you, okay?"

That was followed immediately by a message from Dr. D. "Jillian, Paul Danner here. I'd like to take you to dinner tonight, if you're feeling up to it. I'll call you at six."

She rolled her eyes as she carried a tray to the living room. Men. Seemed like they were only interested in you when you weren't interested in them.

The next message, left promptly at six, was his. Sighing, she wrapped herself in the quilt and snuggled onto the couch. The last message was an automated confirmation of her dental appointment Tuesday.

Bitter disappointment churned in her stomach as she ate, barely tasting the food. Nodding off before she'd finished half of it, she put the lid back on the salad and curled up for a nap.

* * * * *

She jerked to a sitting position, groggy and frowning. How long had she been asleep? Must not have been too long—it wasn't quite dark yet.

Ding-dong!

Her frown cleared. It must have been the doorbell that woke her. Gathering the quilt around her, she hurried to the front door and opened it a crack as she flipped on the porch light.

"Hi, Jillian." April and Tessa, the fifteen-year-old twins from next door, stood on the porch wearing nothing but cut-offs and tank tops and clutching boxes that bore the label of her favorite chocolate bars. Chocolate. Good chocolate. With *nuts*. "We're selling candy for our band fundraiser again."

"Bless you," Jillian breathed, throwing the oak door wide and holding open the storm door for them. "Come in and I'll get my checkbook."

The pony-tailed blondes scooted by her, but didn't go beyond the entry hall. "Are you feeling okay?" April asked. "You don't look so hot."

Jillian winced. She probably had a drool track on her cheek or something—she'd been sleeping pretty hard. Thank God she hadn't cried before she fell asleep or she'd really look like hell now. "I always look like this after a nap. I'll be right back."

They left with wide eyes and wider smiles after she handed them a check for seventy-two dollars. She'd bought a dozen of the sinful chocolate-almond bars from each of them, and the best part was, she didn't even have to feel guilty about it. After all, if she didn't support the band boosters, who would?

Grabbing her Frosty out of the freezer, she settled back onto the couch and turned on the TV. After she'd flipped through all sixty million channels twice and found nothing to watch, she put it on ESPN and hit the mute button, then settled back with her treats. Things were out of order tonight. She was supposed to cry first, then comfort herself with chocolate, but oh well. Using the candy bar as a spoon, she scooped up a gob of ice cream and took a big bite. It wasn't Ben and Jerry's, but it worked.

She'd scooped and crunched her way through half the bar when the sobs started. Slamming the cup onto the coffee table, leaving the chocolate bar sunk in the ice cream, she choked down the last bite and began wailing in earnest. She wrapped her arms across her middle and rocked, sick with misery, as the tears poured down her cheeks and dripped onto the quilt. Drops of chocolaty drool escaped the yawning chasm of her mouth, adding their own unique flair to the growing field of wet spots, but she couldn't bring herself to care. God, would this pain never let go of her?

And the regret... Oh, so much worse than the pain of his leaving, so much more bitter, was the regret that she hadn't done everything she could to make him stay. Hadn't said those pathetic words. She should have, and let pride be damned. She should have gotten out of that bed and crawled to him on her hands and knees, dragging the IV pole behind her if she had to, telling him every inch of the way how much she loved him—no matter how much he didn't want to hear it. He'd needed to hear it, even if it didn't change his mind. And she'd *needed* to say it. She could have lived with the pain of rejection—hell, she was living with it anyway—but this relentless feeling that she'd somehow left things unfinished between them was killing her.

Jillian plucked a couple of tissues out of the box at her feet and mopped her face. She needed to finish this. She wasn't her mother—she knew that now. The pain wasn't really going to kill her, wasn't going to send her into a tailspin of depression and substance abuse and suicide. She was just going to suffer for a while. A long, *long* while, apparently. And she was never going to get past it if she didn't let it out. She needed to purge herself of the words.

It took her a minute to remember where she'd left her cell phone. Grabbing it from the bedroom dresser, she fished her address book from the buffet and returned to her cocoon on the sofa. Anthony had given her Barrett's home number, but she'd never looked at it until now. Hadn't memorized it or punched it into the phone's memory because that would have been pathetic, too.

Setting her jaw, she rectified that last mistake. He was going to be a father. She'd need to call him again about that, if nothing else. As far as she knew, he hadn't been back to Kansas City yet. She had no idea where he was, and neither, apparently, did his father. Word from Boston was that he'd left without notice barely ten days after arriving and nobody had heard from him since.

Anthony called her every week, which was bittersweet comfort. He'd stayed in town until after her mother's funeral, had stood with her beside the casket when her brother refused to request a furlough. Talk about one, bitter, screwed-up guy...

But Anthony had been there for her. He'd held her while she cried and somehow become the father she'd always wanted. Barrett might be in for a rude shock when he reappeared, because there were ties between them now that he had no control over. The thought scared her even while it empowered her.

Without giving herself time to reconsider, she dialed his number with a trembling finger.

Chapter Eighteen

"Remind me to let you pick the movie from now on," Jillian said, leaning back against the headrest with a big sigh of contentment. "That was amazing."

"Told you so," Cherry grinned, wheeling them into the Saturday afternoon traffic.

"Well, how was I supposed to know I'd like a pirate love story?"

"Who wouldn't?"

Jillian just smiled. She'd wept a little during the movie, but they'd been easy tears. It was the first time she'd cried since leaving that message on Barrett's voice mail almost three months ago. It had felt so good, so freeing, to finally lay out what was in her heart that she hadn't needed to cry since. Not that losing him didn't still hurt in a very big way—it hurt more than she cared to think about. But the loss didn't consume her now.

And she'd finally put that purple vibrator back to work after Bay's last visit. It had been kind of a rude shock when his comforting hug had sent hormones careening through her system. His arms had tightened when she tried to pull away and she'd felt an answering surge in the front of his pants, but instead of acting embarrassed, he'd dropped a kiss on her forehead and said, "It's okay—I love him, too."

The idea that she could be turned on by another man had upset her for just a heartbeat before common sense had regained control. After what they'd shared with Barrett, such a reaction was only natural, but love for him kept them both from acting on the attraction. That was another pivotal moment in her life, realizing that she could be sexually drawn to a man and yet walk away, knowing full well the kind of release he could give her. There was no longer any doubt that she would never be her mother.

A half-hour after he left, she'd put new batteries in the vibrator and taken care of the hormone rush by herself. Barrett would have been better, but Barrett wasn't around.

She had to wonder if it was her own resilient nature or the little life growing inside her that enabled her to cope so well. Whatever the reason, she was grateful to feel more like herself these days. The laundry was caught up, the garden long cleaned out, and she had plenty of healthy food in the house now, even if she didn't feel like eating it sometimes. And unbelievably, there were still eighteen of the candy bars in the cupboard. She'd managed to rein in her chocolate craving, both for her sake and the baby's, limiting herself to bite or two a day.

"Hey, do you want to learn how to quilt?"

Cherry's look said it all.

"I know, I know," Jillian said, smiling. "That's about the last thing I expected to be doing at this point in my life. But Tiell—you know, that widow who lives two doors down, the one with the Pomeranians?—she's starting a class next week and they're making baby blankets, and I thought, hey, what the heck? Gotta have something to do 'til the baby comes."

"Getting pretty friendly with the neighbors lately."

That was true. They'd really come out of the woodwork after her mother's obituary ran in the paper, and much to her surprise, Jillian had found that she had a lot in common with several of them, mostly the single and widowed women. A group of them played Pitch every Thursday night, and she'd even talked Meg into joining them. Cherry, though, had even less interest in Pitch than she had in quilting.

"You never told me why Baylen Butcher was at your house last week," Cherry said. Jillian looked at her sharply. Her tone was too casual.

"He was just being friendly. Why?" Cherry's look was frankly disbelieving. "What, you don't believe I can be friends with a man?"

"It's not you I doubt—it's him."

"Well, believe it."

"And you don't think he wants you sexually?"

Jillian turned her face away, hoping to hide the heat that flowed into her ears and cheeks. She'd never told Cherry about her little indiscretion. "No, he doesn't want me."

"If you say so."

"Why don't you like him?"

"Because he's a player."

"Aren't you a player?"

Cherry speared her with a look. "Hardly. Not on his level, anyway."

"How do you know?"

"Word around the circuit is that he's into a lot of kinky stuff, so just be careful around him, okay?"

Jillian just nodded.

"Uh, Jillian..."

She looked at Cherry, then followed her gaze down the street, to the white Suburban in front of her house. And then to the bearded man raking leaves in her yard.

And felt her heartbeat stutter.

* * * * *

He couldn't see her through the tinted windows, but he knew Jillian was in the tan Acura that stopped at the corner. The sudden thickness in his throat, the heavy thumping of his heart, the sweat that sprang to his palms as he raked, all told him so.

Out of the corner of his eye, he monitored the car as it sat at the stop sign. There was no cross traffic, yet it remained at the corner.

Barrett couldn't let himself think about what might be going on inside. Without missing a beat, he continued to pull the sparse yard waste into a pile, letting the repetitive motions and the cold, flat light of late afternoon lull his over-amped senses. He'd made a copy of Jillian's house key without telling her last summer and, needing something to do while he waited for her, he'd used it to let himself into her garage to get the rake. Probably not the best way to try to win her back. Maybe she'd forgive the unauthorized entry if he cleaned up the stray leaves well enough. Getting her to forgive the rest…

Still the car sat there. He turned away and kept raking.

Tension gathered in his shoulders, curled in his gut. Hell, his hands were starting to shake. Were they going to drive off? Was she never going to speak to him again, never give him a chance to make any of it up to her? He didn't think Jillian had it in her to be so—

Barrett swallowed, raking harder, his pulse pounding in his ears. She'd be stupid not to protect herself from him. He'd hurt her badly and there was no guarantee he wouldn't do it again. Remembering the look in her eyes right before he'd walked out on her made him sick with regret. She had no way of knowing that he'd changed, or at least started to change. That he'd been working hard to shovel out all the scary, painful shit, all the rage and guilt he'd carried around in his head all these years. That he'd actually found himself a shrink, and that he'd actually talked to him—twice a week for the past four months.

All so he could find his way back to her. So that he could get down on his knees and beg her to marry him.

And so that he could handle it if she kicked him to the curb.

Lost in his stressful thoughts, Barrett didn't realize he was bearing down too hard until the prongs of the rake started to bend backward. Grunting, he eased off the pressure to keep from stripping up the grass. That was just great. Breaking into her house, destroying her property... How else could he impress her with the New Barrett?

He took a few deep breaths to calm himself, to try to release some of the tension. The scent of her stopped him in his tracks.

"Barrett?"

He stiffened at the soft touch on his back. Even through the quilted flannel and the tee shirt, it seared him. Fuck. The moment was here and he didn't know if he could even turn around and face her. Every muscle had turned to stone.

"I take it you got my message?" Her voice was even softer than her touch, tremulous. Encouraging.

He half-turned and looked down at her out of the corner of his eye. *Chickenshit.* "What message?"

Her head tilted slightly and she looked puzzled. Worried. Tired. The black turtleneck made her look thin and washed out, and the bulky winter coat over it practically swallowed her. She was still beautiful enough to make his cock strain against his jeans. *Down, you asshole!*

"What message?" he repeated, turning to face her fully, habit firming the command in his voice.

"I... um..." Deep red surged up her neck into her face.

"You called my house?" Shit, he hadn't stopped at home or checked his messages. It hadn't even occurred to him that she might try to call, after the way he'd left her.

Jillian was definitely flustered. She'd backed up a step and her fingers were fiddling with the zipper pull on her purse. The Acura was nowhere to be seen. She must have walked from the corner.

She'd left him a message.

"Jill, what message did you leave me?" he asked, dropping the rake. The effort he was making to keep a lid on his hope roughened his voice a little more than he intended.

Her lip trembled and she bit it, shaking her head. Her chest was rising and falling rapidly, and not with lust. Tears hovered in her eyes.

She was afraid.

Choking back his own sudden fear, he pulled out his cell phone and dialed his home number. Her eyes widened in alarm and she took another step away.

Barrett grabbed her wrist. "Stay."

She was trembling. Hard. Barrett tightened his fingers, trying to offer some comfort even as he punched in the code to call up his messages. Nine of them. Not a whole hell of a lot for so many months.

He forwarded through the first six. The seventh was left almost two months ago.

"Hi, Barrett, it's me. I'm sorry to have to say this to you over the phone, on voice mail, no less." His blood froze. Her voice was weary and nasal, like she'd been sleeping. Or crying. Fuck, he was about to hear what a jerk she thought he was. "I should have said it at the hospital, but I was... Well, never mind. I don't know how much time I have to leave a message, so I'll get to the point. I know you don't want to hear this, but I love you, Barrett Isaiah George. You're the most beautiful man I've ever—"

Barrett's cell phone hit the ground and his heart cantered crazily as he stared at her.

"Jillian..." He grabbed her other wrist. "Jilli—" His voice broke and he squeezed his eyes shut as relief blew through him.

"Oh God." Her voice quivered as she tried to shake him off, but he held her fast, trying to get himself under control. "Please let me go!"

He opened his eyes. Incredibly, she was even paler now. "Jillian, what's wrong?"

"I'm so sorry, Barrett," she whispered, her eyes searching his. "I didn't mean for it to happen, truly I didn't."

"You're sorry?" Why the hell was she sorry about loving him?

"I know that's no excuse—although really it was just as much your fault as mine, if not more so," she added, sniffling. "But you don't have to worry about me trapping you into marriage the way my mother did. I know you never wanted to be a father, and honestly, I'm strong enough to—"

"Be a father?" Barrett tried to wrap his head around what she was saying—

"Barrett, are you okay?"—but the words were starting to sound kind of funny. And his heart was racing. Coffee, he'd had too much coffee on the drive down. Man, he was gonna have to cut *way*—

Chapter Nineteen
ಸಾ

Making breakfast for the man in her bed was the sweetest kind of torture she could imagine.

Jillian stood at the stove in her flannel nightgown and fuzzy socks, scrambling half a carton of eggs with a fork while hope and doubt waged a vicious war in her gut. Hands trembling, she paused long enough to pluck the last of the bacon from the skillet and blot it with a wadded-up paper towel. There were a dozen strips in all, thick-sliced and chewy, just the way Barrett liked them. A bowl of almond icing sat on the counter waiting for the cinnamon rolls, which would be out of the oven in six minutes. She'd made up the dough from scratch last night, keeping her fingers crossed that the just-expired dry yeast would rise to the occasion.

God knew she'd needed something to keep her busy, something to keep her from going crazy thinking about Barrett's extreme reaction to the news of her pregnancy. The big lug had actually passed out! He keeled over in her yard, landing face-down in the leaf pile he'd raked up for her, and Jillian was on him in a flash, screaming for help while she tried to shove him over so he wouldn't suffocate. Fortunately, the twins' mother Carolyn, a physician assistant, was on her back porch grilling burgers at the time and raced to the rescue. Barrett was already coming around by the time she reached them, but she checked him over thoroughly while Jillian sat holding his head in her lap, clutching his glasses and plucking bits of dried leaf from his hair and beard.

Carolyn wanted him to go to the hospital for a complete physical, but he refused, sitting up on the crispy brown grass and rubbing the back of his neck with a confused look.

"Tired," he said. "Drove straight through."

"From where?" Carolyn asked.

"Maine."

"That'd do it." She shook her head, grinning at him. "Next time you make a drive like that, macho man, do not stop to manicure the lawn, do *not* even unpack your car—just go directly to bed before you kill yourself or someone else."

Nodding, he let each of them take a hand and pull him to his feet. After thanking her profusely, Jillian unlocked the front door with shaking fingers and led him to her bedroom. Then, since he couldn't seem to do anything but watch her, she stripped him to his boxers and shoved him onto the bed.

"Can I fuck you when I wake up?" he asked as she pulled the quilt over him, startling a laugh out of her. Usually he just demanded sex rather than asking for it.

"I'd be pretty put out if you didn't," she assured him, brushing his hair back and laying her lips on his forehead.

"Will you marry me?"

Lungs frozen in disbelief, she drew back and stared. Watching her through his long lashes, barely awake, he nudged, "Jill?"

"I..." She swallowed hard before continuing, "If that's what you want."

He'd closed his eyes with a sigh and been asleep ever since.

Jillian drained the excess bacon grease into an empty coffee can and then poured the eggs into the drippings, heaving a big sigh of her own. His impromptu proposal had obliterated her remaining control and she'd stumbled to the garage for a nice, long howl, sitting in her car with the windows rolled up so Barrett wouldn't hear her. The wild flood of emotions battering through her had left her almost as exhausted as the man who inspired them, but she'd been too wired to sleep. Hence, the cinnamon rolls. And the lemon bars. And the foil-covered pans of meatloaf and scalloped potatoes in the refrigerator. She'd had to do something while the dough was rising, after all, and making his favorite foods had seemed like a good idea at the time.

The way to a man's heart…

Like her cooking was enough to keep him here. Jillian frowned as she expertly folded the eggs over and over, feeling slightly nauseated. Her domestic goddess routine hadn't kept him from leaving before, but she couldn't seem to help trying it again. She hated the desperation driving her actions. Could she accept his proposal—if he'd meant it—and marry him, knowing he'd been trapped into it by circumstance? It didn't seem wise, or fair to either of them, but she didn't think she could help herself. She wanted him any way she could get him.

Pathetic.

Love him, love him, love him…

Pathetic!

I need him. And he needs me!

Path—

A long arm reached in front of her and turned off the burner.

"What—"

"I missed you." Barrett slid one strong hand around her neck and urged her toward him.

The timer went off.

"I need to get the rolls out before they burn."

"Screw the rolls."

Heart pounding, Jillian ducked out of his grasp. "Nothing doing! These took forever to make. Here." She shoved the plate of bacon into his hand without looking at him and grabbed the oven mitts. God, if he got her into bed before they talked, they *wouldn't* talk, and there were things that needed to be said.

But oh, the temptation!

She pulled the pan out of the oven and slid it onto the wooden doily trivet. Vibrating with tension, she dropped her mitts and snatched up the bowl and a spatula, then slapped a big gob of icing right in the middle of the pan and started spreading.

"I love you, too, Jill."

* * * * *

His palms were sweaty.

Jillian stood motionless at the counter, her hand poised over the roll pan. Just a second ago she was slinging the white stuff around like she was being timed, but his declaration had put an immediate stop to that.

Damn it, he should have waited until they were at least looking at each other. Instead, he'd done it the lame-o way, mumbling his tender feelings to the back of her curly head like a ten-year-old with his toe in the dirt and a frog in his pocket.

He felt like a ten-year-old, damn it, and he hated it. Hated being vulnerable again, hated needing something so badly. Needing *someone* so badly. But need her, he did. And love her? God, he'd never even known what love was 'til he walked away from Jillian Fox and left such a huge chunk of himself behind.

"You don't—" She sagged against the cabinet and dropped her hands to the counter, one still wearing the mitt and the other clutching the spatula. "You don't have to say that, Barrett."

His name emerged as a broken whisper, grinding Barrett's heart to hamburger. He wrapped his arms around her and pressed the side of his face against hers. A few of her hot tears trickled into his beard. The rest plopped onto the rolls, making tiny craters in the icing.

"I'm so sorry, Jill," he whispered thickly. "I didn't want to leave you, but I just…"

Jesus, even if he could find the words, how the hell was he ever going to get them out?

"It's okay."

"No, damn it, it's not." He squeezed her harder, trying to absorb the silent sobs racking her, trying to soak up the pain rolling off her in waves. "Can you ever forgive me?"

The mitt and spatula fell to the floor as she turned in his arms and suddenly they were clutching at each other, grappling to see who could get the tightest hold. Her sobs poured out against his ear and the harsh scraping sound of them was almost more than he could take.

"There's nothing to forgive!" she finally choked out. "You never promised me—"

"I knew I was hurting you—"

"But I knew you didn't—"

Barrett reared back. "Goddamn it, Jillian, stop trying to make excuses for me! I was a fucking..." He frowned, lowering his voice. "I didn't...think I deserved you."

Jillian gave a watery laugh and laid her palms against his cheeks. "Oh, you deserve me, all right—swollen ankles, weepy spells, and all."

The love shining in her eyes made it even tougher to say this, but he had to get it out there. "I didn't deserve you. I was scared out of my mind—scared of loving you, scared of losing you. So I ran." He closed his eyes and sighed at the softness of her skin on his. "But like they say, wherever you go, there you are. And there I was."

He looked at her again, taking a deep breath to steady his nerves. "I tried to go back, Jill. I thought all I had to do was get back into my safety zone, where I didn't feel anything, didn't fear anything. You have a right to know that I tried to fuck my way through Boston in the first couple of weeks."

Unbelievably, she gave a choked laugh as more tears dripped down her cheeks. "Of course you did."

"Why are you smiling?" he demanded. "I screwed other women, Jill. Hookers, too."

"Did you use a condom?"

Barrett stared at her. "What the hell kind of question is that? Of course I used a condom!"

"Well, then...are you still screwing around?"

Stung, he stepped away from her, backing up 'til his ass hit the counter. Then he crossed his arms, breathing deeply. *Calm down.* "I deserve that, I guess. And no, I haven't been with anyone else since..." He shook his head.

She watched him with patient, understanding eyes. "Since...?"

"Since that ulcer you were always bitching about perforated on me."

"Oh, Barrett!"

"Yeah, I know. Fucked me up pretty good. Like I wasn't fucked up enough already." He shifted uncomfortably but didn't look away. "I don't know if it was the pain or the sepsis or—" Shit, he didn't want to tell her all this, but she needed to know. "That night was...it was really bad, Jill."

"It's all right. You don't have to tell me."

"I think I do."

Standing there in her kitchen, Barrett relived his final descent into hell—the Jill at the bar, the hooker and her red-haired pussy, the pain and craziness that had followed. "It mostly just seems like a dream to me now, but I do remember thinking that I was about to die and I'd never told you how I felt about you. It tore me up to know you'd live the rest of your life believing I..." He closed his eyes and tried to swallow the golf ball in his throat. "That you'd never know how much... Aw, fuck, give me a minute here."

She sniffled but didn't say anything, just let him pull himself together.

"Anyway, I woke up two days later with tubes running out of me every which way," he finally continued. "That redhaired hooker came by and told me she'd given the motel manager some cash out of my wallet to cover the damages so that he wouldn't call the cops. Without the wig and all that makeup, she looked like a kid." A plain little redheaded kid whose mouth he'd fucked. It still made him feel like shit to think about it. She'd probably saved his life and he'd been too doped up on pain meds and too hoarse from the tubes down his throat to offer more than a raspy Thanks. He should have gotten her name, tried to repay her somehow.

"When the doctors discharged me, I ran some more, just got in the truck and drove around for a few days, trying not to think. Stopped in northern Maine, rented a beach house, and spent a few weeks just walking up and down the shoreline."

Staggering was more like it—still recovering from emergency surgery, he'd barely had the energy to get around, but he'd felt driven to move and keep on moving, to keep on hiding from the pathetically inadequate man he knew himself to be. When he finally collapsed in front of a neighboring cabin, the owner had come right out and scraped him up off the rocks—and then become the first shrink he'd ever been able to open up to.

"At first I thought Dr. Kestor must be the greatest therapist ever, but now I think I was just...ready. It was time to either deal with it or die." Scary shit, realizing how close he'd come. Again. And this time, he would have cared, would've hated like hell to check out of life when he had so much to live for—a father who loved him, a little brother who was getting married, and a soft, sensuous, sweet-hearted woman who carried his child.

"Oh, Barrett, I'm so glad he was there!"

"Yeah, me too." His stomach still twisted to think about it, but he forged ahead. "I knew there had to be something bad about me, Jill. No matter how many times they told me it wasn't my fault, I knew I must have done something really,

really bad to make Mom think killing herself was better than staying with me. And I'd compounded my sins by waiting. I'd stood outside her door knocking forever before I finally worked up the nerve to call my dad. If I'd called sooner..."

"Barrett, no!" Suddenly her arms were around his waist, squeezing him urgently.

"I know, I know," he sighed. "My head knows, anyway. But when I remember my father on his knees, crying into my neck and telling me how sorry he was, I still wonder why he was sorry. He came home right away. I was the one who should be saying I was sorry. But I didn't. I thought if he ever realized how long I'd waited, he'd..."

Jillian took his clenched jaw in her palms and looked at him hard. "Barrett, you know there was nothing you could do, right?"

He looked back for a second, but finally let his eyes drop. "I knocked on that door for a long time before I called him, Jill."

"Barrett!" Her horrified look made his stomach contract painfully and he tried to back away, but she wouldn't let go of his face. "Listen to me, sweetheart, your father said she'd been gone hours when he found her. Hours! There was nothing you or anyone could do."

Barrett frowned.

"Think about it," she insisted. "Your father's office was still open when you called, right?" When he nodded, she said, "So it was probably before five o'clock, and if school gets out around three..."

"Three-fifteen. We got out at three-fifteen." He'd ridden his bike that day, and he was starving when he got home. "The Looney Toons were on from three to four, and the Incredible Hulk came on at four. That's what I really wanted to see."

But he never got to watch the Hulk. He'd heard Dusty screaming and found him upstairs. When his mother didn't answer the door, he'd taken the baby downstairs, given him a sippy cup of milk and some cereal, and turned on the Looney Toons for him. Then he'd gone back upstairs and started knocking.

When his dad raced through the front door, Wyle E. Coyote was up to his usual hilarity, but Barrett hadn't been able to laugh because he kept looking up the stairs.

It couldn't even have been four o'clock yet. Dad had gotten home less than half an hour after he did.

"She'd been gone for hours?"

Jillian's warm hands slid down to rest on his chest as she nodded. "The reason your father said he was sorry was because you'd seen her like that. He was sick about it. Losing her would have been hard enough for you without having to carry around a memory like that."

"Wow."

Barrett didn't know what else to say. Maybe he was in shock because, although relief was there, it was nothing compared to the relief of knowing that Jillian still loved him. Or maybe he'd already started to accept that he wasn't to blame for his mother's death.

Either way, he'd have to talk to his father later and really clear the air between them, once and for all. But right now, making Jillian his was all he wanted to think about.

"I kind of screwed everything up yesterday, didn't I?" he asked. It was blurry, but he was pretty sure he remembered asking if he could fuck her. And then, as an afterthought, asking her to marry him. *Way to let your dick do the talking, asshole.*

She cocked her head with a smile. "What did you screw up?"

"Something I promised myself I'd do right."

Setting her away from him, he sank awkwardly to his knees on the vinyl floor in front of her and squeezed a hand into his jeans pocket. Jillian clutched the edge of the counter behind her with both hands as he pulled out the gray jeweler's box.

Her wary expression stopped him cold.

"Oh Christ, I'm sorry, honey." Could he do anything without screwing up? Hurrying to snap open the lid, he took the delicate ring in his fingers and stuffed the box back in his pocket. "I'd give my right nut not to have hurt you like that, but I just wasn't thinking about anything that day except getting away."

Her face crumpled. "Barrett..."

"Jillian Irene Fox, will you marry me?"

She wiped her eyes with the heel of her hand. "You already had it?" she whispered. "Before you knew? About the baby?"

"I bought it before I left Maine." He swallowed and held out his empty hand.

The feeling that pounded through him when she laid her shaking fingers in his was like nothing he'd ever known. All those days he'd wandered the rocky, desolate beaches, oblivious to the cold and the raging wind and the prickles of ice and sea spray against his face, he'd thought about this very thing. Of holding her hand. He'd never held hands with her or anyone else. It had always been too uncomfortable—too intimate, somehow. More intimate, even, than sex.

He slid their palms together. *Together.* Squeezing, he prodded, "So...?"

"Of course I'll marry you," she laughed, wiping away more tears as she tugged at him.

He tugged back, pulling her to him and sliding her ring onto the proper finger. A little loose, maybe a little overstated—he'd wanted something that said *I love you* in a big way—but it didn't matter. He was whole now.

Sighing, he wrapped his arms around her and laid his head against her breast. God, she smelled good. "No *of course* about it." Barrett rubbed her lower back. "I've made some progress, Jill, but I think I probably have a long way to go before I'm decent husband material. Father material." His arms tightened convulsively. "Are you feeling okay? No problems or anything?"

Her fingers sifted through his hair and tilted his head back. She didn't say anything, just stared into his eyes, her lips curved into a smile that made him feel about ten feet tall.

Jesus, what had he ever done to earn a look like that?

"I love you, Barrett. I think I always have, from the first time I saw you."

He closed his eyes and leaned into her fingers as she combed through his hair.

"I think the feeling was mutual—I was just too stupid to realize it at the time."

"Guess we were stupid together then, huh?"

Barrett opened his eyes and his breath backed up in his chest. Her breasts hung before him, unfettered beneath the flannel nightgown, and her hips were warm beneath his fingers, and she smelled like baking bread and feminine musk, like sustenance of the most basic kind. And he was starving for her.

His hands slid down over her ass as a wave of pure desire crashed over him, squeezing the air from his lungs.

"Will you make love with me?" The words were rough, rusty—didn't sound quite right coming from his lips. Love. It was going to take some getting used to, in more ways than one.

It was Jillian's turn to sigh. "I thought you'd never ask."

* * * * *

She gave their breakfast a passing thought when Barrett snagged two strips of bacon on the way out of the kitchen, but her stomach was too fluttery to eat now anyway. Hand-in-hand, they walked through the living room, and Jillian's thighs tightened when he stopped in the hallway and stuffed the last bite of bacon into his mouth before nudging the thermostat down.

Make love with me.

"Sixty okay?"

The familiarity of his action closed her throat and she could only nod. Sixty actually sounded pretty darn cold, but Barrett would keep her warm. Hot. *Scorching.*

God, she was dripping already.

Once inside the door, though, Barrett hesitated. Taking her other hand, he looked down at her.

"I've never done anything but nasty, Jill. I don't know how good I'll be at nice."

"Barrett!" she started to laugh. His pensive look drew her up short. "That's really, really sweet, honey, but you know better than anyone what nasty does for me."

"I don't want to fuck you this time," he said doggedly, his chin thrust out. "I want to make love to you. Like you made love to me after we came back from Kansas City."

She smiled at the memory.

"I did, didn't I? But you know what?" She searched his eyes, anxious for him to see the truth in hers. "I knew I loved you then, and the knowing made it…easy. Honestly, Barrett, I think when you love someone, *making* love just comes naturally."

"No, what comes naturally," he growled, releasing her hands, "is shoving up your nightgown to see if your pussy is still bare." His fingers settled on her hips and started gathering up the fabric, baring her legs to the cooling air little by little.

"Hard to make love with flannel between us," Jillian breathed, swaying a little. She was ready for nasty. Oh, was she ready.

"I never got to see it except in that picture you sent me. I loaded it as wallpaper so I could look at you every time I turned on my laptop."

Heat blistered her cheeks. "Barrett George, you'd better be kidding."

"Sorry," he grinned, then ducked out of the way when she tried to smack him. "Hey, it was all I had!"

"That's more than I had," she muttered, eyes narrowed. Oh, he looked so good!

"I promise I'll replace it with our wedding picture." Taking her in his arms again, he planted a kiss on her forehead. Jillian remained stiff for, oh, about two nanoseconds, and then leaned into him. His lips touched the bridge of her nose, and then the tip, and then his mouth was hovering over hers.

"I've never kissed a man with a beard before," she whispered, caressing the short crinkly hair with her fingers. There was a lot of gray in it, much more than on his head, but it looked right on him.

"I'll shave it, if you'd like."

"Nah." She looked at him from under her lashes. "I've already done enough shaving for the both of us this morning."

Barrett's arms squeezed her hard as he groaned, "Oh, fuck…"

Twining her arms around his neck, Jillian pulled his head down. "Kiss me, Barrett."

* * * * *

The brush of her lips sent a tremor through him. He wanted this kiss to be fairy tale-perfect, but he suddenly wondered if he could pull it off.

"I love you so much, Jill." It sprang forth unbidden, and as if he'd said the magic words, his neck muscles relaxed and their lips met with exquisite tenderness. Jesus, could he survive anything more perfect than this? His heart raced, his knees wobbled... Jillian's lips parted, sucking his lower lip into her mouth, and his blood pressure skyrocketed.

Then her hands slid down between them and shoved his tee shirt up to his neck, and the time for tenderness was over.

He broke the kiss just long enough to yank the shirt over his head, sending his glasses somewhere, and then there was no stopping either of them. Her nightgown split right down the front when he yanked at two handfuls of the neckline, and she somehow managed to shove his jeans and his underwear down over his ass without undoing anything, and then they were falling onto the bed in a tangle of ravenous passion.

Barrett couldn't get enough of her. His hands roamed urgently, savoring the smooth, silky skin of her back and hips and the gentle swelling of her abdomen as he devoured her sweet mouth. When his palms found her breasts, they both moaned harshly.

She was definitely pregnant.

"Are they sore?" he asked roughly, amazed by the changes that had already taken place.

"Yes, but don't hold back. I need you."

Barrett stilled as the skin on the back of his neck prickled and his stomach pitched like he was on a roller coaster. *I need you.* Jillian needed him, his baby needed him, and the weight of that responsibility threatened to suffocate him. Every cell in his body screamed for him to run, to get out before someone got hurt.

Dropping his forehead to her breastbone, he closed his eyes and took a few deep breaths. *Old tapes, old tapes,* he chanted silently.

"Barrett." Her warm, soft hands curved under his jaw and pulled him up to face her. She wasn't smiling. "Yes, I *need* you," she repeated. "And I want you. And I love you. But I won't die without you. If you need to go, then go. I can wait until you're ready, because I know you will be—if not today, then next week. Or next year. But one day you *will* be ready, because you need me, too."

Speaking of magic words...

Barrett sighed as all the tension drained right out of him.

"You're right," he said, rolling to his back and pulling her over him. "I do need you, probably more than you need me."

"That's the scariest part, isn't it?"

"Always. But I'll get over it, because there's no way in hell I'm leaving now."

He stared, mesmerized by the heavy globes suspended over his mouth, their areolas wider, darker, their nipples hard and long.

With a tender smile, she plumped one breast in her hand and guided it to his lips. Then she held his head as he suckled hungrily. When her cries grew urgent, he drew her upward and took his fill of her smooth, fragrant pussy, lapping at the wetness that rained out of her until she screamed with need. Then he filled her with his fingers and pulled hard at her clit with his lips while he watched her come unglued. She bucked over his face, her hands locked on the headboard, her head thrown back in sensual abandon, and something inside Barrett burst. This was how she was supposed to look. How she was *born* to look.

And she only looked like this for him.

Buoyed by a power beyond anything he'd ever felt, Barrett shoved her to her back and claimed her, gently at first, then with rising greed as she wrapped her legs around his thighs and raked her nails over his ass. Bracing himself up on his hands, he drove into her again and again, awed by the energy that swirled between them. The emotion. When she broke, her cry echoed in his ears.

"Oh God, Barrett, I love you!"

Unable to speak, he groaned as the clenching of her muscles pulled him headlong into the rush.

When he collapsed, Barrett managed to catch some of his weight with his elbows and laid his forehead on her shoulder, his chest heaving like he'd just done a hundred stadiums. Then he smiled. Jillian's hips were still undulating beneath his.

"Are you trying to tell me something?" he panted, raising his head.

"I was just wondering…"

He brushed damp curl back from her temple. "Yes, sweet Jill?"

Mischief mingled with the love in her eyes.

"Can I have some nasty now?"

Epilogue

✽

"Oh, no way!" Barrett yelled, leaning forward and pointing at the TV. "Watch the replay, you stupid maggots! He was out of bounds by a mile!"

Dustin punched his shoulder. "You're just pissed because I'm going to win the pot."

"Fu—I mean, screw that! There's no way in hell that was good." Then he brightened. "Ha! There's a flag on the play."

"Give it up, bro. The Irish are dead in the water."

Barrett looked at his dad, who was grinning at the two of them. "Is he ever going to face reality?"

"Oh, I'd say he'll have to in about six weeks."

Barrett smirked. "Yeah, getting married kind of does that to a guy, doesn't it?"

Slender fingers smoothed over his shoulder and around his neck. "Why do I feel like I've just been insulted?"

"No way, babe." He grabbed Jillian's hand and pressed a kiss into her palm, his eyes wandering to their official wedding portrait propped on the piano. It was good, but not as good as the large one that hung over their mantel at home—and, as promised, served as wallpaper for his laptop. That one the photographer had snapped after the session was officially done, when he'd started tickling Jill's neck with his beard. The tickling had turned to something else and the canny photographer had kept right on snapping.

He'd sent her a large bouquet and a hefty bonus for her initiative.

"Facing reality was the best thing that ever happened to me."

He ignored Dustin's snicker and groaned when the officials let the completion stand.

"Are you ready to go?"

"Go?" Finally looking up, he was startled to see Jillian wearing her coat. "Now? It's not even halftime yet."

"I'm ready to go," she said softly.

Okay, something was going on here and he needed to figure it out quick. He glanced around and saw Sheila rocking gently in the recliner by the Christmas tree, still rubbing Amity's little back, though she'd burped and conked out about an hour ago. Her thumb had fallen out of her mouth and she was sucking at empty air. The sight tightened his throat.

"She's spending the night with Grandma and Grandpa," Jillian said.

Barrett blinked. "Oh, yeah?"

Craning his head, he stared at her. Jillian's eyes fell away and a blush worked its way up her neck into her cheeks as she pulled the two sides of her coat together. His own eyes widening, he turned and examined the nearly empty baby bottle on the coffee table. *Oh, fuck yeah...*

Studiously looking anywhere but at Jill's chest, Barrett wiped the graphic images from his mind before lust turned him into a slobbering beast. He needed to get out of here before his boner became too obvious.

Standing, he said, "Guess I'll have to collect the pot tomorrow, Dusty. Jillian says I have to go home now."

"You're whipped, man," Dusty swore, shaking his head.

"Dustin, you said you'd help me with these, remember?" Amber called from the dining room. "Wedding invitations don't address themselves."

"Speaking of whipped," Barrett grinned at him.

Dusty rolled his eyes and hunched deeper into the couch. "After the game!"

"Isn't there another game after this one?"

He obviously knew when to fold. "Coming, sweetheart."

They said their goodbyes quietly, Jillian teary-eyed at this first night away from their daughter. Barrett got a little choked up himself when he stroked Amity's soft, flaming ringlets and kissed her rosy cheek. Then he surprised himself by planting a kiss on Sheila's cheek while he was in the vicinity.

"Thanks for everything," he told her.

He grabbed Jill by the hand and blasted out of there before things got any mushier.

"Don't do anything I wouldn't do," Dusty yelled after him.

When the front door had closed behind them, Barrett slid his hands into the open front of Jillian's coat and pulled her to him, driving his tongue into her mouth and letting his imagination go berserk. The first time her breasts had leaked during sex, they struck a deal—he'd leave all her milk for the baby until she was weaned to formula, and in return...

He groaned, lifting his head to look down at her tits. For the rest of this afternoon and tonight, they were his—all his—and he intended to make the most of it. His new therapist would probably have a field day with some of what he had planned, but that was what she got paid the big bucks for.

"You could have given me a little warning," he rumbled, sliding his hands up over the heavy mounds. His cock jerked to full attention as he imagined the screams of pleasure he would wring from her. That was the one thing he regretted about having a baby in the house—they had to moderate the volume when they fucked and he really missed hearing his wife scream out her orgasms.

As soon as Amity could get around on her own, they'd have to confine their activities to the bedroom, which would really be a test of his willpower. He loved jumping Jillian when she least expected it.

"Barrett!" She backed away, swatting at him. "Save it 'til we get home!"

"Oh no." He yanked her hips against his and palmed her ass. "There's only so much temptation I can stand. You have to give me a sample in the car or we'll never make it home."

"It's not dark yet!"

Barrett grinned. She sounded scandalized, but her breath was coming in short, excited puffs.

"In the car or right here," he said. "You choose."

A pickup roared down the street and she gasped.

"Fine! In the car, Mr. Domination Freak." Her cheeks were a brilliant red as she grabbed his wrists and pulled his hands away from her backside.

"I thought you'd see things my way," he grinned, taking her hand as they walked down the front steps.

"Don't I always?" she groused.

He stopped and pulled her face up to look into her eyes. "Come on, admit it—you love being dominated."

She stared up at him for a moment and then her smile took his breath away. "Only by you, Barrett. Only by you."

The End

Also by Robin L. Rotham

☙

Alien Overnight
Carnal Harvest
Seniorella

About the Author

A bookworm from the age of ten, Robin L. Rotham lived vicariously through daring, romantic heroines for nearly twenty years, dreaming all the while of one day writing her own romance novels, as well as her own happily ever after. When she finally found her real-life hero, he wasn't quite what--or where--she expected. Undaunted, she chased him over three states and four years before he finally swept her off her feet. He's been more than worth the effort.

The realities of home and family kept her from fulfilling her other dream for ten more years, but Robin finally succumbed to the writing bug in 2005 and cranked out her first novel on a used laptop from eBay in less than seven weeks. Alien Overnight is her second completed novel.

Robin welcomes comments from readers. You can find her website and email address on her author bio page at www.ellorascave.com.

Tell Us What You Think

We appreciate hearing reader opinions about our books. You can email us at Comments@EllorasCave.com.

Why an electronic book?

We live in the Information Age—an exciting time in the history of human civilization, in which technology rules supreme and continues to progress in leaps and bounds every minute of every day. For a multitude of reasons, more and more avid literary fans are opting to purchase e-books instead of paper books. The question from those not yet initiated into the world of electronic reading is simply: *Why?*

1. ***Price.*** An electronic title at Ellora's Cave Publishing and Cerridwen Press runs anywhere from 40% to 75% less than the cover price of the exact same title in paperback format. Why? Basic mathematics and cost. It is less expensive to publish an e-book (no paper and printing, no warehousing and shipping) than it is to publish a paperback, so the savings are passed along to the consumer.
2. ***Space.*** Running out of room in your house for your books? That is one worry you will never have with electronic books. For a low one-time cost, you can purchase a handheld device specifically designed for e-reading. Many e-readers have large, convenient screens for viewing. Better yet, hundreds of titles can be stored within your new library—on a single microchip. There are a variety of e-readers from different manufacturers. You can also read e-books on your PC or laptop computer. (Please note that Ellora's Cave does not endorse any specific brands.

You can check our websites at www.ellorascave.com or www.cerridwenpress.com for information we make available to new consumers.)

3. ***Mobility.*** Because your new e-library consists of only a microchip within a small, easily transportable e-reader, your entire cache of books can be taken with you wherever you go.

4. ***Personal Viewing Preferences.*** Are the words you are currently reading too small? Too large? Too... ANNOYING? Paperback books cannot be modified according to personal preferences, but e-books can.

5. ***Instant Gratification.*** Is it the middle of the night and all the bookstores near you are closed? Are you tired of waiting days, sometimes weeks, for bookstores to ship the novels you bought? Ellora's Cave Publishing sells instantaneous downloads twenty-four hours a day, seven days a week, every day of the year. Our webstore is never closed. Our e-book delivery system is 100% automated, meaning your order is filled as soon as you pay for it.

Those are a few of the top reasons why electronic books are replacing paperbacks for many avid readers.

As always, Ellora's Cave and Cerridwen Press welcome your questions and comments. We invite you to email us at Comments@ellorascave.com or write to us directly at Ellora's Cave Publishing Inc., 1056 Home Avenue, Akron, OH 44310-3502.

Cerridwen, the Celtic Goddess of wisdom, was the muse who brought inspiration to storytellers and those in the creative arts. Cerridwen Press encompasses the best and most innovative stories in all genres of today's fiction. Visit our site and discover the newest titles by talented authors who still get inspired - much like the ancient storytellers did, once upon a time.

Cerridwen Press
www.cerridwenpress.com

Discover for yourself why readers can't get enough of the multiple award-winning publisher
Ellora's Cave.
Whether you prefer e-books or paperbacks,
be sure to visit EC on the web at
www.ellorascave.com
for an erotic reading experience that will leave you breathless.

Made in the USA